The Friend, Conducted by S.T. Coleridge, No

Samuel Taylor Coleridge

Nabu Public Domain Reprints:

You are holding a reproduction of an original work published before 1923 that is in the public domain in the United States of America, and possibly other countries. You may freely copy and distribute this work as no entity (individual or corporate) has a copyright on the body of the work. This book may contain prior copyright references, and library stamps (as most of these works were scanned from library copies). These have been scanned and retained as part of the historical artifact.

This book may have occasional imperfections such as missing or blurred pages, poor pictures, errant marks, etc. that were either part of the original artifact, or were introduced by the scanning process. We believe this work is culturally important, and despite the imperfections, have elected to bring it back into print as part of our continuing commitment to the preservation of printed works worldwide. We appreciate your understanding of the imperfections in the preservation process, and hope you enjoy this valuable book.

THE FRIEND:

In Three Volumes.

VOL. I.

FOURTH EDITION:

With the Author's laſt Corrections and an Appendix, and with a Synoptical Table of the Contents of the Work.

BY HENRY NELSON COLERIDGE, M.A.

THE FRIEND:

A SERIES OF ESSAYS

To aid in the Formation of fixed Principles in Politics,
Morals, and Religion, with Literary
Amuſements interſperſed:

BY SAMUEL TAYLOR COLERIDGE.

VOL. I.

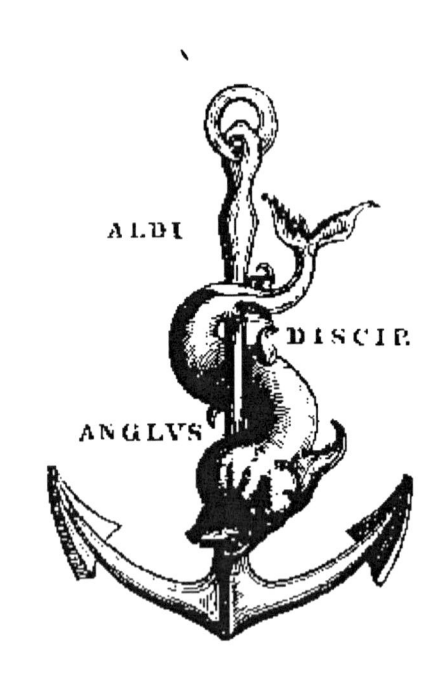

ALDI DISCIP. ANGLVS

LONDON
WILLIAM PICKERING
1850

Now for the writing of this werke,
I, who am a lonesome clerke,
Purposed for to write a book
After the world, that whilome took
Its course in oldè days long passed:
But for men sayn, it is now lassed
In worser plight than it was tho,
I thought me for to touch also
The world which neweth every day—
So as I can, so as I may,
Albeit I sickness have and pain,
And long have had, yet would I fain
Do my mind's hest and besiness,
That in some part, so as I guess,
The gentle mind may be advised.

   GOWER, *Pro. to the Confess. Amantis.*

ADVERTISEMENT.

THE present edition of THE FRIEND comprises all the corrections, and most of the notes, found in the author's handwriting in an interleaved copy of the work, bequeathed by him to his daughter-in-law. The Editor has revised the text with as much care as circumstances would permit, and has added a preliminary sketch of the plan and details of the whole, with an appendix, containing several passages, parts of the scattered essays originally published in 1809, and omitted in the recast of the work in 1818, but which seem worthy of separate preservation. It is earnestly hoped that what has thus been done may further the more general acceptance of a work, which, with all its imperfections, is, perhaps, the most vigorous of Mr. Coleridge's compositions; and which, if it had contained nothing but the essays, in the first volume, on the duty and conditions of communicating truth, and those in the third, on the principles of scientific method, with the reconcilement of the Platonic and Baconian processes of investigation, would still, as the Editor conceives, have constituted one of the most signal benefits conferred in this age on the cause of morals and sound philosophy.

Lincoln's Inn,
11th September, 1837.

OBJECT AND PLAN OF THE WORK

THE FRIEND consists of a methodical series of essays, the principal purpose of which is to assist the mind in the formation for itself of sound, and therefore permanent and universal, principles in regard to the investigation, perception, and retention of truth, in what direction soever it may be pursued; but pre-eminently with reference to the three great relations in which we are placed in this world,—as citizens to the state, as men to our neighbours, and as creatures to our Creator,—in other words, to politics, to morals, and to religion. The author does not exhibit any perfect scheme of action or system of belief in any one of these relations; and that he has not done so, nor meant to do so, are points which must be borne in mind by every reader who would understand and fairly appreciate the work. For its scope is to prepare and discipline the student's moral and intellectual being,—not to propound dogmas or theories for his adoption. The book is not the plan of a palace, but a manual of the rules of architecture. It is a προπαίδευμα,—something to set the mind in a state of pure recipiency for the specific truths of philosophy, and to arm its faculties with power to recognise and endure their presence.

In pursuing, however, this main design, the author has examined with more or less minuteness many particular systems and codes of opinion lying in his way; and in stating the grounds of his rejection of some, and entire or partial admission of others of them, he has in effect expressed his own convictions upon several of the most important questions, yet disputed in moral and political philosophy. But it is not so much to any given conclusion so expressed that the reader's attention seems to be invited, as to the reasoning founded on principles of universal application, by which such conclusion has been evolved;—the primary and prevailing aim throughout the work being, as well under the forms of criticism, biography, local description, or personal anecdote, as of direct moral, political, or metaphysical disquisition, to lay down and illustrate certain fundamental distinctions and rules of intellectual action, which, if well grounded and thoroughly taken up and appropriated, will give to every one the power of working out, under any circumstances, the conclusions of truth for himself. The game from time to time started and run down may be rich and curious; but still at the end of the day it is the chase itself, the quickened eye, the lengthened breath, the firmer nerve, that must ever be the huntsman's best reward.

The Friend is divided into two main sections; the first comprising a discussion of the principles of political knowledge; the second treating of the grounds of morals and religion, and revealing the systematic discipline of mind requisite for a true understanding of the same. To these is prefixed a general introduction, for the greater part devoted to a statement of the duty of communicating the truth, and of the conditions under which it may be communicated safely; and three several collections of essays, in some degree miscellaneous and called Landing-Places — interposed in different places for amusement, retrospect, and preparation —complete the work.

TABLE OF CONTENTS.

THE following synoptical view of the plan and contents of The Friend may prove useful to those who read the work for the first time in the present edition.

GENERAL INTRODUCTION.

VOL. I. ESSAYS I—XVI. pp. 1—162.

Essay

Particular Introduction. Essays I—IV. pp. 1—36.
- I. Design of the work.
- II. Ditto continued: necessity of attention and thought, and distinction between them.
- III. Style: author's hopes and expectations.
- IV. Defence against charges of arrogance and presumption.

Duty of the communication of truth, and the conditions under which it may be safely communicated. Essays V—XIII. pp. 37—125.
- V. Inexpediency of pious frauds: indifference of truth and falsehood denied: objection from the impossibility of conveying an adequate notion answered.
- VI. Conditions, under which right, though inadequate, notions may be taught.
- VII.
- VIII. } Application of those conditions to publications by the press;— 1. as between an individual
- IX. and his own conscience.
- X. Ditto.—2. as between the publisher and the state: free press.
- XI. Law of libel: its anomalies and peculiar difficulties.
- XII. Despotism and insecurity without a free press: Charlemagne and Buonaparte.
- XIII. Only solution of the difficulties of the law of libel compatible with a free press: toleration and tolerance.

Necessity of principles founded in the reason as the basis of all genuine expedience. Essays XIV—XVI. pp. 126—162.

Essay
- XIV. Clearness of conceptions in the understanding essential to purity in the will: duty of communicating knowledge.
- XV. Right use of metaphysic reasoning: principles founded in reason the sole root of prudence: distinctive powers of the human mind.
- XVI. Supremacy of the reason: power given by acting on principle: falsehood and unworthiness of modern principles in taste, morals, and religion.

FIRST LANDING-PLACE.

VOL. I. ESSAYS I—V. pp. 165—212.

Historic parallels. Essays I. & II. pp. 165—186.

Essay
- I. Voltaire and Erasmus: Rousseau and Luther.
- II. Luther's visions in the Warteburg.

Theory of Apparitions. Essay III. pp. 187—191.
- III. Theory to explain Luther's visions: apostrophe on Thomas Wedgwood.

Review of the work and prospect. Essay IV. pp. 192—200.
- IV. Purpose of the Landing-Places: summary of the preceding essays: use of the term 'reason.'

On the Reason and the Understanding. Essay V. pp. 201—212.
- V. Do. continued: the reason and the understanding distinguished: their mutual and necessary relation: eduction of the conscience.

FIRST SECTION.

On the Principles of Political Knowledge.

VOL. I. ESSAYS I—IV. pp. 215—270.

VOL. II. ESSAYS I—XII. pp. 1—196.

Essay

Three systems of political justice, or Three theories on the origin of Government.
Vol. I.
Essays I—IV.
pp. 215—270.
Vol. II.
Essay I.
pp. 1—26.

I. System of Hobbes: fear and the force of custom: confutation.
II. Do. continued: spirit of law: use of the phrase, 'original contract.'
III. System of expedience and prudence —adopted: system of the pure reason: motives for exposing its falsehood.
IV. Statement of the system: Rousseau's 'Social Contract,' and Paine's 'Rights of Man:' French physiocratic philosophers: Cartwright: confutation.
I. Cartwright: party-spirit: Jacobins and Anti-Jacobins: injudicious treatment of the former by the latter.

Personal retrospect.
Essay II.
pp. 27—33.

II. The author never a Jacobin: pantisocracy: peace of Amiens, its character and good effects.

Political Reform.
Essays III—V.
pp. 34—83.

III. Vulgar errors respecting taxes and taxation: true principles: national debt.
IV. Classes of political reformers: elective franchise.
V. Catechism preparatory to examination of the principles of the English Government: letter of Decatur's, and anecdotes illustrative of principles

FIRST SECTION.

International Law.
Essays VI—X.
pp. 84—159.

Essay
- VI. Review of circumstances which led to the peace of Amiens, and recommencement of the war, especially with regard to the occupation of Malta, — introductory to, and as commentary on, the subject of international law.
- VII.
- VIII. Interposed in vindication of freedom of thought, and of the duty of searching out, and abiding by, the truth: reason and faith: extracts from Taylor and Bedell.
- IX. Law of nations: cosmopolitism and nationality.
- X. Law of nations continued: modern political economy: balance of European power: allegoric fable on the seizure of the Danish fleet: defence of the principle.

Principles of political conduct.
Essay XI.
pp. 160—178.

- XI. Doctrine of general consequences as the best criterion of the right or wrong of particular actions not tenable in reason, or safe in practice.

True love of liberty.
Essay XII.
pp. 179—196.

- XII. Address delivered at Bristol in 1795.

SECOND LANDING-PLACE.

VOL. II. ESSAYS I—IV. pp. 207—261.

Miseries of misgovernment in a country nominally free.
Essay I.
pp. 199—223.

Essay
- I. Tale of Maria Eleonora Schöning.

Principles of true biography.
Essay II.
pp. 224—234.

- II. Spirit of anecdote-mongering condemned: extract from R. North's Life of Lord Keeper Guilford.

TABLE OF CONTENTS.

Miscellaneous. Essays III. and IV. pp. 235—250.
- Essay
- III. Fable of Irus (Buonaparte) and Toxaris: Christmas within, and out of, doors in North Germany: extract from Mr. Wordsworth's MS. poem.
- IV. Rabbinical tales.

SECOND SECTION.

On the Grounds of Morals and Religion, and the Discipline of the Mind requisite for a true Understanding of the same.

VOL. III. ESSAYS I—XI. pp. 1—206.

Introduction. pp. 1—48.
- Letter from Mathetes (Professor Wilson and Mr. A. Blair): internal and external difficulties to a mind endeavouring to establish itself on sure principles, moral and intellectual: answer by The Friend (Mr. Wordsworth): advice and caution.

Dignity and necessity of speculative philosophy, and a history of its decline. Essays I—III. pp. 51—102.
- Essay
- I. Relation of morality and religion: pamphlets of the age of Charles I.: extract: sanity of true genius: distinction between genius, talent, sense, and cleverness: relative character of the national mind of Germany, England, and France.
- II. Self-interest and conscience: ethics not founded on utility: honour: universal assent a presumption of truth: ground of belief in miracles: true Christian enthusiasm: mysteries of faith not to be explained by mere human analogies: Taylor's latitudinarianism.
- III. Greek sophists: their character and principles: separation of ethics

SECOND SECTION.

Essay

{ from religion: the author's convictions of the nature and results of the history of the last century and a half.

Principles of the Science of Method. Essays IV—XI. pp. 103—206.

IV. Method, in the will and in the understanding: illustrated from Shakspeare: founded on observation of relations of things: want and excess of generalization: necessity of a mental initiative: definition of method.

V. Two kinds of relations in which objects of mind may be considered: 1. Law: synthetic and analytic process: Plato's view.

VI. 2.—Theory: method in the fine arts intermediate: poetry and music: mental initiative in botany: history and estimate of the science: in chemistry.

VII. Intention of Plato's writings: zoology and John Hunter: theory cannot supply the principle of method: nor hypothesis: necessity of an idea: contrast between the state of science as to electricity and magnetism: law of polarity.

VIII. True character of Plato: Aristotle: unpleasant side of Bacon's character: Hooke: Kepler: Tycho Brahe: reconcilement of the Platonic and Baconian methods.

IX. Investigation of the Baconian method: shown to be essentially one with the Platonic, but in a different direction: method the guiding light in education and cultivation.

X. Existence of a self-organizing purpose in nature and man: illustrated: operation of this idea in the history of mankind: patriarchal state: corrupted into a polytheism: early Greeks: their idolatry checked by the physical theology of the mysteries: portion which they represented of the education of man: their discoveries in the region

Principles of the Science of Method (*continued*).

Essay

of the pure intellect and success in the arts of imagination contrasted with their crude essays in the investigation of physical laws and phænomena: Romans: Hebrews the mid-point of a line, toward which the Greeks as the ideal, and the Romans as the material, pole were approximating, — Christianity the synthesis.

XI. Trade and Literature essential to a nation: consequences of the commercial spirit preponderating: difference of ultimate aims in men and nations: evidence of objective reality in man himself: nature and man, union and difference: mere being in its essence: the idea, whence originated: revelation: God: the material world made for man: universal laws for the whole tempered by particular laws for the individual in nature and man: causation: invisible nexus: ground of union: difference between the reason and the understanding: what they can respectively achieve: method of the will: religious faith.

THIRD LANDING-PLACE.

VOL. III. ESSAYS I—VI. pp. 209—286.

Existence of luck or fortune under the Christian scheme. Essay I. pp. 209—214.

Essay

I. Fortune favours fools: different meanings of the proverb: luck has a real existence in human affairs: how: invidious use of the phrase.

THIRD LANDING-PLACE.

Notices of the life and character of Sir Alexander Ball, and of the circumstances of the English occupation of Malta. Essays II—VI. pp. 215—286.

Essay

II. Impression left by Sir A. B. on the author: state of Malta: corruption.

III. Personal memoir of Sir A. B.: anecdotes of him.

IV. Ball and Nelson: Nelson's reliance on him: Ball at the battle of the Nile: explosion of the ship *L'Orient*: anecdote.

V. Ball's habits of mind: conduct during siege of Valetta: behaviour of English to foreigners: Ball's decisive conduct with the court of Naples: unjust and unwise treatment of the Maltese by the British government.

VI. Ball's popularity in Malta: jealousy of him in the government: discussion of the importance of Malta to this country.

*FRIEND! were an author privileged to name his own judge,—in addition to moral and intellectual competence I should look round for some man, whose knowledge and opinions had for the greater part been acquired experimentally; and the practical habits of whose life had put him on his guard with respect to all speculative reasoning, without rendering him insensible to the desirableness of principles more secure than the shifting rules and theories generalized from observations merely empirical, or unconscious in how many departments of knowledge, and with how large a portion even of professional men, such principles are still a *desideratum*. I would select, too, one who felt kindly, nay, even partially, toward me; but one whose partiality had its strongest foundations in hope, and more prospective than retrospective would make him quick-sighted in the detection, and unreserved in the exposure, of the de-

---

* Dedication to the second edition.—*Ed.*

ficiencies and defects of each present work, in the anticipation of a more developed future. In you, honoured friend! I have found all these requisites combined and realized: and the improvement, which these essays have derived from your judgment and judicious suggestions, would, of itself, have justified me in accompanying them with a public acknowledgment of the same. But knowing, as you cannot but know, that I owe in great measure the power of having written at all to your medical skill, and to the characteristic good sense which directed its exertion in my behalf; and whatever I may have written in happier vein to the influence of your society and to the daily proofs of your disinterested attachment;—knowing too, in how entire a sympathy with your feelings in this respect the partner of your name has blended the affectionate regards of a sister or daughter with almost a mother's watchful and unwearied solicitudes alike for my health, interest, and tranquillity;—you will not, I trust, be pained,—you ought not, I am sure, to be surprised—that

TO

MR. AND MRS. GILLMAN,

OF HIGHGATE,

Thefe Volumes are Dedicated, in teftimony of high

refpect and grateful affection, by

their Friend,

S. T. COLERIDGE.

October 7, 1818.
   Highgate.

THE FRIEND.

ESSAY I.

Crede mihi, non est parvæ fiduciæ, polliceri opem decertantibus, consilium dubiis, lumen cæcis, spem dejectis, refrigerium fessis. Magna quidem hæc sunt, si fiant; parva, si promittantur. Verum ego non tam aliis legem ponam, quam legem vobis meæ propriæ mentis exponam; quam qui probaverit, teneat; cui non placuerit, abjiciat. Optarem, fateor, talis esse, qui prodesse possem quam plurimis.
PETRARCH. *De vita solitaria.**

Believe me, it requires no little confidence, to promise help to the struggling, counsel to the doubtful, light to the blind, hope to the despondent, refreshment to the weary. These are indeed great things, if they be accomplished; trifles if they exist but in a promise. I, however, aim not so much to prescribe a law for others, as to set forth the law of my own mind; which let the man, who shall have approved of it, abide by; and let him, to whom it shall appear not reasonable, reject it. It is my earnest wish, I confess, to employ my understanding and acquirements in that mode and direction, in which I may be enabled to benefit the largest number possible of my fellow-creatures.

ANTECEDENTLY to all history, and long glimmering through it as a holy tradition, there presents itself to our imagination an indefinite period,

---

* Lib. I. tract. iv. c. 4. Some clauses in the original

dateless as eternity; a state rather than a time. For even the sense of succession is lost in the uniformity of the stream.

It was toward the close of this golden age (the memory of which the self-dissatisfied race of men have everywhere preserved and cherished) when conscience acted in man with the ease and uniformity of instinct; when labour was a sweet name for the activity of sane minds in healthful bodies, and all enjoyed in common the bounteous harvest produced, and gathered in, by common effort; when there existed in the sexes, and in the individuals of each sex, just variety enough to permit and call forth the gentle restlessness and final union of chaste love and individual attachment, each seeking and finding the beloved one by the natural affinity of their beings; when the dread Sovereign of the universe was known only as the universal parent, no altar but the pure heart, and thanksgiving and grateful love the sole sacrifice.——

In this blest age of dignified innocence one of their honoured elders, whose absence they were beginning to notice, entered with hurrying steps the place of their common assemblage at noon, and instantly attracted the general attention and wonder by the perturbation of his gestures, and by a strange trouble both in his eyes and over his whole countenance. After a short but deep silence, when the

---

are omitted, and one or two changes of words have been made, by the Author, in this quotation.—*Ed.*

first buzz of varied inquiry was becoming audible, the old man moved toward a small eminence, and having ascended it, he thus addressed the hushed and listening company :—

"In the warmth of the approaching mid-day, as I was reposing in the vast cavern, out of which, from its northern portal, issues the river that winds through our vale, a voice powerful, yet not from its loudness, suddenly hailed me. Guided by my ear I looked toward the supposed place of the sound for some form, from which it had proceeded. I beheld nothing but the glimmering walls of the cavern. Again, as I was turning round, the same voice hailed me: and whithersoever I turned my face, thence did the voice seem to proceed. I stood still therefore, and in reverence awaited its continuation. 'Sojourner of earth!' (these were its words) 'hasten to the meeting of thy brethren, and the words which thou now hearest, the same do thou repeat unto them. On the thirtieth morn from the morrow's sun-rising, and during the space of thrice three days and thrice three nights, a thick cloud will cover the sky, and a heavy rain fall on the earth. Go ye therefore, ere the thirtieth sun arise, retreat to the cavern of the river and there abide, till the clouds have passed away and the rain be over and gone. For know ye of a certainty that whomever that rain wetteth, on him, yea, on him and on his children's children will fall—the spirit of madness.' Yes! madness was the word of the voice: what this be, I know not! But at the sound of the word trembling came upon me, and a feeling which I would not have had; and I remained even as ye beheld and now behold me."

The old man ended, and retired. Confused murmurs succeeded, and wonder, and doubt. Day followed day, and every day brought with it a diminution of the awe impressed. They could attach no image, no remembered sensations, to the threat. The ominous morn arrived, the prophet had retired to the appointed cavern, and there remained alone during the appointed time. On the tenth morning, he emerged from his place of shelter, and sought his friends and brethren. But alas! how affrightful the change! Instead of the common children of one great family, working towards the same aim by reason, even as the bees in their hives by instinct, he looked and beheld, here a miserable wretch watching over a heap of hard and innutritious small substances, which he had dug out of the earth, at the cost of mangled limbs and exhausted faculties. This he appeared to worship, at this he gazed, even as the youths of the vale had been accustomed to gaze at their chosen virgins in the first season of their choice. There he saw a former companion speeding on and panting after a butterfly, or a withered leaf whirling onward in the breeze; and another with pale and distorted countenance following close behind, and still stretching forth a dagger to stab his precursor in the back. In another place he observed a whole troop of his fellowmen famished and in fetters, yet led by one of their brethren who had enslaved them, and pressing furiously onwards in the hope of famishing and enslaving another troop moving in an opposite direction. For the first time, the prophet missed his accustomed power of distinguishing between his dreams and his waking perceptions. He stood gazing and motionless, when several of the race gathered around him, and inquired of each other, Who is this man? how strangely he looks! how wild!—a worthless idler! exclaims one: assuredly, a very dangerous madman! cries a second. In short, from words they proceeded to violence: till harassed, endangered, solitary in a world of forms like his own, without sympathy, without object of love, he at length espied in some fofs or furrow a quantity of the maddening water still unevaporated, and uttering the last words of reason, IT IS IN VAIN TO BE SANE IN A WORLD OF MADMEN, plunged and rolled himself in the liquid poison, and came out as mad as, and not more wretched than, his neighbours and acquaintances.

The plan of The Friend is comprised in the motto to this essay. This tale or allegory seems to me to contain the objections to its practicability in all their strength. Either, says the sceptic, you are the blind offering to lead the blind, or you are talking the language of sight to those who do not possess the sense of seeing. If you mean to be read, try to entertain and do not pretend to instruct. To such objections it would be amply sufficient, on my system of faith, to answer, that we are not all blind, but all subject to distempers of the mental sight, differing in kind and in degree; that though all men are in error, they are not all in the same error, nor at the same time; and that each therefore may possibly heal the other, even as two or more physicians, all diseased in their general health, yet under the immediate action of the disease on different days, may remove or alleviate the complaints of each other. But in respect to the entertainingness of moral writings, if in entertainment be included whatever delights the imagination or affects the generous passions, so far from rejecting such a mean of persuading the human soul, my very system compels me to defend not only the propriety, but the absolute necessity, of adopting it, if we really intend to render our fellow-creatures better or wiser.

But it is with dulness as with obscurity. It may be positive, and the author's fault; but it may likewise be relative, and if the author has presented his bill of fare at the portal, the reader has himself only to blame. The main question then is, of what class are the persons to be entertained?—" One of the later school of the Grecians (says Lord Bacon) examineth the matter, and is at a stand to think what should be in it that men should love lies, where neither they make for pleasure, as with poets; nor for advantage, as with the merchant; but for the lie's sake. But I cannot tell: this same truth is a naked and open day-light, that doth not shew the masques and mummeries and triumphs of the world half so stately and daintily, as candle-lights. Truth may perhaps come to the price of a pearl, that sheweth best by day; but it will not rise to the price of a diamond or carbuncle, that sheweth best in varied lights. A mixture of a lie doth ever add pleasure. Doth any man doubt, that if there were taken from men's minds, vain opinions, flattering hopes, false valuations, imaginations as one would, and the like, but it would leave the minds of a number of men, poor shrunken things, full of melancholy and indisposition, and unpleasing to themselves?" *

A melancholy, a too general, but not, I trust, a universal truth!—and even where it does apply, yet in many instances not irremediable. Such at least must have been my persuasion: or the present volumes must have been wittingly written to no purpose. If I believed our nature fettered to all this wretchedness of head and heart by an absolute and innate necessity, at least by a necessity which no human power, no efforts of reason or eloquence, could remove or lessen; I should deem it even presumptuous to aim at other or higher object than that of amusing a small portion of the reading public.

And why not? whispers worldly prudence. To amuse, though only to amuse, our visitors, is wisdom as well as good-nature, where it is presumption to attempt their amendment. And truly it

---

* Essays. I. Of Truth.—*Ed.*

would be most convenient to me in respects of no trifling importance, if I could persuade myself to take the advice. Released by these principles from all moral obligation, and ambitious of procuring pastime and self-oblivion for a race, which could have nothing noble to remember, nothing desirable to anticipate, I might aspire even to the praise of the critics and *dilettanti* of the higher circles of society; of some trusty guide of blind fashion; some pleasant analyst of taste, as it exists both in the palate and the soul; some living gauge and mete-wand of past and present genius. But alas! my former studies would still have left a wrong bias! If instead of perplexing my common sense with the flights of Plato, and of stiffening over the meditations of the imperial Stoic, I had been labouring to imbibe the gay spirit of a Casti, or had employed my erudition, for the benefit of the favoured few, in elucidating the interesting deformities of ancient Greece and India, what might I not have hoped from the suffrage of those, who turn in weariness from the Paradise Lost, because compared with the prurient heroes and grotesque monsters of Italian romance, or even with the narrative dialogues of the melodious Metastasio, that adventurous song,

> Which justifies the ways of God to man,—

has been found a poor substitute for a Grimaldi, a most inapt medicine for an occasional propensity to yawn! For, as hath been decided, to fill up pleasantly the brief intervals of fashionable pleasures, and above all to charm away the dusky gnome of *ennui*, is the chief and appropriate business of the poet and — the novelist! This duty unfulfilled, Apollo will have lavished his best gifts in vain; and Urania henceforth must be content to inspire astronomers alone, and leave the sons of verse to more amusing patronesses. And yet — and yet — but it will be time to be serious, when my visitors have sat down.

ESSAY II.

Sic oportet ad librum, presertim miscellanei generis, legendum accedere lectorem, ut solet ad convivium conviva civilis. Convivator annititur omnibus satisfacere: et tamen si quid apponitur, quod hujus aut illius palato non respondeat, et hic et ille urbane dissimulant, et alia fercula probant, ne quid contristent convivatorem. Quis enim eum convivam ferat, qui tantum hoc animo veniat ad mensam, ut carpens quæ apponuntur, nec vescatur ipse, nec alios vesci sinat? Et tamen his quoque reperias inciviliores, qui palam, qui sine fine damnent ac lacerent opus, quod nunquam legerint. Ast hoc plusquam sycophanticum est damnare quod nescias.

ERASMUS.

A reader should sit down to a book, especially of the miscellaneous kind, as a well-behaved visitor does to a banquet. The master of the feast exerts himself to satisfy all his guests; but if after all his care and pains there should still be something or other put on the table that does not suit this or that person's taste, they politely pass it over without noticing the circumstance, and commend other dishes, that they may not distress their kind host, or throw any damp on his spirits. For who could tolerate a guest that accepted an invitation to your table with no other purpose but that of finding fault with every thing put before him, neither eating himself, nor suffering others to eat in comfort. And yet you may fall in with a still worse set than even these, with churls that in all companies and without stop or stay, will condemn and pull to pieces a work which they have never read. But this sinks below the baseness of an informer, yea, though he were a false witness to boot! The man, who abuses a thing of which he is utterly ignorant, unites the infamy of both—and in addition to this, makes himself the pander and sycophant of his own and other men's envy and malignity.

THE musician may tune his instrument in private, ere his audience have yet assembled: the architect conceals the foundation of his building beneath the superstructure. But an author's harp must be tuned in the hearing of those, who are to understand its after harmonies; the foundation stones of his edifice must lie open to common view, or his friends will hesitate to trust themselves beneath the roof.

From periodical literature the general reader deems himself entitled to expect amusement, and some degree of information, and if the writer can convey any instruction at the same time and without demanding any additional thought (as the Irishman, in the hackneyed jest, is said to have passed off a light guinea between two good halfpence), this supererogatory merit will not perhaps be taken amiss. Now amusement in and for itself may be afforded by the gratification either of the curiosity or of the passions. I use the former word as distinguished from the love of knowledge, and the latter in distinction from those emotions which arise in well-ordered minds, from the perception of truth or falsehood, virtue or vice:—emotions, which are always preceded by thought, and linked with improvement. Again, all information pursued without any wish of becoming wiser or better thereby, I class among the gratifications of mere curiosity, whether it be sought for in a light novel or a grave history. We may therefore omit the word information, as included either in amusement or instruction.

The present work is an experiment; not whether a writer may honestly overlook the one, or successfully omit the other, of the two elements themselves, which serious readers at least persuade themselves that they pursue; but whether a change might not be hazarded of the usual order, in which periodical writers have in general attempted to convey them. Having myself experienced that no delight either in kind or degree is equal to that which accompanies the distinct perception of a fundamental truth, relative to our moral being; having, long after the completion of what is ordinarily called a learned education, discovered a new world of intellectual profit opening on me—not from any new opinions, but lying, as it were, at the roots of those which I had been taught in childhood in my catechism and spelling-book; there arose a soothing hope in my mind that a lesser public might be found, composed of persons susceptible of the same delight, and desirous of attaining it by the same process. I heard a whisper too from within, (I trust that it proceeded from conscience not vanity) that a duty was performed in the endeavour to render it as much easier to them, than it had been to me, as could be effected by the united efforts of my understanding and imagination.

Actuated by this impulse, the writer wishes, in the following essays, to convey not instruction merely, but fundamental instruction; not so much to show the reader this or that fact, as to kindle his own torch for him, and leave it to himself to choose the particular objects, which he might wish to examine by its light. The Friend does not indeed exclude from his plan occasional interludes, and vacations of innocent entertainment and promiscuous information, but still in the main he proposes to himself the communication of such delight as rewards the march of truth, rather than to collect the flowers which diversify its track, in order to present them apart from the homely, yet foodful or medicinable, herbs, among which they had grown. To refer men's opinions to their absolute principles, and thence their feelings to the appropriate objects, and in their due degrees; and finally, to apply the principles thus ascertained, to the formation of stedfast convictions concerning the most important questions of politics, morality, and religion — these are to be the objects and the contents of his work.

Themes like these not even the genius of a Plato or a Bacon could render intelligible, without demanding from the reader thought sometimes, and attention generally. By thought I here mean the voluntary production in our own minds of those states of consciousness, to which, as to his fundamental facts, the writer has referred us: while attention has for its object the order and connection of thoughts and images, each of which is in itself already and familiarly known. Thus the elements of geometry require attention only; but the analysis of our primary faculties, and the investigation of all the absolute grounds of religion and morals, are impossible without energies of thought in addition to the effort of attention. The Friend will not attempt to disguise from his readers that both attention and thought are efforts, and the latter a most difficult and laborious effort; nor from himself, that to require it often or for any continuance of time, is incompatible with the nature of the present publication, even were it less incongruous than it unfortunately is with the present habits and pursuits of Englishmen. Accordingly I shall be on my guard to make the essays as few as possible, which would require from a well educated reader any energy of thought and voluntary abstraction.

But attention, I confess, will be requisite throughout, except in the excursive and miscellaneous essays that will be found interposed between each of the three main divisions of the work. On whatever subject the mind feels a lively interest, attention, though always an effort, becomes a delightful effort. I should be quite at ease, could I secure for the whole work as much of it, as a card party of earnest whist-players often expend in a single evening, or a lady in the making-up of a fashionable dress. But where no interest previously exists, attention (as every schoolmaster knows) can be procured only by terror: which is the true reason why the majority of mankind learn nothing systematically, except as schoolboys or apprentices.

Happy shall I be, from other motives besides those of self-interest, if no fault or deficiency on my part shall prevent the work from furnishing a presumptive proof, that there are still to be found among us a respectable number of readers who are desirous to derive pleasure from the consciousness of being instructed or meliorated: and who feel a sufficient interest as to the foundations of their own opinions in literature, politics, morals, and religion, to afford that degree of attention, without which, however men may deceive themselves, no actual progress ever was or ever can be made in that knowledge, which supplies at once both strength and nourishment.

ESSAY III.

Ἀλλ' ὡς παρέλαβον τὴν τέχνην παρὰ σοῦ, τὸ πρῶτον μὲν εὐθὺς
Οἰδοῦσαν ὑπὸ κομπασμάτων, καὶ ῥημάτων ἐπαχθῶν,
Ἴσχνανα μὲν πρώτιστον αὐτὴν, καὶ τὸ βάρος ἀφεῖλον,
Ἐπυλλίοις καὶ περιπάτοις καὶ τευτλίοισι μικροῖς
Χυλὸν διδοὺς στωμυλμάτων, ἀπὸ βιβλίων, ἀπ' ἠθῶν.

ARISTOPH. RANÆ. 939.

IMITATION. *

When I received the Muse from you, I found her puffed
    and pampered,
With pompous sentences and terms, a cumbrous huge vi-
    rago.
My first attention was applied to make her look genteelly,
And bring her to a moderate bulk by dint of lighter diet,
I fed her with plain household phrase, and cool familiar
    sallad,
With water-gruel episode, with sentimental jelly,
With moral mince-meat: till at length I brought her within
    compass.   FRERE.

IN the preceding essay I named the present undertaking an experiment. The explanation will be found in the following letter, written to a correspondent during the first attempt, and before the

---

* This imitation is printed here by permission of the author, from a series of free translations of selected scenes from Aristophanes: a work, of which (should the author be

plan was discontinued from an original error in the mode of circulation.

TO ⸺

WHEN I first undertook the present publication for the sake and with the avowed object of referring men in all things to principles or fundamental truths, I was well aware of the obstacles which the plan itself would oppose to my success. For in order to the regular attainment of this object, all the driest and least attractive essays must appear in the beginning, and thus subject me to the necessity of demanding effort or soliciting patience in that part of the work, where it was most my interest to secure the confidence of my readers by winning their favour. Though I dared warrant for the pleasantness of the journey on the whole; though I might promise that the road would, for the far greater part of it, be found plain and easy, that it would pass through countries of various prospect, and that at every stage there would be a change of company; it still remained a heavy disadvantage, that I had to start at the foot of a high and steep hill: and I foresaw, not without occasional feelings of despondency, that during the slow

---

persuaded to make it public) it is my deliberate judgment, that it will form an important epoch in English literature, and open out sources of metrical and rhythmical wealth in the very heart of our language, of which few, if any, among us are aware.

and laborious ascent it would require no common management to keep my passengers in good humour with the vehicle and its driver. As far as this inconvenience could be palliated by sincerity and previous confession, I have no reason to accuse myself of neglect. In the prospectus* of The Friend, which for this cause I reprinted and annexed to the first essay, I felt it my duty to inform such as might be inclined to patronize the publication, that I must submit to be esteemed dull by those who sought chiefly for amusement: and this I hazarded as a general confession, though in my own mind I felt a cheerful confidence that it would apply almost exclusively to the earlier essays. I could not therefore be surprised, however much I may have been depressed, by the frequency with which you hear The Friend complained of for its abstruseness and obscurity; nor did the highly flattering expressions, with which you accompanied your communication, prevent me from feeling its truth to the whole extent.

An author's pen, like children's legs, improves by exercise. That part of the blame which rests on myself, I am exerting my best faculties to remove. A man long accustomed to silent and solitary meditation, in proportion as he increases the power of thinking in long and connected trains, is apt to lose or lessen the talent of communicating his thoughts with grace and perspicuity. Doubt-

---

* See Appendix to Vol. III. *Ed.*

less too, I have in some measure injured my style, in respect to its facility and popularity, from having almost confined my reading, of late years, to the works of the ancients and those of the elder writers in the modern languages. We insensibly imitate what we habitually admire; and an aversion to the epigrammatic unconnected periods of the fashionable Anglo-Gallican taste has too often made me willing to forget, that the stately march and difficult evolutions, which characterize the eloquence of Hooker, Bacon, Milton, and Jeremy Taylor, are, notwithstanding their intrinsic excellence, still less suited to a periodical essay. This fault I am now endeavouring to correct; though I can never so far sacrifice my judgment to the desire of being immediately popular, as to cast my sentences in the French moulds, or affect a style which an ancient critic would have deemed purposely invented for persons troubled with the asthma to read, and for those to comprehend who labour under the more pitiable asthma of a short-witted intellect. It cannot but be injurious to the human mind never to be called into effort: the habit of receiving pleasure without any exertion of thought, by the mere excitement of curiosity and sensibility, may be justly ranked among the worst effects of habitual novel reading. It is true that these short and unconnected sentences are easily and instantly understood: but it is equally true, that wanting all the cement of thought as well as of style, all the connections, and (if you will forgive so trivial a metaphor) all the hooks-and-eyes of the memory, they are as easily forgotten : or rather, it is scarcely possible that they should be remembered.—Nor is it less true, that those who confine their reading to such books dwarf their own faculties, and finally reduce their understandings to a deplorable imbecility: the fact you mention, and which I shall hereafter make use of, is a fair instance and a striking illustration. Like idle morning visiters, the brisk and breathless periods hurry in and hurry off in quick and profitless succession; each indeed for the moments of its stay prevents the pain of vacancy, while it indulges the love of sloth ; but all together they leave the mistress of the house (the soul, I mean) flat and exhausted, incapable of attending to her own concerns, and unfitted for the conversation of more rational guests.

I know you will not suspect me of fostering so idle a hope, as that of obtaining acquittal by recrimination; or think that I am attacking one fault, in order that its opposite may escape notice in the noise and smoke of the battery. On the contrary, I shall do my best, and even make all allowable sacrifices, to render my manner more attractive and my matter more generally interesting. In the establishment of principles and fundamental doctrines, I must of necessity require the attention of my reader to become my fellow-labourer. The primary facts essential to the intelligibility of my principles I can prove to others only as far as I can prevail on them to retire into themselves and make their own minds the objects of their stedfast attention. But, on the other hand, I feel too deeply the importance of the convictions, which first impelled me to the present undertaking, to leave unattempted any honourable means of recommending them to as wide a circle as possible.

Hitherto I have been employed in laying the foundation of my work. But the proper merit of a foundation is its massiveness and solidity. The conveniences and ornaments, the gilding and stucco work, the sunshine and sunny prospects, will come with the superstructure. Yet I dare not flatter myself, that any endeavours of mine, compatible with the duty I owe to truth and the hope of permanent utility, will render The Friend agreeable to the majority of what is called the reading public. I never expected it. How indeed could I, when I was to borrow so little from the influence of passing events, and when I had absolutely excluded from my plan all appeals to personal curiosity and personal interests? Yet even this is not my greatest impediment. No real information can be conveyed, no important errors rectified, no widely injurious prejudices rooted up, without requiring some effort of thought on the part of the reader. But the obstinate (and toward a contemporary writer, the contemptuous) aversion to intellectual effort is the mother evil of all which I had proposed to war against, the queen bee in the hive of our errors and misfortunes, both private and national. To solicit the attention of those, on whom these debilitating causes have acted to their full extent, would be no less absurd than to recommend exercise with the dumb bells, as the only mode of cure, to a patient paralytic in both arms. You well know, that my expectations were more modest as well as more rational. I hoped, that my readers in general would be aware of the impracticability of suiting every essay to every taste in any period of the work; and that they would not attribute wholly to the author, but in part to the necessity of his plan, the austerity and absence of the lighter graces in the first fifteen or twenty numbers. In my cheerful moods I sometimes flattered myself, that a few even among those, who foresaw that my lucubrations would at all times require more attention than from the nature of their own employments they could afford them, might yet find a pleasure in supporting The Friend during its infancy, so as to give it a chance of attracting the notice of others, to whom its style and subjects might be better adapted. But my main anchor was the hope, that when circumstances gradually enabled me to adopt the ordinary means of making the publication generally known, there might be found throughout the kingdom a sufficient number of meditative minds, who, entertaining similar convictions with myself, and gratified by the prospect of seeing them reduced to form and system, would take a warm interest in the work from the very circumstance, that it wanted those allurements of transitory interests, which render particular patronage superfluous, and for the brief season of their blow and fragrance attract the eye of thousands, who would pass unregarded

——————————— flowers
Of sober tint, and herbs of med'cinable powers.

———

In these three introductory essays, the Friend has endeavoured to realize his promise of giving an honest bill of fare, both as to the objects and the style of the work. With reference to both I conclude with a prophecy of Simon Grynæus, from his premonition to the candid reader, prefixed to Ficinus's translation of Plato, published at Leyden, 1557. How far it has been gradually fulfilled in this country since the Revolution in 1688, I leave to my candid and intelligent readers to determine :—

Ac dolet mihi quidem deliciis literarum inescatos subito jam homines adeo esse, præsertim qui Christianos se profitentur, ut legere nisi quod ad presentem gustum *facit, sustineant nihil: unde et disciplinæ et philosophia ipsa jam fere prorsus etiam a doctis negliguntur. Quod quidem propositum studiorum nisi mature corrigetur, tam magnum rebus incommodum dabit, quam dedit barbaries olim. Pertinax res barbaries est, fateor; sed minus potest tamen, quam illa persuasa prudentia literarum si ratione caret, sapientiæ virtutisque specie misere* lectores *circumducens.* * * *

Succedet igitur, ut arbitror, haud ita multo post, pro rusticana sæculi nostri ruditate, captatrix illa blandiloquentia, robur animi virilis omne, omnem virtutem masculam, profligatura, nisi cavetur.*

In very truth, it grieveth me that men, those especially who profess themselves to be Christians, should be so taken with the sweet baits of literature that they can endure to read nothing but what gives them immediate gratification, no matter how low or sensual it may be. Consequently, the more austere and disciplinary branches of philosophy itself are almost wholly neglected, even by the learned.—A course of study (if such reading, with such a purpose in view, could deserve that name) which, if not corrected in time, will occasion worse consequences than even barbarism did in the times of our forefathers. Barbarism is, I own, a wilful headstrong thing; but with all its blind obstinacy it has less power of doing harm than this self-sufficient, self-satisfied plain good common sense sort of writing, this prudent saleable popular style of composition, if it be deserted by reason and scientific insight; pitiably decoying the minds of men by an imposing shew of amiableness, and practical wisdom, so that the delighted reader knowing nothing knows all about almost everything. There will succeed, therefore, in my opinion, and that too

---

* In the original of this passage, the words *gulam* and *mortales* stand respectively for *præsentem gustum* and *lectores*. *Ed.*

within no long time, to the rudeness and rusticity of our age, that ensnaring meretricious popularness in literature, with all the tricksy humilities of the ambitious candidates for the favourable suffrages of the judicious public, which if we do not take good care will break up and scatter before it all robustness and manly vigour of intellect, all masculine fortitude of virtue.

ESSAY IV.

Si modo quæ natura et ratione concessa sint, assumpserimus, præsumptionis suspicio a nobis quam longissime abesse debet. Multa antiquitati, nobismet nihil, arrogamus. Nihilne vos? Nihil mehercule, nisi quod omnia omni animo veritati arrogamus et sanctimoniæ. ULR. RINOV. De Controversiis.

If we assume only what nature and reason have granted, with no shadow of right can we be suspected of presumption. To antiquity we arrogate many things, to ourselves nothing. Nothing? Aye nothing: unless indeed it be, that with all our strength we arrogate all things to truth and moral purity.

IT has been remarked by the celebrated Haller, that we are deaf while we are yawning. The same act of drowsiness that stretches open our mouths, closes our ears. It is much the same in acts of the understanding. A lazy half-attention amounts to a mental yawn. Where then a subject, that demands thought, has been thoughtfully treated, and with an exact and patient derivation from its principles, we must be willing to exert a portion of the same effort, and to think with the author, or the author will have thought in vain for us. It makes little difference for the time being, whether there be an *hiatus oscitans* in the reader's attention, or an *hiatus lacrymabilis* in the author's manuscript. When this occurs during the perusal of a work of known authority and established fame, we honestly lay the fault on our own deficiency, or on the unfitness of our present mood; but when it is a contemporary production, over which we have been nodding, it is far more pleasant to pronounce it insufferably dull and obscure. Indeed, as charity begins at home, it would be unreasonable to expect that a reader should charge himself with lack of intellect, when the effect may be equally well accounted for by declaring the author unintelligible; or that he should accuse his own inattention, when by half a dozen phrases of abuse, as ' heavy stuff, metaphysical jargon, &c.' he can at once excuse his laziness, and gratify his pride, scorn, and envy. To similar impulses we must attribute the praises of a true modern reader, when he meets with a work in the true modern taste: namely, either in skipping, unconnected, short-winded, asthmatic sentences, as easy to be understood as impossible to be remembered, in which the merest common-place acquires a momentary poignancy, a petty titillating sting, from affected point and wilful antithesis; or else in strutting and rounded periods, in which the emptiest truisms are blown up into illustrious bubbles by help of film and inflation. " Aye ! " (quoth the delighted reader) " this is sense, this is genius! this I understand and admire ! I have thought the very same a hundred times myself ! " In other words, this man has reminded me of my own cleverness, and therefore I admire him. Oh! for one piece of egotism that presents itself under its own honest bare face of I myself I, there are fifty that steal out in the mask of *tu-isms* and *ille-isms!*

It has ever been my opinion, that an excessive solicitude to avoid the use of our first personal pronoun more often has its source in conscious selfishness than in true self-oblivion. A quiet observer of human follies may often amuse or sadden his thoughts by detecting a perpetual feeling of purest egotism through a long masquerade of disguises, the half of which, had old Proteus been master of as many, would have wearied out the patience of Menelaus. I say, the patience only: for it would ask more than the simplicity of Polypheme, with his one eye extinguished, to be deceived by so poor a repetition of Nobody. Yet I can with strictest truth assure my readers that with a pleasure combined with a sense of weariness I see the nigh approach of that point of my labours, in which I can convey my opinions and the workings of my heart without reminding the reader obtrusively of myself. But the frequency, with which I have spoken in my own person, recalls my apprehensions to the second danger, which it was my hope to guard against; the probable charge of arrogance, or presumption, both for daring to dissent from the opinions of great authorities, and, in my following numbers perhaps, from the general opinion concerning the true value of certain authorities deemed great. The word, presumption, I appropriate to the internal feeling, and arrogance to the way and manner of outwardly expressing ourselves.

As no man can rightfully be condemned without reference to some definite law, by the knowledge of which he might have avoided the given fault, it is necessary so to define the constituent qualities and conditions of arrogance, that a reason may be assignable why we pronounce one man guilty and acquit another. For merely to call a person arrogant or most arrogant, can convict no one of the vice except perhaps the accuser. I remember, when a young man who had left his books and a glass of water to join a convivial party, each of whom had nearly finished his second bottle, was pronounced very drunk by the whole party — he looked so strange and pale! Many a man, who has contrived to hide his ruling passion or predominant defect from himself, will betray the same to dispassionate observers, by his proneness on all occasions to suspect or accuse others of it. Now arrogance and presumption, like all other moral qualities, must be shewn by some act or conduct: and this too must be an act that implies, if not an immediate concurrence of the will, yet some faulty constitution of the moral habits. For all criminality supposes its essentials to have been within the power of the agent. Either therefore the facts adduced do of themselves convey the whole proof of the charge, and the question rests on the truth or accuracy with which they have been stated; or they acquire their character from the circumstances. I have looked into a ponderous review of the corpuscular philosophy by a Sicilian Jesuit, in which the acrimonious Father frequently expresses his doubt, whether he should pronounce Boyle or Newton more impious than presumptuous, or more presumptuous than impious. They had both attacked the reigning opinions on most important subjects, opinions sanctioned by the greatest names of antiquity, and by the general suffrage of their learned contemporaries or immediate predecessors. Locke was assailed with a full cry for his presumption in having deserted the philosophical system at that time generally received by the universities of Europe; and of late years Dr. Priestley bestowed the epithets of arrogant and insolent on Reid, Beattie, &c. for presuming to arraign certain opinions of Mr. Locke, himself repaid in kind by many of his own countrymen for his theological novelties. It will scarcely be affirmed, that these accusations were all of them just, or that any of them were fit or courteous. Must we therefore say, that in order to avow doubt or disbelief of a popular persuasion without arrogance, it is required that the dissentient should know himself to possess the genius, and foreknow that he should acquire the reputation, of Locke, Newton, Boyle, or even of a Reid or Beattie? But as this knowledge and prescience are impossible in the strict sense of the words, and could mean no more than a strong inward conviction, it is manifest that such a rule, if it were universally established, would encourage the presumptuous, and condemn modest and humble minds alone to silence. And as this silence could not acquit the individual's own mind of presumption, unless it were accompanied by conscious acquiescence; modesty itself must become an inert quality, which even in private society never displays its charms more unequivocally than in its mode of reconciling moral deference with intellectual courage, and general diffidence with sincerity in the avowal of the particular conviction.

We must seek then elsewhere for the true marks, by which presumption or arrogance may be detected, and on which the charge may be grounded with little hazard of mistake or injustice. And as I confine my present observations to literature, I deem such *criteria* neither difficult to determine nor to apply. The first mark, as it appears to me, is a frequent bare assertion of opinions not generally received, without condescending to prefix or annex the facts and reasons on which such opinions were formed; especially if this absence of logical courtesy is supplied by contemptuous or abusive treatment of such as happen to doubt of, or oppose, the decisive *ipse dixi*. But to assert, however nakedly, that a passage in a lewd novel, in which the Sacred Writings are denounced as more likely to pollute the young and innocent mind than a romance notorious for its indecency — to assert, I say, that such a passage argues equal impudence and ignorance in its author, at the time of writing and publishing it—this is not arrogance; although to a vast majority of the decent part of our countrymen it would be superfluous as a truism, if it were exclusively an author's business to convey or revive knowledge, and not sometimes his duty to awaken the indignation of his reader by the expression of his own.

A second species of this unamiable quality, which has been often distinguished by the name of Warburtonian arrogance, betrays itself, not as in the former, by proud or petulant omission of proof or argument, but by the habit of ascribing weakness of intellect, or want of taste and sensibility, or hardness of heart, or corruption of moral principle, to all who deny the truth of the doctrine, or the sufficiency of the evidence, or the fairness of the reasoning adduced in its support. This is indeed not essentially different from the first, but assumes a separate character from its accompaniments: for though both the doctrine and its proofs may have been legitimately supplied by the understanding, yet the bitterness of personal crimination will resolve itself into naked assertion. We are, therefore, authorized by experience, and justified on the principle of self-defence and by the law of fair retaliation, in attributing it to a vicious temper arrogant from irritability, or irritable from arrogance. This learned arrogance admits of many gradations, and is aggravated or palliated, accordingly as the point in dispute has been more or less

ESSAY IV.

controverted, as the reasoning bears a smaller or greater proportion to the virulence of the personal detraction, and as the person or parties, who are the objects of it, are more or less respected, more or less worthy of respect.*

Lastly, it must be admitted as a just imputation of presumption when an individual obtrudes on the public eye, with all the high pretensions of originality, opinions and observations, in regard to which he must plead wilful ignorance in order to be acquitted of dishonest plagiarism. On the same seat must the writer be placed, who in a disquisition on any important subject proves, by falsehoods either of omission or of positive error, that he has neglected to possess himself, not only of the information requisite for this particular subject; but even of those acquirements, and that general knowledge, which could alone authorize him to commence a public instructor. This is an office which

---

* Had the author of the Divine Legation of Moses more skilfully appropriated his coarse eloquence of abuse, his customary assurances of the idiotcy, both in head and heart, of all his opponents; if he had employed those vigorous arguments of his own vehement humour in the defence of truths acknowledged and reverenced by learned men in general; or if he had confined them to the names of Chubb, Woolston, and other precursors of Thomas Payne; we should perhaps still characterize his mode of controversy by its rude violence, but not so often have heard his name used, even by those who have never read his writings, as a proverbial expression for learned arrogance. But when a novel and doubtful hypothesis of his own formation was the citadel to be defended, and his mephitic hand-granados were thrown with the fury of lawless despotism at the fair

cannot be procured *gratis*. The industry, necessary for the due exercise of its functions, is its purchase-money; and the absence or insufficiency of the same is so far a species of dishonesty, and implies a presumption in the literal as well as the ordinary sense of the word. He has taken a thing before he had acquired any right or title thereto.

If in addition to this unfitness which every man possesses the means of ascertaining, his aim should be to unsettle a general belief closely connected with public and private quiet; and if his language and manner be avowedly calculated for the illiterate, and perhaps licentious, part of his countrymen; disgusting as his presumption must appear, it is yet lost or evanescent in the close neighbourhood of his guilt. That Hobbes translated Homer into English verse and published his translation, furnishes no positive evidence of his self-conceit, though it implies a great lack of self-knowledge

---

reputation of a Sykes and a Lardner, we not only confirm the verdict of his independent contemporaries, but cease to wonder, that arrogance should render men objects of contempt in many, and of aversion in all, instances, when it was capable of hurrying a Christian teacher of equal talents and learning into a slanderous vulgarity, which escapes our disgust only when we see the writer's own reputation the sole victim. But throughout his great work, and the pamphlets in which he supported it, he always seems to write as if he had deemed it a duty of decorum to publish his fancies on the Mosaic Law as the Law itself was delivered, that is, in thunders and lightnings: or as if he had applied to his own book instead of the sacred mount, the menace — *There shall not a hand touch it but he shall surely be stoned or shot through.*

and of acquaintance with the nature of poetry.*
A strong wish often imposes itself on the mind for an actual power: the mistake is favoured by the innocent pleasure derived from the exercise of versification, perhaps by the approbation of intimates; and the candidate asks from more impartial readers that sentence, which nature has not enabled him to anticipate. But when the philosopher of Malmesbury waged war with Wallis and the fundamental truths of pure geometry, every instance of his gross ignorance and utter misconception of the very elements of the science he proposed to confute, furnished an unanswerable fact in proof of his high presumption; and the confident and insulting language of the attack leaves the judicious reader in as little doubt of his gross arrogance. An illiterate mechanic, who mistaking some disturbance of his nerves for a miraculous call proceeds alone to convert a tribe of savages, whose language he can have no natural means of acquiring, may have been misled by impulses very different from those of high self-opinion; but the illiterate perpetrator of the 'Age of Reason' must have had his very conscience stupified by the habitual intoxication of presumptuous

---

* At the time I wrote this essay, and indeed till the present month, December, 1818, I had never seen Hobbes' translation of the Odyssey, which, I now find, is by no means to be spoken of contemptuously. It is doubtless as much too ballad-like, as the later versions are too epic; but still, on the whole, it leaves a much truer impression of the original.

arrogance, and his common-sense over-clouded by the vapours from his heart.

As long therefore as I obtrude no unsupported assertions on my readers; and as long as I state my opinions and the evidence which induced or compelled me to adopt them, with calmness and that diffidence in myself, which is by no means incompatible with a firm belief in the justness of the opinions themselves; while I attack no man's private life from any cause, and detract from no man's honours in his public character, from the truth of his doctrines, or the merits of his compositions, without detailing all my reasons and resting the result solely on the arguments adduced; while I moreover explain fully the motives of duty, which influenced me in resolving to institute such investigation; while I confine all asperity of censure, and all expressions of contempt, to gross violations of truth, honour, and decency, to the base corrupter and the detected slanderer; while I write on no subject, which I have not studied with my best attention, on no subject which my education and acquirements have incapacitated me from properly understanding; and above all while I approve myself, alike in praise and in blame, in close reasoning and in impassioned declamation, a steady friend to the two best and surest friends of all men, truth and honesty; I will not fear an accusation of either presumption or arrogance from the good and the wise, I shall pity it from the weak, and welcome it from the wicked.

ESSAY V.

In eodem pectore nullum est honestorum turpiumque consortium: et cogitare optima simul ac deterrima non magis est unius animi quam ejusdem hominis bonum esse ac malum.

QUINCTILIAN.*

There is no fellowship of honour and baseness in the same breast; and to combine the best and the worst designs is no more possible in one mind, than it is for the same man to be at the same instant virtuous and vicious.

Cognitio veritatis omnia falsa, si modo proferantur, etiam quæ prius inaudita erant, et dijudicare et subvertere idonea est. AUGUSTIN.

A knowledge of the truth is equal to the task both of discerning and of confuting all false assertions and erroneous arguments, though never before met with, if only they may freely be brought forward.

I HAVE said, that my very system compels me to make every fair appeal to the feelings, the imagination, and even the fancy. If these are to be withholden from the service of truth, virtue, and happiness, to what purpose were they given? In whose service are they retained? I have indeed considered the disproportion of human passions to

---
* XII. 1. 4.—*Ed.*

their ordinary objects among the strongest internal evidence of our future destination, and the attempt to restore them to their rightful claimants, the most imperious duty and the noblest task of genius. The verbal enunciation of this master truth could scarcely be new to me at any period of my life since earliest youth; but I well remember the particular time, when the words first became more than words to me, when they incorporated with a living conviction, and took their place among the realities of my being. On some wide common or open heath, peopled with anthills, during some one of the gray cloudy days of late autumn, many of my readers may have noticed the effect of a sudden and momentary flash of sunshine on all the countless little animals within his view, aware too that the selfsame influence was darted co-instantaneously over all their swarming cities as far as his eye could reach; may have observed, with what a kindly force the gleam stirs and quickens them all, and will have experienced no unpleasurable shock of feeling in seeing myriads of myriads of living and sentient beings united at the same moment in one gay sensation, one joyous activity! But awful indeed is the same appearance in a multitude of rational beings, our fellow-men, in whom too the effect is produced not so much by the external occasion as from the active quality of their own thoughts. I had walked from Göttingen in the year 1799, to witness the arrival of the Queen of Prussia, on her visit to the

Baron Von Hartzberg's seat, five miles from the University. The spacious outer court of the palace was crowded with men and women, a sea of heads, with a number of children rising out of it from their fathers' shoulders. After a buzz of two hours expectation, the avant-courier rode at full speed into the court. At the loud cracks of his long whip and the trampling of his horse's hoofs, the universal shock and thrill of emotion — I have not language to convey it — expressed as it was in such manifold looks, gestures, and attitudes, yet with one and the same feeling in the eyes of all! Recovering from the first inevitable contagion of sympathy, I involuntarily exclaimed, though in a language to myself alone intelligible, " O man! ever nobler than thy circumstances! Spread but the mist of obscure feeling over any form, and even a woman incapable of blessing or of injuring thee shall be welcomed with an intensity of emotion adequate to the reception of the Redeemer of the world!"

To a creature so highly, so fearfully gifted, — who, alienated as he is by a sorcery scarcely less mysterious than the nature on which it is exercised, yet, like the fabled son of Jove in the evil day of his sensual bewitchment, lifts the spindles and distaffs of Omphale with the arm of a giant — to such a creature truth is self-restoration: for that which is the correlative of truth, the existence of absolute life, is the only object which can attract toward it the whole depth and mass of his fluctuating being, and alone therefore can unite calmness with elevation. But it must be truth without alloy and unsophisticated. It is by the agency of indistinct conceptions, as the counterfeits of the ideal and transcendant, that evil and vanity exercise their tyranny on the feelings of man. The powers of darkness are politic if not wise; but surely nothing can be more irrational in the pretended children of light, than to enlist themselves under the banners of truth, and yet rest their hopes on an alliance with delusion.

As one among the numerous artifices, by which austere truths are to be softened down into palatable falsehoods, and virtue and vice, like the atoms of Epicurus, to receive that insensible *clinamen* which is to make them meet each other half way, I have an especial dislike to the expression, pious frauds. Piety indeed shrinks from the very phrase, as an attempt to mix poison with the cup of blessing: while the expediency of the measures which the words were intended to recommend or palliate, appears more and more suspicious, as the range of our experience widens, and our acquaintance with the records of history becomes more extensive and accurate. One of the most seductive arguments of infidelity grounds itself on the numerous passages in the works of the Christian Fathers, asserting the lawfulness of deceit for a good purpose. For how can we rely on their testimony concerning the supernatural facts? That the Fathers held, almost without exception, that

" wholly without breach of duty it is allowed to the teachers and heads of the Christian Church to employ artifices, to intermix falsehoods with truths, and especially to deceive the enemies of the faith, provided only they hereby serve the interests of truth and the advantage of mankind," * is the unwilling confession of RIBOF. St. Jerome, as is shewn by the citations of this learned theologian, boldly attributes this management—*falsitatem dispensativam*—even to the Apostles themselves. But why speak I of the advantage given to the opponents of Christianity? Alas! to this doctrine chiefly, and to the practices derived from it, we must attribute the utter corruption of the religion itself for so many ages, and even now over so large a portion of the civilized world. By a system of accommodating truth to falsehood, the pastors of the Church gradually changed the life and light of

---

* *De œconom. Patrum. Integrum omnino doctoribus et cœtus Christiani antistitibus esse, ut dolos versent, falsa veris intermisceant, et imprimis religionis hostes fallant, dummodo veritatis commodis et utilitati inserviant.*—I trust, I need not add, that the imputation of such principles of action to the first inspired propagators of Christianity, is founded on a gross misconstruction of those passages in the writings of St. Paul, in which the necessity of employing different arguments to men of different capacities and prejudices, is supposed and acceded to. In other words, St. Paul strove to speak intelligibly, willingly sacrificed indifferent things to matters of importance, and acted courteously as a man, in order to win attention as an Apostle. A traveller prefers for daily use the coin of the nation through which he is passing, to bullion or the mintage of his own country: and is this to justify a succeeding traveller in the use of counterfeit coin?

the Gospel into the very superstitions which they were commissioned to disperse, and thus paganized Christianity in order to christen Paganism. At this very hour Europe groans and bleeds in consequence.

So much in proof and exemplification of the probable expediency of pious deception, as suggested by its known and recorded consequences. An honest man, however, possesses a clearer light than that of history. He knows, that by sacrificing the law of his reason to the maxim of pretended prudence, he purchases the sword with the loss of the arm that is to wield it. The duties which we owe to our own moral being, are the ground and condition of all other duties; and to set our nature at strife with itself for a good purpose, implies the same sort of prudence, as a priest of Diana would have manifested, who should have proposed to dig up the celebrated charcoal foundations of the mighty temple of Ephesus, in order to furnish fuel for the burnt-offerings on its altars. Truth, virtue, and happiness, may be distinguished from each other, but cannot be divided. They subsist by a mutual co-inherence, which gives a shadow of divinity even to our human nature. *Will ye speak wickedly for God; and talk deceitfully for him?** is a searching question, which most affectingly represents the grief and impatience of an uncorrupted mind at perceiving a good cause

---

* Job xiii. 7.—*Ed.*

defended by ill means: and assuredly if any temptation can provoke a well regulated temper to intolerance, it is the shameless assertion, that truth and falsehood are indifferent in their own natures; that the former is as often injurious (and therefore criminal) as the latter, and the latter on many occasions as beneficial (and consequently meritorious) as the former.

I feel it incumbent on me, therefore, to place immediately before my readers in the fullest and clearest light, the whole question of moral obligation respecting the communication of truth, its extent and conditions. I would fain obviate all apprehensions either of my incaution on the one hand, or of any insincere reserve on the other, by proving that the more strictly we adhere to the letter of the moral law in this respect, the more completely shall we reconcile that law with prudence; thus securing a purity in the principle without mischief from the practice. I would not, I could not dare, address my countrymen as a friend, if I might not justify the assumption of that sacred title by more than mere veracity, by open-heartedness. Pleasure, most often delusive, may be born of delusion. Pleasure, herself a sorceress, may pitch her tents on enchanted ground. But happiness (or, to use a far more accurate as well as more comprehensive term, solid well-being) can be built on virtue alone, and must of necessity have truth for its foundation. Add, too, the known fact that the meanest of men feels himself insulted by an unsuccessful attempt to deceive him; and hates and despises the man who has attempted it. What place then is left in the heart for virtue to build on, if in any case we may dare practise on others what we should feel as a cruel and contemptuous wrong in our own persons? Every parent possesses the opportunity of observing how deeply children resent the injury of a delusion; and if men laugh at the falsehoods that were imposed on themselves during their childhood, it is because they are not good and wise enough to contemplate the past in the present, and so to produce by a virtuous and thoughtful sensibility that continuity in their self-consciousness, which nature has made the law of their animal life. Ingratitude, sensuality, and hardness of heart, all flow from this source. Men are ungrateful to others only when they have ceased to look back on their former selves with joy and tenderness. They exist in fragments. Annihilated as to the past, they are dead to the future, or seek for the proofs of it everywhere, only not (where alone they can be found) in themselves. A contemporary poet has expressed and illustrated this sentiment with equal fineness of thought and tenderness of feeling:—

> My heart leaps up when I behold
>   A rain-bow in the sky!
> So was it, when my life began;
> So is it now I am a man;
> So let it be, when I grow old,
>   Or let me die.
> The child is father of the man,

ESSAY V.

And I would wish my days to be
Bound each to each by natural piety.*
WORDSWORTH.

Alas! the pernicious influence of this lax morality extends from the nursery and the school to the cabinet and senate. It is a common weakness with men in power, who have used dissimulation successfully, to form a passion for the use of it, dupes to the love of duping! A pride is flattered by these lies. He who fancies that he must be perpetually stooping down to the prejudices of his fellow-creatures, is perpetually reminding and re-assuring himself of his own vast superiority to them. But no real greatness can long co-exist with deceit. The whole faculties of man must be exerted in order to noble energies; and he who is not earnestly sincere, lives in but half his being, self-mutilated, self-paralyzed.

---

* I am informed, that these very lines have been cited, as a specimen of despicable puerility. So much the worse for the citer. Not willingly in his presence would I behold the sun setting behind our mountains, or listen to a tale of distress or virtue; I should be ashamed of the quiet tear on my own cheek. But let the dead bury the dead! The poet sang for the living. Of what value indeed, to a sane mind, are the likings or dislikings of one man, grounded on the mere assertions of another? Opinions formed from opinions — what are they, but clouds sailing under clouds, which impress shadows upon shadows?

*Fungum pelle procul, jubeo; nam quid mihi fungo?
Conveniunt stomacho non minus ista suo.*

I was always pleased with the motto placed under the figure of the rosemary in old herbals:—

Apage, sus! Haud tibi spiro.

The latter part of the proposition, which has drawn me into this discussion, that, I mean, in which the morality of intentional falsehood is asserted, may safely be trusted to the reader's own moral sense. Is it a groundless apprehension, that the patrons and admirers of such publications may receive the punishment of their indiscretion in the conduct of their sons and daughters? The suspicion of Methodism must be expected by every man of rank and fortune, who carries his examination respecting the books which are to lie on his breakfast-table, farther than to their freedom from gross verbal indecencies, and broad avowals of Atheism in the title-page. For the existence of an intelligent First Cause may be ridiculed in the notes of one poem, or placed doubtfully as one of two or three possible hypotheses, in the very opening of another poem, and both be considered as works of safe promiscuous reading *virginibus puerisque:* and this, too, by many a father of a family, who would hold himself highly culpable in permitting his child to form habits of familiar acquaintance with a person of loose habits, and think it even criminal to receive into his house a private tutor without a previous inquiry concerning his opinions and principles, as well as his manners and outward conduct. How little I am an enemy to free inquiry of the boldest kind, and in which the authors have differed the most widely from my own convictions and the general faith, provided only, the inquiry be conducted with that seriousness, which naturally accompanies the love of truth, and be evidently intended for the perufal of thofe only, who may be prefumed capable of weighing the arguments,—I fhall have abundant occafion of proving in the courfe of this work. *Quin ipfa philofophia talibus e difputationibus non nifi beneficium recipit. Nam fi vera proponit homo ingeniofus veritatifque amans, nova ad eam acceffio fiet: fin falfa, refutatione eorum priores tanto magis ftabilientur.**

The affertion, that truth is often no lefs dangerous than falfehood, founds lefs offenfively at the firft hearing, only becaufe it hides its deformity in an equivocation, or double meaning of the word truth. What may be rightly affirmed of truth, ufed as fynonimous with verbal accuracy, is transferred to it in its higher fenfe of veracity. By verbal truth we mean no more than the correfpondence of a given fact to given words. In moral

---

* GALILÆI *Syft. Cofm.* p. 42.— Moreover, philofophy itfelf cannot but derive benefit from fuch difcuffions. For if a man of genius and a lover of truth brings juft pofitions before the public, there is a frefh acceffion to the ftock of philofophic infight; but if erroneous pofitions, the former truths will by their confutation be eftablifhed fo much the more firmly.

The original is in the following words:—

La filofofia medefima non può fe non ricever benefixio dalle noftre difpute; perchè fe i noftri penfieri faranno veri, nuovi acquifti fi faranno fatti; fe falfi, col ributtargli, maggiormente verranno confermate le prime dottrine.

Dial. I. 44. Padov. 1774.—*Ed.*

truth, we involve likewise the intention of the speaker, that his words should correspond to his thoughts in the sense in which he expects them to be understood by others: and in this latter import we are always supposed to use the word, whenever we speak of truth absolutely, or as a possible subject of moral merit or demerit. It is verbally true, that in the sacred Scriptures it is written: *As is the good, so is the sinner, and he that sweareth as he that feareth an oath. A man hath no better thing under the sun, than to eat, and to drink, and to be merry. There is one event unto all: the living know they shall die, but the dead know not any thing, neither have they any more a reward.** But he who should repeat these words, with this assurance, to an ignorant man in the hour of his temptation, lingering at the door of the alehouse, or hesitating as to the testimony required of him in the court of justice, would, spite of this verbal truth, be a liar, and the murderer of his brother's conscience. Veracity, therefore, not mere accuracy; to convey truth, not merely to say it, is the point of duty in dispute: and the only difficulty in the mind of an honest man arises from the doubt, whether more than veracity, that is, the truth and nothing but the truth—is not demanded of him by the law of conscience; whether it does not exact simplicity; that is, the truth only, and the whole truth. If we can solve this difficulty, if we

---

* Eccles. viii. 15; ix. 2, 5.—*Ed.*

can determine the conditions under which the law of univerſal reaſon commands the communication of the truth independently of conſequences, we ſhall then be enabled to judge whether there is any ſuch probability of evil conſequences from ſuch communication, as can juſtify the aſſertion of its occaſional criminality, as can perplex us in the conception, or diſturb us in the performance, of our duty.

The conſcience, or effective reaſon, commands the deſign of conveying an adequate notion of the thing ſpoken of, when this is practicable: but at all events a right notion, or none at all. A ſchoolmaſter is under the neceſſity of teaching a certain rule in ſimple arithmetic empirically,—(do ſo and ſo, and the ſum will always prove true);—the neceſſary truth of the rule—that is, that the rule having been adhered to, the ſum muſt always prove true—requiring a knowledge of the higher mathematics for its demonſtration. He, however, conveys a right notion, though he cannot convey the adequate one.

ESSAY VI.

Πολυμαθίη κάρτα μὲν ὠφελέει, κάρτα δὲ βλάπτει τὸν ἔχοντα. Ὠφελέει μὲν τὸν δεξιὸν ἄνδρα, βλάπτει δὲ τὸν ῥηϊδίως φωνεῦντα πᾶς ἔπος καὶ ἐν παντὶ δήμῳ. Χρὴ δὲ καιροῦ μέτρα εἰδέναι· σοφίης γὰρ οὗτος ὅρος. Εἰ δὲ οἱ ἔξω καιροῦ ῥῆσιν μουσικὴν πεπνυμένως ἀείσουσιν, οὐ παρα δέχονται ἐν ἀργίῃ γνώμῃ, αἰτίην δ᾽ ἔχουσι μωρίας.

ANAXARCHUS, apud Stobæum, Serm. xxxiv.*

General knowledge and ready talent may be of very great benefit, but they may likewife be of very great diſſervice, to the poſſeſſor. They are highly advantageous to the man of ſound judgment, and dexterous in applying them; but they injure your fluent holder-forth on all ſubjects in all companies. It is neceſſary to know the meaſures of the time and occaſion: for this is the very boundary of wiſdom — (that by which it is defined, and diſtinguiſhed from mere ability). But he, who without regard to the unfitneſs of the time and the audience will ſoar in the high region of his fancies with his garland and ſinging robes about him, will not acquire the credit of ſeriouſneſs amidſt frivolity, but will be condemned for his ſillineſs, as the greateſt idler of the company becauſe the moſt unſeaſonable.

THE moral law, it has been ſhewn, permits an inadequate communication of unſophiſticated truth, on the condition that it alone is practicable, and binds us to ſilence when neither an adequate, nor

---

* Edit. Gaisford.—*Ed.*

even a right, exposition of the truth is in our power. We must first inquire then,—what is necessary to constitute, and what may allowably accompany, a right though inadequate notion,—and, secondly, what are the circumstances, from which we may deduce the impracticability of conveying even a right notion; the presence or absence of which circumstances it therefore becomes our duty to ascertain. In answer to the first question, the conscience demands: 1. That it should be the wish and design of the mind to convey the truth only; that if in addition to the negative loss implied in its inadequateness, the notion communicated should lead to any positive error, the cause should lie in the fault or defect of the recipient, not of the communicator, whose paramount duty, whose inalienable right, it is to preserve his own integrity,* the integral character of his own moral being. Self-respect; the reverence which he owes

---

* The best and most forcible sense of a word is often that, which is contained in its etymology. The author of the poems, the Synagogue, frequently affixed to Herbert's Temple, gives the original purport of the word 'integrity,' in the following lines of the fourth stanza of the eighth poem;*

    Next to sincerity, remember still,
    Thou must resolve upon integrity.
    God will have all thou hast, thy mind, thy will,
    Thy thoughts, thy words, thy works.—

And again, after some verses on constancy and humility, the poem concludes with—

---

* Church-Porch.—*Ed.*

to the presence of humanity in the person of his neighbour; the reverential upholding of the faith of man in man; gratitude for the particular act of confidence; and religious awe for the divine purposes in the gift of language; are duties too sacred and important to be sacrificed to the guesses of an individual, concerning the advantages to be gained by the breach of them. 2. It is further required, that the supposed error shall not be such as will pervert or materially vitiate the imperfect truth, in communicating which we had unwillingly, though not perhaps unwittingly, occasioned it. A barbarian so instructed in the power and intelligence of the infinite Being as to be left wholly ignorant of his moral attributes, would have acquired none but erroneous notions even of the former. At the very best, he would gain only a theory to satisfy his curiosity with; but more probably, would deduce the belief of a Moloch or a Baal. For the idea of an irresistible, invisible, Being naturally produces terror in the mind of uninstructed and unprotected man, and with terror there will be

---

He that desires to see
The face of God, in his religion must
Sincere, entire, constant, and humble be.

Having mentioned the name of Herbert, that model of a man, a gentleman, and a clergyman, let me add, that the quaintness of some of his thoughts, not of his diction, than which nothing can be more pure, manly, and unaffected, has blinded modern readers to the great general merit of his poems, which are for the most part exquisite in their kind.

associated whatever has been accustomed to excite it, anger, vengeance, &c.; as is proved by the mythology of all barbarous nations. This must be the case with all organized truths; the component parts derive their significance from the idea of the whole. Bolingbroke removed love, justice, and choice, from power and intelligence, and yet pretended to have left unimpaired the conviction of a Deity. He might as consistently have paralyzed the optic nerve, and then excused himself by affirming, that he had, however, not touched the eye.

The third condition of a right though inadequate notion is, that the error occasioned be greatly outweighed by the importance of the truth communicated. The rustic would have little reason to thank the philosopher, who should give him true conceptions of the folly of believing in ghosts, omens, dreams, &c. at the price of abandoning his faith in divine providence, and in the continued existence of his fellow-creatures after their death. The teeth of the old serpent planted by the Cadmuses of French literature, under Lewis XV., produced a plenteous crop of philosophers and truth-trumpeters of this kind, in the reign of his successor. They taught many truths, historical, political, physiological, and ecclesiastical, and diffused their notions so widely, that the very ladies and hair-dressers of Paris became fluent encyclopedists: and the sole price which their scholars paid for these treasures of new information, was to believe Christianity an imposture, the Scriptures a forgery, the worship, if not the belief, of God superstition, hell a fable, heaven a dream, our life without providence, and our death without hope. They became as gods as soon as the fruit of this Upas tree of knowledge and liberty had opened their eyes to perceive that they were no more than beasts—somewhat more cunning, perhaps, and abundantly more mischievous. What can be conceived more natural than the result,—that self-acknowledged beasts should first act, and next suffer themselves to be treated, as beasts. We judge by comparison. To exclude the great is to magnify the little. The disbelief of essential wisdom and goodness, necessarily prepares the imagination for the supremacy of cunning with malignity. Folly and vice have their appropriate religions, as well as virtue and true knowledge: and in some way or other fools will dance round the golden calf, and wicked men beat their timbrels and kettle-drums to,—

—Moloch, horrid king, besmeared with blood
Of human sacrifice and parents' tears.

My feelings have led me on, and in my illustration I had almost lost from my view the subject to be illustrated. One condition yet remains: that the error foreseen shall not be of a kind to prevent or impede the after acquirement of that knowledge which will remove it. Observe, how graciously nature instructs her human children. She cannot give us the knowledge derived from sight without occasioning us at first to mistake images of reflection for substances. But the very consequences of the delusion lead inevitably to its detection; and out of the ashes of the error rises a new ~~flower~~ of knowledge. We not only see, but are enabled to discover by what means we see. So, too, we are under the necessity, in given circumstances, of mistaking a square for a round object: but ere the mistake can have any practical consequences, it is not only removed, but in its removal gives us the symbol of a new fact, that of distance. In a similar train of thought, though more fancifully, I might have elucidated the preceding condition, and have referred our hurrying enlighteners and revolutionary amputators to the gentleness of nature, in the oak and the beech, the dry foliage of which she pushes off only by the propulsion of the new buds, that supply its place. My friends! a clothing even of withered leaves is better than bareness.

Having thus determined the nature and conditions of a right notion, it remains to consider the circumstances which tend to render the communication of it impracticable, and oblige us of course, to abstain from the attempt—oblige us not to convey falsehood under the pretext of saying truth. These circumstances, it is plain, must consist either in natural or moral impediments. The former, including the obvious gradations of constitutional insensibility and derangement, preclude all temptation to misconduct, as well as all probability of ill-consequences from accidental oversight, on the part of the communicator. Far otherwise is it with the impediments from moral causes. These demand all the attention and forecast of the genuine lovers of truth in the matter, the manner, and the time of their communications public and private; and these are the ordinary materials of the vain and the factious, determine them in the choice of their audiences and of their arguments, and to each argument give powers not its own. They are distinguishable into two sources, the streams from which, however, most often become confluent, namely, hindrances from ignorance,—(I here use the word in relation to the habits of reasoning as well as to the previous knowledge requisite for the due comprehension of the subject,)—and hindrances from predominant passions.*

From both these the law of conscience commands us to abstain, because such being the ignorance and such the passions of the supposed auditors, we ought to deduce the impracticability of conveying not only adequate but even right notions of our own convictions: much less does it permit us to avail ourselves of the causes of this impracticability in order to procure nominal proselytes, each of whom will have a different, and all a false, conception of those notions that were to be conveyed for their truth's sake alone. What-

---

* See Lay Sermon addressed to the higher and middle classes, p. 16.

ever is, or but for some defect in our moral character would have been, foreseen as preventing the conveyance of ourthoughts, makes the attempt an act of self-contradiction: and whether the faulty cause exist in our choice of unfit words or our choice of unfit auditors, the result is the same and so is the guilt. We have voluntarily communicated falsehood.

Thus, without reference to consequences,—if only one short digression be excepted—from the sole principle of self-consistence or moral integrity, we have evolved the clue of right reason, which we are bound to follow in the communication of truth. Now then let me appeal to the judgment and experience of the reader, whether he who most faithfully adheres to the letter of the law of conscience will not likewise act in strictest correspondence to the maxims of prudence and sound policy. I am at least unable to recollect a single instance, either in history or in my personal experience, of a preponderance of injurious consequences from the publication of any truth, under the observance of the moral conditions above stated: much less can I even imagine any case, in which truth, as truth, can be pernicious. But if the assertor of the indifferency of truth and falsehood in their own natures, attempt to justify his position by confining the word truth, in the first instance, to the correspondence of given words to given facts, without reference to the total impression left by such words,—what is this more than to assert, that articulated sounds are things of moral indifferency;—and that we may relate a fact accurately, and nevertheless deceive grossly and wickedly? Blifil related accurately Tom Jones's riotous joy during his benefactor's illness, only omitting that this joy was occasioned by the physician's having pronounced him out of danger. Blifil was not the less a liar for being an accurate matter-of-fact liar. Tell-truths in the service of falsehood we find everywhere, of various names and various occupations, from the elderly young women that discuss the love affairs of their friends and acquaintances at the village tea-tables, to the anonymous calumniators of literary merit in reviews, and the more daring malignants, who dole out discontent, innovation and panic, in political journals: and a most pernicious race of liars they are! But who ever doubted it?—Why should our moral feelings be shocked, and the holiest words with all their venerable associations be profaned, in order to bring forth a truism! But thus it is for the most part with the venders of startling paradoxes. In the sense in which they are to gain for their author the character of a bold and original thinker, they are false even to absurdity; and the sense in which they are true and harmless, conveys so mere a truism, that it even borders on nonsense. How often have we heard " The rights of man—hurra!—— The sovereignty of the people — hurra!"——roared out by men who, if called upon in another place and before another audience, to explain themselves, would give to the words a meaning, in which the moſt monarchical of their political opponents would admit them to be true, but which would contain nothing new, or ſtrange, or ſtimulant, nothing to flatter the pride, or kindle the paſſions, of the populace!

ESSAY VII.

At profanum vulgus lectorum quomodo arcendum est? Librisne nostris jubeamus, ut coram indignis obmutescant? Si linguis, ut dicitur, emortuis utamur, eheu! ingenium quoque nobis emortuum jacet: sin aliter, — Minervæ secreta crassis ludibrium divulgamus, et Dianam nostram impuris hujus sæculi Actæonibus nudam proferimus. Respondeo: — ad incommoditates hujusmodi evitandas, nec Græce nec Latine scribere opus est. Sufficiet, nos sicca luce usos fuisse et strictiore argumentandi methodo. Sufficiet, innocenter, utiliter scripsisse: eventus est apud lectorem. Nuper emptum est a nobis Ciceronianum istud De Officiis, opus quod semper pæne Christiano dignum putabamus. Mirum! libellus factus fuerat famosissimus. Credisne? Vix: at quomodo? Maligno quodam, nescio quem, plena margine et super tergo, annotatum est, et exemplis, calumniis potius, superfœtatum! Sic et qui introrsum uritur inflammationes animi vel Catonianis (ne dicam, sacrosanctis) paginis accipit. Omni aura mons, omnibus scriptis mens ignita, vescitur.

Rudolphi Langii Epist. ad amicum quemdam
Italicum, in qua linguæ patriæ et hodiernæ
usum defendit et eruditis commendat.

Nec me fallit, ut in corporibus hominum sic in animis multiplici passione affectis, medicamenta verborum multis inefficacia visum iri. Sed nec illud quoque me præterit, ut invisibiles animorum morbos, sic invisibilia esse remedia. Falsis opinionibus circumventi veris sententiis liberandi sunt, ut qui audiendo ceciderant audiendo consurgant.

Petrarch. Prefat. in lib. de remed. utriusque
fortunæ, sub fin.

But how are we to guard against the herd of promiscuous readers? Can we bid our books be silent in the prefence of the unworthy? If we employ what are called the dead languages, our own genius, alas! becomes flat and dead: and if we embody our thoughts in the words native to them or in which they were conceived, we divulge the secrets of Minerva to the ridicule of blockheads, and expose our Diana to the Actæons of a sensual age. I reply: that in order to avoid inconveniences of this kind, we need write neither in Greek nor in Latin. It will be enough, if we abstain from appealing to the bad passions and low appetites, and confine ourselves to a strictly consequent method of reasoning.

To have written innocently, and for wise purposes, is all that can be required of us: the event lies with the reader. I purchased lately Cicero's work, *De Officiis*, which I had always considered as almost worthy of a Christian. To my surprise it had become a most flagrant libel. Nay! but how? —Some one, I know not who, out of the fruitfulness of his own malignity, had filled all the margins and other blank spaces with annotations—a true superfœtation of examples, that is, of false and slanderous tales! In like manner, the slave of impure desires will turn the pages of Cato, not to say, Scripture itself, into occasions and excitements of wanton imaginations. There is no wind but fans a volcano, no work but feeds a combustible mind.

I am well aware, that words will appear to many as inefficacious medicines when administered to minds agitated with manifold passions, as when they are muttered by way of charm over bodily ailments. But neither does it escape me, on the other hand, that as the diseases of the mind are invisible, invisible must the remedies likewise be. Those who have been entrapped by false opinions are to be liberated by convincing truths: that thus having imbibed the poison through the ear they may receive the antidote by the same channel.

THAT our elder writers to Jeremy Taylor inclusively quoted to excess, it would be the very blindness of partiality to deny. More than one might be mentioned, whose works are well characterized in the words of Milton, as a paroxysm of citations, pampered metaphors, and aphorifming pedantry. On the other hand, it seems to me that we now avoid quotations with an anxiety that offends in the contrary extreme. Yet it is the beauty and independent worth of the citations far more than their appropriateness which have made Johnson's Dictionary popular even as a reading book—and the mottos with the translations of them are known to add confiderably to the value of the Spectator. With this conviction I have taken more than common pains in the selection of the mottos for the Friend: and of two mottos equally appropriate prefer always that from the book which is least likely to have come into my readers' hands. For I often please myself with the fancy, now that I may have saved from oblivion the only striking paffage in a whole volume, and now that I may have attracted notice to a writer undefervedly forgotten. If this should be attributed to a filly ambition in the difplay of various reading, I can do no more than deny any confcioufnefs of having been fo actuated: and for the rest, I must confole myself by the reflection, that if it be one of the moft foolish, it is at the same time one of the moft harmless, of human vanities.

The paffages prefixed lead at once to the queftion, which will probably have more than once occurred to the reflecting reader of the preceding effay. How will thefe rules apply to the moft important mode of communication? to that, in which one man may utter his thoughts to myriads of men at the same time, and to myriads of myriads at various times and through successions of generations? How do they apply to authors, whose foreknowledge assuredly does not inform them who, or how many, or of what description, their readers will be? How do these rules apply to books, which once published, are as likely to fall in the way of the incompetent as of the judicious, and will be fortunate indeed if they are not many times looked at through the thick mists of ignorance, or amid the glare of prejudice and passion? — I answer in the first place, that this is not universally true. The readers are not seldom picked and chosen. Relations of certain pretended miracles performed a few years ago, at Holywell, in consequence of prayers to the Virgin Mary, on female servants, and these relations moralized by the old Roman Catholic arguments without the old Protestant answers, have to my knowledge been sold by travelling pedlars in villages and farm-houses, not only in a form which placed them within the reach of the narrowest means, but sold at a price less than their prime cost, and doubtless, thrown in occasionally as the make-weight in a bargain of pins and stay-tape. Shall I be told, that the publishers and reverend authorizers of these base and vulgar delusions had exerted no choice as to the purchasers and readers? But waiving this, or rather having first pointed it out, as an important exception, I further reply, — that if the author have clearly and rightly established in his own mind the class of readers, to which he means to address his communications; and if both in this choice, and in the particulars of the manner and matter of his work, he conscientiously observe all the conditions which reason and conscience have been shewn to dictate, in relation to those for whom the work was designed; he will, in most instances, have effected his design and realized the desired circumscription. The posthumous work of Spinoza —(*Ethica ordine geometrico demonstrata*)—may, indeed, accidentally fall into the hands of an incompetent reader. But, (not to mention, that it is written in a dead language), it will be entirely harmless, because it must needs be utterly unintelligible. I venture to assert, that the whole first book, *De Deo*, might be read in a literal English translation to any congregation in the kingdom, and that no individual who had not been habituated to the strictest and most laborious processes of reasoning, would even suspect its orthodoxy or piety, however heavily the few who listened might complain of its obscurity and want of interest.

This, it may be objected, is an extreme case. But it is not so for the present purpose. I am speaking of the probability of injurious consequences from the communication of truth. This I have denied, if the right means have been adopted, and the necessary conditions adhered to, for its actual communication. Now the truths — that is, the positions believed by the author to be truths—

conveyed in a book are either evident of themselves, or such as require a train of deductions in proof: and the latter will be either such truths as are authorized and generally received; or such as are in opposition to received and authorized opinions; or lastly, positions presented as truths for the appropriate test of examination, and still under trial, *adhuc in lite*. Of this latter class I affirm, that in no one of the three sorts can an instance be brought of a preponderance of ill-consequences, or even of an equilibrium of advantage and injury from a work, in which the understanding alone has been appealed to, by results fairly deduced from just premisses, in terms strictly appropriate. Alas! legitimate reasoning is impossible without severe thinking, and thinking is neither an easy nor an amusing employment. The reader, who would follow a close reasoner to the summit and absolute principle of any one important subject, has chosen a chamois-hunter for his guide. Our guide will, indeed, take us the shortest way, will save us many a wearisome and perilous wandering, and warn us of many a mock road that had formerly led himself to the brink of chasms and precipices, or at best in an idle circle to the spot from which he started. But he cannot carry us on his shoulders: we must strain our own sinews, as he has strained his; and make firm footing on the smooth rock for ourselves, by the blood of toil from our own feet. Examine the journals of our humane and zealous missionaries in Hindoſtan. How often and how feelingly do they deſcribe the difficulty of making the ſimpleſt chain of reaſoning intelligible to the ordinary natives: the rapid exhauſtion of their whole power of attention, and with what pain and diſtreſsful effort it is exerted, while it laſts. Yet it is amongſt individuals of this claſs, that the hideous practices of ſelf-torture chiefly, indeed almoſt excluſively, prevail. O! if folly were no eaſier than wiſdom, it being often ſo very much more grievous, how certainly might not theſe miſerable men be converted to Chriſtianity? But alas! to ſwing by hooks paſſed through the back, or to walk on ſhoes with nails of iron pointed upward on the ſoles, all this is ſo much leſs difficult, demands ſo very inferior an exertion of the will than to think, and by thought to gain knowledge and tranquillity!

It is not true, that ignorant perſons have no notion of the advantages of truth and knowledge. They ſee and confeſs thoſe advantages in the conduct, the immunities, and the ſuperior powers of the poſſeſſors. Were theſe attainable by pilgrimages the moſt toilſome, or penances the moſt painful, we ſhould aſſuredly have as many pilgrims and as many ſelf-tormentors in the ſervice of true religion and virtue, as now exiſt under the tyranny of Papal or Brahman ſuperſtition. This inefficacy of legitimate reaſon, from the want of fit objects,—this its relative weakneſs, and how narrow at all times its immediate ſphere of action muſt be,—is proved to us by the impoſtors of all profeſſions. What, I pray, is their fortreſs, the rock which is both their quarry and their foundation, from which and on which they are built?— The deſire of arriving at the end without the effort of thought and will, which are the appointed means. Let us look backward three or four centuries. Then, as now, the great maſs of mankind were governed by the three main wiſhes, the wiſh for vigour of body, including the abſence of painful feelings;—for wealth, or the power of procuring the external conditions of bodily enjoyment,—theſe during life; and ſecurity from pain and continuance of happineſs after death. Then, as now, men were deſirous to attain them by ſome eaſier means than thoſe of temperance, induſtry, and ſtrict juſtice. They gladly therefore applied to the prieſt, who could inſure them happineſs hereafter without the performance of their duties here; to the lawyer who could make money a ſubſtitute for a right cauſe; to the phyſician, whoſe medicines promiſed to take the ſting out of the tail of their ſenſual indulgences, and let them fondle and play with vice, as with a charmed ſerpent; to the alchemiſt, whoſe gold-tincture would enrich them without toil or economy; and to the aſtrologer, from whom they could purchaſe foreſight without knowledge or reflection. The eſtabliſhed profeſſions were, without exception, no other than licenſed modes of witchcraft. The wizards, who would now find their due reward in

Bridewell, and their appropriate honours in the pillory, sat then on episcopal thrones, candidates for saintship, and already canonized in the belief of their deluded contemporaries; while the one or two real teachers and discoverers of truth were exposed to the hazard of fire and faggot,—a dungeon the best shrine that was vouchsafed to a Roger Bacon * and a Galileo!

---

* " It is for his country, not his order, to glory in the man whom that order condemned to imprisonment, not for his supposed skill in magic, but for those opinions which he derived from studying the Scriptures, wherein he was versed beyond any other person of his age."

SOUTHEY's *Colloquies*, viii.

And see the note there.—*Ed.*

ESSAY VIII.

Pray, why is it, that people say that men are not such fools now-a-days as they were in the days of yore? I would fain know, whether you would have us understand by this same saying, as indeed you logically may, that formerly, men were fools, and in this generation are grown wise? How many and what dispositions made them fools? How many and what dispositions were wanting to make 'em wise? Why were those fools? How should these be wise? Pray, how came you to know that men were formerly fools? How did you find that they are now wise? Who made them fools? Who in Heaven's name made us wise? Who d'ye think are most, those that loved mankind foolish, or those that love it wise? How long has it been wise? How long otherwise? Whence proceeded the foregoing folly? Whence the following wisdom? Why did the old folly end now and no later? Why did the modern wisdom begin now and no sooner? What were we the worse for the former folly? What the better for the succeeding wisdom? How should the ancient folly have come to nothing? How should this same new wisdom be started up and established? Now answer me, an't please you!

RABELAIS' *Preface to his 5th Book.*

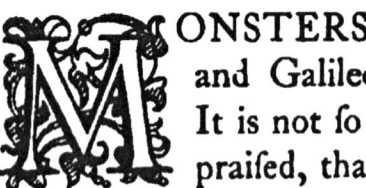

MONSTERS and madmen canonized and Galileo blind in a dungeon![*] It is not so in our times. Heaven be praised, that in this respect, at least,

---

[*] This is not strictly accurate. Galileo was sentenced by the Inquisition at Rome, on the 22nd of June, 1633;

we are, if not better, yet better off, than our forefathers. But to what, and to whom (under Providence) do we owe the improvement? To any radical change in the moral affections of mankind in general? Perhaps the great majority of men are now fully conscious that they are born with the god-like faculty of reason, and that it is the business of life to develope and apply it?— The Jacob's ladder of truth, let down from heaven, with all its numerous rounds, is now the common highway, on which we are content to toil upward to the objects of our desires?— We are ashamed of expecting the end without the means?—In order to answer these questions in the affirmative, I must have forgotten the animal magnetists;* the proselytes of Brothers, and of Joanna Southcote; and some thousand fanatics less original in their creeds, but not a whit more rational in their expectations; I must forget the infamous empirics, whose advertisements pollute and disgrace all our newspapers, and almost paper the walls of our cities; and the vending of whose poisons and poisonous drams — with shame and anguish be it spoken — supports a

---

and, although his right eye had been formerly affected, he did not become blind till the end of 1637. His confinement, likewise, in the proper prison of the Inquisition, was merely nominal, although the restrictions under which he was kept to the end of his life, were of the most distressing and injurious description.—*Ed.*

* Recanted since 1817. After subtracting all exaggerated or doubtful testimonies, the undeniable facts are as important as they are surprizing.

shop in every market-town! I must forget that other reproach of the nation, that mother-vice, the lottery! I must forget, that a numerous class plead prudence for keeping their fellow-men ignorant and incapable of intellectual enjoyments, and the revenue for upholding such temptations as men so ignorant will not withstand,—yes! that even senators and officers of state put forth the revenue as a sufficient reason for upholding, at every fiftieth door throughout the kingdom, temptations to the most pernicious vices, which fill the land with mourning, and fit the labouring classes for sedition and religious fanaticism! Above all I must forget the first years of the French revolution, and the millions throughout Europe who confidently expected the best and choicest results of knowledge and virtue, namely, liberty and universal peace, from the votes of a tumultuous assembly—that is, from the mechanical agitation of the air in a large room at Paris—and this too in the most light, unthinking, sensual, and profligate, of the European nations,—a nation, the very phrases of whose language are so composed, that they can scarcely speak without lying!—No! Let us not deceive ourselves. Like the man who used to pull off his hat with great demonstration of respect whenever he spoke of himself, we are fond of styling our own the enlightened age: though as Jortin, I think, has wittily remarked, the golden age would be more appropriate. But in spite of our great scientific discoveries, for which praise be given to whom the praise is due, and in spite of that general indifference to all the truths and all the principles of truth, that belong to our permanent being, and therefore do not lie within the sphere of our senses,—that same indifference which makes toleration so easy a virtue with us, and constitutes nine-tenths of our pretended illumination,—it still remains the character of the mass of mankind to seek for the attainment of their necessary ends by any means rather than the appointed ones; and for this cause only, that the latter imply the exertion of the reason and the will. But of all things this demands the longest apprenticeship, even an apprenticeship from infancy; which is generally neglected, because an excellence, that may and should belong to all men, is expected to come to every man of its own accord.

To whom then do we owe our meliorated condition?—To the successive few in every age,—more indeed in one generation than in another, but relatively to the mass of mankind always few,—who by the intensity and permanence of their action have compensated for the limited sphere, within which it is at any one time intelligible; and whose good deeds posterity reverences in their results; though the mode, in which we repair the inevitable waste of time, and the style of our additions, too generally furnish a sad proof, how little we understand the principles. I appeal to the histories of the Jewish, the Grecian, and the Roman republics, to the records of the Christian

ESSAY VIII.

Church, to the history of Europe from the treaty of Westphalia, 1648. What do they contain but accounts of noble structures raised by the wisdom of the few, and gradually undermined by the ignorance and profligacy of the many? If therefore the deficiency of good, which everywhere surrounds us, originate in the general unfitness and aversion of men to the process of thought, that is, to continuous reasoning, it must surely be absurd to apprehend a preponderance of evil from works which cannot act at all except as far as they call the reasoning faculties into full co-exertion with them.

Still, however, there are truths so self-evident, or so immediately and palpably deduced from those that are, or are acknowledged for such, that they are at once intelligible to all men, who possess the common advantages of the social state; although by sophistry, by evil habits, by the neglect, false persuasions, and impostures of an anti-Christian priesthood joined in one conspiracy with the violence of tyrannical governors, the understandings of men may become so darkened and their consciences so lethargic, that a necessity will arise for the republication of these truths, and this too with a voice of loud alarm, and impassioned warning. Such were the doctrines proclaimed by the first Christians to the Pagan world; such were the lightnings flashed by Wickliff, Huss, Luther, Calvin, Zuinglius, Latimer, and others, across the Papal darkness; and such in our own times the agitating truths, with which Thomas Clarkson, and his excellent confederates, the Quakers, fought and conquered the legalized *banditti* of men-stealers, the numerous and powerful perpetrators and advocates of rapine, murder, and (of blacker guilt than either) slavery. Truths of this kind being indispensable to man, considered as a moral being, are above all expedience, all accidental consequences: for as sure as God is holy, and man immortal, there can be no evil so great as the ignorance or disregard of them. It is the very madness of mock prudence to oppose the removal of a poisoned dish on account of the pleasant sauces or nutritious viands which would be lost with it! The dish contains destruction to that, for which alone we ought to wish the palate to be gratified, or the body to be nourished.

The sole condition, therefore, imposed on us by the law of conscience in these cases is, that we employ no unworthy and heterogeneous means to realize the necessary end, — that we entrust the event wholly to the full and adequate promulgation of the truth, and to those generous affections which the constitution of our moral nature has linked to the full perception of it. Yet evil may, nay it will, be occasioned. Weak men may take offence, and wicked men avail themselves of it; though we must not attribute to the promulgation, or to the truth promulgated, all the evil, of which wicked men—predetermined, like the wolf in the fable, to create some occasion — may choose to make it the pretext. But that there ever was, or ever can be, a preponderance of evil, I defy either the historian to instance, or the philosopher to prove. "Let it fly away, all that chaff of light faith that can fly off at any breath of temptation; the cleaner will the true grain be stored up in the granary of the Lord,"—we are entitled to say with Tertullian :[*] and to exclaim with heroic Luther,—"Scandal and offence! Talk not to me of scandal and offence. Need breaks through stone walls, and recks not of scandal. It is my duty to spare weak consciences as far as it may be done without hazard of my soul. Where not, I must take counsel for my soul, though half or the whole world should be scandalized thereby."[†]

Luther felt and preached and wrote and acted, as beseemed a Luther to feel and utter and act. The truths, which had been outraged, he re-proclaimed in the spirit of outraged truth, at the behest of his conscience and in the service of the God of truth. He did his duty, come good, come evil! and made no question, on which side the preponderance would be. In the one scale there

---

[*] *Avolent, quantum volent, paleæ leves fidei quocunque afflatu tentationum! eo purior massa frumenti in horrea Domini reponetur.* De Præscript. adverf. Hæretic. I. c. 3.—Ed.

[†] *Aergerniss hin, Aergerniss her! Noth bricht Eisen, und hat kein Aergerniss. Ich soll der schwachen Gewissen schonen so fern es ohne Gefahr meiner Seelen geschehen mag. Wo nicht, so soll ich meiner Seelen rathen, es aergere sich daran die ganze oder halbe Welt.*

was gold, and impressed thereon the image and superscription of the universal Sovereign. In all the wide and ever-widening commerce of mind with mind throughout the world, it is treason to refuse it. Can this have a counter-weight? The other scale indeed might have seemed full up to the very balance-yard; but of what worth and substance were its contents? Were they capable of being counted or weighed against the former? The conscience, indeed, is already violated when to moral good or evil we oppose things possessing no moral interest. Even if the conscience dared waive this her preventive *veto*, yet before we could consider the twofold results in the relation of loss and gain, it must be known whether their kind is the same or equivalent. They must first be valued, and then they may be weighed or counted, if they are worth it. But in the particular case at present before us, the loss is contingent and alien; the gain essential and the tree's own natural produce. The gain is permanent, and spreads through all times and places; the loss but temporary, and owing its very being to vice or ignorance, vanishes at the approach of knowledge and moral improvement. The gain reaches all good men, belongs to all that love light and desire an increase of light: to all and of all times, who thank Heaven for the gracious dawn, and expect the noon-day; who welcome the first gleams of spring, and sow their fields in confident faith of the ripening summer and the rewarding harvest-tide! But the loss is confined to the unenlightened and the prejudiced—say rather, to the weak and the prejudiced of a single generation. The prejudices of one age are condemned even by the prejudiced of the succeeding ages: for endless are the modes of folly, and the fool joins with the wise in passing sentence on all modes but his own. Who cried out with greater horror against the murderers of the Prophets, than those who likewise cried out, Crucify him! Crucify him!—Prophet and Saviour, and Lord of life, Crucify him! Crucify him!—The truth-haters of every future generation will call the truth-haters of the preceding ages by their true names: for even these the stream of time carries onward. In fine, truth considered in itself and in the effects natural to it, may be conceived as a gentle spring or water-source, warm from the genial earth, and breathing up into the snow drift that is piled over and around its outlet. It turns the obstacle into its own form and character, and as it makes its way increases its stream. And should it be arrested in its course by a chilling season, it suffers delay, not loss, and waits only for a change in the wind to awaken and again roll onwards:—

> *I semplici pastori*
> *Sul Vesolo nevoso*
> *Fatti curvi e canuti,*
> *D' alto stupor son muti,*
> *Mirando al fonte ombroso*
> *Il Po con pochi umori;*
> *Poscia udendo gli onori*
> *Dell' urna angusta e stretta,*

Che 'l Adda, che 'l Tesino
Soverchia in suo cammino,
Che ampio al mar 's affretta,
Che si spuma, e si suona,
Che gli si da corona! *

'The simple shepherds grown bent and hoary-headed on the snowy Vesolo, are mute with deep astonishment, gazing in the overshadowed fountain on the Po with his scanty waters; then hearing of the honours of his confined and narrow urn, how he receives as a sovereign the ADDA and the TESINO in his course, how ample he hastens on to the sea, how he foams, how mighty his voice, and that to him the crown is assigned.'

---

* *Chiabrera Rime*, xxviii. "But falsehood," continues Mr. C., " is fire in stubble; it likewise turns all the light stuff around it into its own substance for a moment, one crackling blazing moment,—and then dies; and all its converts are scattered in the wind, without place or evidence of their existence, as viewless as the wind which scatters them."—Lit. Rem. vol. I. *Omniana.—Ed.*

ESSAY IX.

Great men have liv'd among us, heads that plann'd
And tongues that utter'd wifdom—better none.
 * * * * *
Even fo doth Heaven protect us!
WORDSWORTH.

IN the preceding effay I have explained the good, that is, the natural confequences of the promulgation to all of truths which all are bound to know and to make known. The evils occafioned by it, with few and rare exceptions, have their origin in the attempts to fupprefs or pervert it; in the fury and violence of impofture attacked or undermined in her ftrong holds, or in the extravagances of ignorance and credulity roufed from their lethargy, and angry at the medicinal difturbance—awaking, not yet broad awake, and thus blending the monfters of uneafy dreams with the real objects, on which the drowfy eye had alternately half-opened and clofed, again half-opened and again clofed. This re-action of deceit and fuperftition, with all the trouble and tumult incident, I would compare to a fire which burfts forth from fome ftifled and fermenting mafs on the firft admiffion of light and air. It roars and blazes, and converts the already spoilt or damaged stuff with all the straw and straw-like matter near it, first into flame and the next moment into ashes. The fire dies away, the ashes are scattered on all the winds, and what began in worthlessness ends in nothingness. Such are the evil, that is, the casual consequences of the same promulgation.

It argues a narrow or corrupt nature to lose sight of the general and lasting consequences of rare and virtuous energy, in the brief accidents, which accompanied its first movements—to set lightly by the emancipation of the human reason from a legion of devils, in our complaints and lamentations over the loss of a herd of swine! The Cranmers, Hampdens, and Sidneys,—the counsellors of our Elizabeth, and the friends of our other great deliverer, the third William,—is it in vain, that these have been our countrymen? Are we not the heirs of their good deeds? And what are noble deeds but noble truths realized? As Protestants, as Englishmen, as the inheritors of so ample an estate of might and right, an estate so strongly fenced, so richly planted, by the sinewy arms and dauntless hearts of our forefathers, we of all others have good cause to trust in the truth, yea, to follow its pillar of fire through the darkness and the desert, even though its light should but suffice to make us certain of its own presence. If there be elsewhere men jealous of the light, who prophesy an excess of evil over good from its manifestation, we are entitled to ask them, on what experience they ground their bodings? Our own country bears no traces, our own history contains no records, to justify them. From the great æras of national illumination we date the commencement of our main national advantages. The tangle of delusions, which stifled and distorted the growing tree, have been torn away; the parasite weeds, that fed on its very roots, have been plucked up with a salutary violence. To us there remain only quiet duties, the constant care, the gradual improvement, the cautious, unhazardous, labours of the industrious though contented gardener—to prune, to engraft, and one by one to remove from its leaves and fresh shoots the slug and the caterpillar. But far be it from us to undervalue with light and senseless detraction the conscientious hardihood of our predecessors, or even to condemn in them that vehemence, to which the blessings it won for us leave us now neither temptation nor pretext. That the very terms, with which the bigot or the hireling would blacken the first publishers of political and religious truth, are, and deserve to be, hateful to us, we owe to the effects of its publication. We ante-date the feelings in order to criminate the authors of our tranquillity, opulence, and security. But let us be aware. Effects will not, indeed, immediately disappear with their causes; but neither can they long continue without them. If by the reception of truth in the spirit of truth, we became what we are; only by the retention of it in the same spirit, can we remain what we are. The narrow seas that form our boundaries,—what were they in times of old? The convenient highway for Danish and Norman pirates. What are they now? Still but "a span of waters." Yet they roll at the base of the inisled Ararat, on which the ark of the hope of Europe and of civilization rested!

> Even so doth God protect us, if we be
> Virtuous and wise. Winds blow and waters roll,
> Strength to the brave, and power and deity:
> Yet in themselves are nothing! One decree
> Spake laws to them, and said that by the soul
> Only the nations shall be great and free!
> WORDSWORTH.

ESSAY X.

I deny not but that it is of greatest concernment in the church and commonwealth to have a vigilant eye how books demean themselves as well as men; and thereafter to confine, imprison, and do sharpest justice on them as malefactors. For books are not absolutely dead things, but do contain a potency of life in them to be as active as that soul was whose progeny they are; nay, they do preserve as in a vial the purest efficacy and extraction of that living intellect that bred them. I know they are as lively and as vigorously productive as those fabulous dragon's teeth: and being sown up and down may chance to spring up armed men. And yet on the other hand, unless wariness be used, as good almost kill a man as kill a good book. Who kills a man, kills a reasonable creature, God's image; but he who destroys a good book, kills reason itself, kills the image of God, as it were in the eye. Many a man lives a burthen to the earth; but a good book is the precious life-blood of a master spirit, embalmed and treasured up on purpose to a life beyond life.

MILTON's *Speech for the liberty of unlicensed printing.*

THUS far then I have been conducting a cause between an individual and his own mind. Proceeding on the conviction, that to man is entrusted the nature, not the result, of his actions, I have presupposed no calculations; I have presumed no foresight.—Introduce no contradiction into thy own consciousness. Acting, or abstaining from action, delivering or withholding thy thoughts, whatsoever thou doeſt, do it in ſingleneſs of heart. In all things, therefore, let thy means correſpond to thy purpoſe, and let the purpoſe be one with the purport.—To this principle I have referred the ſuppoſed individual, and from this principle ſolely I have deduced each particular of his conduct. As far, therefore, as the court of conſcience extends,—and in this court alone I have been pleading hitherto—I have won the cauſe. It has been decided, that there is no juſt ground for apprehending miſchief from truth communicated conſcientiouſly,—that is, with a ſtrict obſervance of all the conditions required by the conſcience;—that what is not ſo communicated, is falſehood, and that to the falſehood, not to the truth, muſt the ill conſequences be attributed.

Another and altogether different cauſe remains now to be pleaded; a different cauſe, and in a different court. The parties concerned are no longer the well-meaning individual and his conſcience, but the citizen and the ſtate—the citizen, who may be a fanatic as probably as a philoſopher, and the ſtate, which concerns itſelf with the conſcience only as far as it appears in the action, or ſtill more accurately, in the fact; and which muſt determine the nature of the fact not merely by a rule of right formed from the modification of particular by general conſequences,—not merely by a principle of compromiſe, that reduces the freedom of each citizen to the common meaſure in which it becomes compatible with the freedom of all;

but likewise by the relation which the facts bear to its,—the state's,—own instinctive principle of self-preservation. For every depository of the supreme power must presume itself rightful: and as the source of law not legally to be endangered. A form of government may indeed, in reality, be most pernicious to the governed, and the highest moral honour may await the patriot who risks his life in order by its subversion to introduce a better and juster constitution; but it would be absurd to blame the law by which his life is declared forfeit. It were to expect, that by an involved contradiction the law should allow itself not to be law, by allowing the state, of which it is a part, not to be a state. For, as Hooker has well observed, the law of men's actions is one, if they be respected only as men; and another, when they are considered as parts of a body politic.*

But though every government subsisting in law, —for pure lawless despotism grounding itself wholly on terror precludes all consideration of duty— though every government subsisting in law must, and ought to, regard itself as the life of the body politic, of which it is the head, and consequently must punish every attempt against itself as an act of assault or murder, that is, sedition or treason; yet still it ought so to secure the life as not to prevent the conditions of its growth, and of that adaptation to circumstances, without which its very

---

* Eccl. Pol. I. xvi. 6.—*Ed.*

life becomes insecure. In the application, therefore, of these principles to the public communication of opinions by the most efficient mean,—we have to decide, whether consistently with them there should be any liberty of the press; and if this be answered in the affirmative, what shall be declared abuses of that liberty, and made punishable as such; and in what way the general law shall be applied to each particular case.

First, then, ought there to be any liberty of the press? I do not here mean, whether it should be permitted to print books at all;—for this essay has little chance of being read in Turkey, and in any other part of Europe it cannot be supposed questionable—but whether by the appointment of a censorship the government should take upon itself the responsibility of each particular publication. In governments purely monarchical,—that is, oligarchies under one head—the balance of advantage and disadvantage from this monopoly of the press will undoubtedly be affected by the general state of information; though after reading Milton's ' Speech for the liberty of unlicensed printing '* we shall probably be inclined to believe, that the best argument in favour of licensing under any

---

* *Il y a un voile qui doit toujours couvrir tout ce que l'on peut dire et tout ce qu'on peut croire du droit des peuples et de celui des princes, qui ne s'accordent jamais si bien ensemble que dans le silence.* Mém. du Card. de Retz.

How severe a satire where it can be justly applied! how false and calumnious if meant as a general maxim!

constitution is that, which supposing the ruler to have a different interest from that of his country, and even from himself as a reasonable and moral creature, grounds itself on the incompatibility of knowledge with folly, oppression, and degradation. What our prophetic Harrington said of religious, applies equally to literary, toleration :—" If it be said that in France there is liberty of conscience in part, it is also plain that while the hierarchy is standing, this liberty is falling, and that if ever it comes to pull down the hierarchy, it pulls down that monarchy also : wherefore the monarchy or hierarchy will be beforehand with it, if they see their true interest."*—On the other hand, their is no flight danger from general ignorance : and the only choice, which Providence has graciously left to a vicious government, is either to fall by the people, if they are suffered to become enlightened, or with them, if they are kept enslaved and ignorant.

The nature of our constitution, since the Revolution, the state of our literature, and the wide diffusion, if not of intellectual, yet of literary, power, and the almost universal interest in the productions of literature, have set the question at rest relatively to the British press. However great the advantages of previous examination might be under other circumstances, in this country it would be both impracticable and inefficient. I need only suggest

---

* Syst. of Politics, vi. 10.—*Ed.*

in broken sentences — the prodigious number of licensers that would be requisite — the variety of their attainments, and — inasmuch as the scheme must be made consistent with our religious freedom — the ludicrous variety of their principles and creeds — their number being so great, and each appointed censor being himself a man of letters, *quis custodiet ipsos custodes?* If these numerous licensers hold their offices for life, and independently of the ministry *pro tempore*, a new, heterogeneous, and alarming power is introduced, which can never be assimilated to the constitutional powers already existing : — if they are removable at pleasure, that which is heretical and seditious in 1809, may become orthodox and loyal in 1810; — and what man, whose attainments and moral respectability gave him even an endurable claim to this awful trust, would accept a situation at once so invidious and so precarious? And what institution can retain any useful influence in so free a nation when its abuses have made it contemptible? Lastly, and which of itself would suffice to justify the rejection of such a plan — unless all proportion between crime and punishment were abandoned, what penalties could the law attach to the assumption of a liberty, which it had denied, more severe than those which it now attaches to the abuse of the liberty, which it grants? In all those instances at least, which it would be most the inclination — perhaps the duty — of the state to prevent, namely, in seditious and incendiary publications, — (whether actually such, or only such as the existing government chose so to denominate, makes no difference in the argument)—the publisher, who hazards the punishment now assigned to seditious publications, would assuredly hazard the penalties of unlicensed ones, especially as the very practice of licensing would naturally diminish the attention to the contents of the works published, the chance of impunity therefore be so much greater, and the artifice of prefixing an unauthorised licence so likely to escape detection. It is a fact, that in many of the former German states in which literature flourished, notwithstanding the establishment of censors or licensers, three fourths of the books printed were unlicensed—even those, the contents of which were unobjectionable, and where the sole motive for evading the law, must have been either the pride and delicacy of the author, or the indolence of the bookseller. So difficult was the detection, so various the means of evasion, and worse than all, from the nature of the law and the affront it offers to the pride of human nature, such was the merit attached to the breach of it—a merit commencing perhaps with Luther's Bible, and other prohibited works of similar great minds, published with no dissimilar purpose, and thence by many an intermediate link of association finally connected with books, of the very titles of which a good man would wish to remain ignorant. The interdictory catalogues of the Romish hierarchy always present to my fancy the muster-rolls of the two hostile armies of Michael and of Satan printed promiscuously, or extracted at haphazard, save only that the extracts from the former appear somewhat the more numerous. And yet even in Naples, and in Rome itself, whatever difficulty occurs in procuring any article catalogued in these formidable folios, must arise either from the scarcity of the work itself, or the absence of all interest in it. Assuredly there is no difficulty in obtaining from the most respectable booksellers the vilest provocatives to the basest crimes, though intermixed with gross lampoons on the heads of the church, the religious orders, and on religion itself. The stranger is invited into an inner room, and the proscribed wares presented to him with most significant looks and gestures, implying the hazard, and the necessity of secresy. A creditable English bookseller would deem himself insulted, if such works were even inquired after at his shop. It is a well-known fact, that with the mournful exception indeed of political provocatives, and the titillations of vulgar envy provided by our anonymous critics, the loathsome articles are among us vended and offered for sale almost exclusively by foreigners. Such are the salutary effects of a free press, and the generous habit of action imbibed from the blessed air of law and liberty, even by men who neither understand the principle, nor feel the sentiment, of the dignified purity, to which they yield obeisance from the instinct of character. As there is a national guilt which can be charged but gently on each individual, so are there national virtues, which can as little be imputed to the individuals,—no where, however, but in countries where liberty is the presiding influence, the universal *medium* and *menstruum* of all other excellence, moral and intellectual. Admirably doth the admirable Petrarch admonish us :—

Nec sibi vero quisquam falso persuadeat, eos qui pro libertate excubant, atque hactenus desertæ reipublicæ partes suscipiunt, alienum agere negotium; suum agunt. In hac una reposita sibi omnia norint omnes, securitatem mercator, gloriam miles, utilitatem agricola. Postremo, in eadem religiosi cærimonias, otium studiosi, requiem senes, rudimenta disciplinarum pueri, nuptias puellæ, pudicitiam matronæ, gaudium omnes invenient. * * * *Huic uni reliquæ cedant curæ! Si hanc omittitis, in quantalibet occupatione nihil agitis: si huic incumbitis, etsi nihil agere videmini, cumulate tamen et civium et virorum implevistis officia.**

Nor let any one falsely persuade himself, that those who keep watch and ward for liberty, are meddling with things that do not concern them, instead of minding their own business. For all men should know, that all blessings are stored and protected in this one, as in a common repository.

---

* Petrarch. *Epist.* 45, *ad Nicolaum tribunum urbis almæ novissimum et ad populum Romanum.* The translation contains clauses referring to expressions, which in the second edition, were inserted in the Latin quotation by Mr. C. himself.—*Ed.*

Here is the tradesman's security, the soldier's honour, the agriculturist's profit. Lastly, in this one good of liberty the religious will find the permission of their rites and forms of worship, the students their learned leisure, the aged their repose, boys the rudiments of the several branches of their education, maidens their chaste nuptials, matrons their womanly honour and the dignity of their modesty, fathers of families the dues of natural affection and the sacred privileges of their ancient home, every one their hope and their joy. To this one solicitude therefore let all other cares yield the priority. If you omit this, be occupied as much and seduloufly as you may, you are doing nothing: If you apply your heart and strength to this, though you seem to be doing nothing, you will, nevertheless, have been fulfilling the duties of citizens and of men, yea, in a measure pressed down and running over.

I quote Petrarch often in the hope of drawing the attention of scholars to his inestimable Latin writings. Let me add, in the wish likewise of recommending to the London publishers a translation of select passages from his treatises and letters. If I except the German writings and original letters of the heroic Luther, I do not remember a work from which so delightful and instructive a volume might be compiled.

To give the true bent to the above extract, it is necessary to bear in mind, that he who keeps watch and ward for freedom, has to guard against two enemies, the despotism of the few and the despotism of the many — but especially in the present day against the sycophants of the populace.

> License they mean, when they cry liberty!
> For who loves that, must first be wise and good.

ESSAY XI.

Nemo vero fallatur, quasi minora sint animorum contagia quam corporum. Majora sunt; gravius lædunt; altius descendunt, serpuntque latentius.
  PETRARCH. De Vit. Solit. L. 1. tract. 3. c. 4.

And let no man be deceived as if the contagions of the soul were less than those of the body. They are yet greater; they convey more direful diseases; they sink deeper, and creep on more unsuspectedly.

WE have abundant reason then to infer, that the law of England has done well and concluded wisely in proceeding on the principle so clearly worded by Milton: "that a book should be as freely admitted into the world as any other birth; and if it prove a monster, who denies but that it may justly be burnt or sunk into the sea?" We have reason then, I repeat, to rest satisfied with our laws, which no more prevent a book from coming into the world unlicensed, lest it should prove a libel, than a traveller from passing unquestioned through our turnpike-gates, because it is possible he may be a highwayman. Innocence is presumed in both cases. The publication is a part of the offence, and its necessary condition.

Words are moral acts and words deliberately made public the law confiders in the fame light as any other cognizable overt act.

Here however a difficulty prefents itfelf. Theft, robbery, murder, and the like, are eafily defined: the degrees and circumftances likewife of thefe and fimilar actions are definite, and conftitute fpecific offences, defcribed and punifhable each under its own name. We have only to prove the fact and identify the offender. The intention too, in the great majority of cafes, is fo clearly implied in the action, that the law can fafely adopt it as its univerfal maxim, that the proof of the malice is included in the proof of the fact; efpecially as the few occafional exceptions have their remedy provided in the prerogative of pardon entrufted to the fupreme magiftrate. But in the cafe of libel, the degree makes the kind, the circumftances conftitute the criminality; and both degrees and circumftances, like the afcending fhades of colour or the fhooting hues of a dove's neck, die away into each other, incapable of definition or outline. The eye of the underftanding, indeed, fees the determinate difference in each individual cafe, but language is moft often inadequate to exprefs what the eye perceives, much lefs can a general ftatute anticipate and pre-define it. Again: in other overt acts a charge difproved leaves the accufed either guilty of a different fault, or at beft fimply blamelefs. A man having killed a fellow-citizen is acquitted of murder;—the act was manflaughter only, or it was juftifiable homicide. But when we reverfe the iniquitous fentence paffed on Algernon Sidney, during our perufal of his work on government; at the moment we deny it to have been a traitorous libel, our beating hearts declare it to have been a benefaction to our country, and under the circumftances of thofe times the performance of an heroic duty. From this caufe, therefore, as well as from a libel's being a thing made up of degrees and circumftances,—and thefe too, difcriminating offence from merit by fuch dim and ambulant boundaries,—the intention of the agent, wherever it can be independently or inclufively afcertained, muft be allowed a great fhare in determining the character of the action, unlefs the law is not only to be divorced from moral juftice, but to wage open hoftility againft it.*

Add too, that laws in doubtful points are to be interpreted according to the defign of the legiflator, where this can be certainly inferred. But the laws of England, which owe their own prefent fupremacy and abfolutenefs to the good fenfe and generous difpofitions diffufed by the prefs more, far more, than to any other fingle caufe, muft needs be prefumed favourable to its general influence. Even in the penalties attached to its abufe, we muft fuppofe the legiflature to have been actuated

---

* According to the old adage: you are not hanged for ftealing a horfe, but that horfes may not be ftolen. To what extent this is true, I fhall have occafion to examine hereafter.

by the desire of preserving its essential privileges. The press is indifferently the passive instrument of evil and of good: nay, there is some good even in its evil. "Good and evil we know," says Milton, in the Speech from which I have selected the motto of the preceding essay, " in the field of this world, grow up together almost inseparably: and the knowledge of good is so involved and interwoven with the knowledge of evil, and in so many cunning resemblances hardly to be discerned, that those confused seeds which were imposed on Psyche as an incessant labour to cull out and sort asunder, were not more intermixed."—" As, therefore, the state of man now is, what wisdom can there be to choose, what continence to forbear, without the knowledge of evil? He that can apprehend and consider vice with all her baits and seeming pleasures, and yet abstain, and yet distinguish, and yet prefer that which is truly better, he is the true way-faring Christian. I cannot praise a fugitive and cloistered virtue, unexercised and unbreathed, that never sallies out and sees her adversary."— " That virtue, therefore, which is but a youngling in the contemplation of evil, and knows not the utmost that vice promises to her followers, and rejects it, is but a blank virtue, not a pure."—" Since, therefore, the knowledge and survey of vice is in this world so necessary to the constituting of human virtue, and the scanning of error to the confirmation of truth, how can we more safely and with less danger scout into the regions of sin and falsity, than by reading all manner of tractates, and hearing all manner of reason?"—Again—but, indeed the whole treatise is one strain of moral wisdom and political prudence:—"Why should we then affect a rigour contrary to the manner of God and of nature, by abridging or scanting those means, which books, freely permitted, are both to the trial of virtue and the exercise of truth? It would be better done to learn, that the law must needs be frivolous, which goes to restrain things uncertainly, and yet equally, working to good and to evil. And were I the chooser, a dram of well-doing should be preferred before many times as much the forcible hindrance of evil-doing. For God, sure, esteems the growth and completion of one virtuous person, more than the restraint of ten vicious."

The evidence of history is strong in favour of the same principles, even in respect of their expediency. The average result of the press from Henry VIII. to Charles I. was such a diffusion of religious light as first redeemed and afterwards saved this nation from the spiritual and moral death of Popery; and in the following period it is to the press that we owe the gradual ascendancy of those wise political maxims, which casting philosophic truth in the moulds of national laws, customs, and existing orders of society, subverted the tyranny without suspending the government, and at length completed the mild and salutary revolution by the establishment of the house of Brunswick. To what must we attribute this vast over-balance of good in the general effects of the press, but to the over-balance of virtuous intention in those who employed the press? The law, therefore, will not refuse to manifest good intention a certain weight even in cases of apparent error, lest it should discourage and scare away those, to whose efforts we owe the comparative infrequency and weakness of error on the whole. The law may however, nay, it must demand, that the external proofs of the author's honest intentions should be supported by the general style and matter of his work, and by the circumstances and mode of its publication. A passage, which in a grave and regular disquisition would be blameless, might become highly libellous and justly punishable if it were applied to present measures or persons for immediate purposes, in a cheap and popular tract. I have seldom felt greater indignation than at finding in a large manufactory a sixpenny pamphlet, containing a selection of inflammatory paragraphs from the prose-writings of Milton, without a hint given of the time, occasion, state of government, and other circumstances under which they were written—not a hint, that the freedom, which we now enjoy, exceeds all that Milton dared hope for, or deemed practicable; and that his political creed sternly excluded the populace, and indeed the majority of the population, from all pretensions to political power. If the manifest bad intention would constitute this publication a seditious libel, a good intention equally manifest cannot justly be denied its share of influence in producing a contrary verdict.

Here then is the difficulty. From the very nature of a libel it is impossible so to define it, but that the most meritorious works will be found included in the description. Not from any defect or undue severity in the particular law, but from the very nature of the offence to be guarded against, a work recommending reform by the only rational mode of recommendation, that is, by the detection and exposure of corruption, abuse, or incapacity, might, though it should breathe the best and most unadulterated English feelings, be brought within the definition of libel equally with the vilest incendiary pamphlet, that ever aimed at leading and misleading the multitude. Not a paragraph in the Morning Post during the Peace of Amiens, (or rather the experimental truce so called,)—though to the immortal honour of the then editor, that newspaper was the chief secondary means of producing the unexampled national unanimity, with which the war re-commenced and has since been continued,—not a paragraph warning the nation, as need was and most imperious duty commanded, of the perilous designs and unsleeping ambition of our neighbour, the mimic and caricaturist of Charlemagne, but was a punishable libel. The law of libel is a vast aviary, which encages the awakening cock and the geese whose alarum preserved the Capitol, no less than the babbling magpye and ominous screech-owl. And yet will we avoid this seeming injustice, we throw down all fence and bulwark of public decency and public opinion; political calumny will soon join hands with private slander; and every principle, every feeling, that binds the citizen to his country and the spirit to its Creator, will be undermined — not by reasoning, for from that there is no danger; but — by the mere habit of hearing them reviled and scoffed at with impunity. Were we to contemplate the evils of a rank and unweeded press only in its effect on the manners of a people, and on the general tone of thought and conversation, the greater the love which we bore to literature and to all the means and instruments of human improvement, the greater would be the earnestness with which we should solicit the interference of law : the more anxiously should we wish for some Ithuriel spear, that might remove from the ear of the public, and expose in their own fiendish shape those reptiles, which inspiring venom and forging illusions as they list,

————— thence raise
At least distempered, discontented, thoughts,
Vain hopes, vain aims, inordinate desires.
PARADISE LOST.

ESSAY XII.

Quomodo autem id futurum sit, ne quis incredibile arbitretur, ostendam. Imprimis multiplicabitur regnum, et summa rerum potestas per plurimos dissipata et concisa minuetur. Tunc discordiæ civiles in perpetuum serentur, nec ulla requies bellis exitialibus erit, donec reges decem pariter existant qui orbem terræ, non ad regendum, sed ad consumendum, partiantur. Hi exercitibus in immensum coactis, et agrorum cultibus destitutis, quod est principium eversionis et cladis, disperdent omnia, et comminuent, et vorabunt. Tum reperite adversus eos hostis potentissimus ab extremis finibus plagæ septentrionalis orietur, qui tribus ex eo numero deletis qui tunc Asiam obtinebunt, assumetur in societatem a cæteris, ac princeps omnium constituetur. Hic insustentabili dominatione vexabit orbem; divina et humana miscebit; infanda dictu et execrabilia molietur; nova consilia in pectore suo volutabit, ut proprium sibi constituat imperium; leges commutabit, suas sanciet; contaminabit, diripiet, spoliabit, occidet. Denique immutato nomine, atque imperii sede translata, confusio ac perturbatio humani generis consequetur. Tum vere detestabile, atque abominandum tempus existet, quo nulli hominum sit vita jucunda.
LACTANTIUS de Vitâ Beatâ, Lib. vii. c. 16.

But left this should be deemed incredible, I will show the manner in which it is to take place. First, there will be a multiplication of independent sovereignties, and the supreme magistracy of the empire, scattered and cut up into fragments, will be enfeebled in the exercise of power by law and authority. Then will be sown the seeds of civil discords, nor will there be any rest or pause to wasteful and ruinous wars; while the soldiery kept together in immense standing armies, the kings will crush and lay waste at their will;—until at length there will rife up againft them a moft puiffant military chieftain of low birth, who will have conceded to him a fellowfhip with the other fovereigns of the earth, and will finally be conftituted the head of all. This man will harafs the civilized world with an infupportable defpotifm, he will confound and commix all things fpiritual and temporal. He will form plans and preparations of the moft execrable and facrilegious nature. He will be for ever reftleffly turning over new fchemes in his imagination, in order that he may fix the imperial power over all in his own name and poffeffion. He will change the former laws, he will fanction a code of his own, he will contaminate, pillage, lay wafte and maffacre. At length, when he has fucceeded in the change of names and titles, and in the transfer of the feat of empire, there will follow a confufion and perturbation of the human race; then will there be for a while an æra of horror and abomination, during which no man will enjoy his life in quietnefs.*

I INTERPOSE this effay as an hiftorical comment on the words "mimic and caricaturift of Charlemagne," as applied to the defpot, whom fince the time that the words were firft printed, we have, thank Heaven! fucceeded in encaging. The motto contains one of the moft ftriking inftances of an uninfpired prophecy fulfilled even in many of its *minutiæ*, that I recollect ever to have met with: and it is hoped, that as a curiofity it will reconcile my readers to its unufual length. But though my chief motive was that of relieving, by the variety of an hiftorical parallel, the feries of argument on this moft important of all fubjects, the communi-

---

* This tranflation has expreffions referring to fome words inferted by the author in the Latin quotation in the previous editions.—*Ed.*

cability of truth, yet the essay is far from being a digression. Having given utterance to *quicquid in rem tam maleficam indignatio dolorque dictarent*, concerning the mischiefs of a lawless press, I held it an act of justice to give a portrait no less lively of the excess to which the remorseless ambition of a government might go in accumulating its oppressions in the one instance before the discovery of printing, and in the other during the suppression of its freedom.

I have translated the following from a voluminous German work, Michael Ignaz Schmidt's History of the Germans, from Charles the Great to Conrade I.; in which this extract forms the conclusion of the second chapter of the third book. The late tyrant's close imitation of Charlemagne was sufficiently evidenced by his assumption of the iron crown of Italy, by his imperial coronation with the presence and authority of the Holy Father; by his imperial robe embroidered with bees in order to mark him as a successor of Pepin, and even by his ostentatious revocation of Charlemagne's grants to the Bishop of Rome. But that the differences might be felt likewise, I have prefaced the translation with the few following observations.

Let it be remembered then, that Charlemagne, for the greater part, created for himself the means of which he availed himself; that his very education was his own work, and that unlike Peter the Great, he could find no assistants out of his own realm; that the unconquerable courage and heroic dispositions of the nations he conquered, supplied a proof positive of real superiority, indeed the sole positive proof of intellectual power, in a warrior: for how can we measure force but by the resistance to it? But all was prepared for Buonaparte; Europe weakened in the very heart of all human strength, namely, in moral and religious principle, and at the same time accidentally destitute of any one great or commanding mind: the French people, on the other hand, still restless from revolutionary fanaticism; their civic enthusiasm already passed into military passion and the ambition of conquest; and alike by disgust, terror, and characteristic unfitness for freedom, ripe for the reception of a despotism. Add too, that the main obstacles to an unlimited system of conquest, and the pursuit of universal monarchy had been cleared away for him by his pioneers the Jacobins, namely, the influence of the great land-holders, of the privileged and of the commercial classes. Even the naval successes of Great Britain, by destroying the trade, rendering useless the colonies, and almost annihilating the navy of France, were in some respects subservient to his designs by concentrating the powers of the French empire in its armies, and supplying them out of the wrecks of all other employments, save that of agriculture. France had already approximated to the formidable state so prophetically described by Sir James Steuart, in his Political Economy, in which the population should consist chiefly of soldiers and peasantry: at least the interests of no other claſſes were regarded. The great merit of Buonaparte has been that of a ſkilful ſteerſman, who with his boat in the moſt violent ſtorm ſtill keeps himſelf on the ſummit of the waves, which not he, but the winds had raiſed. I will now proceed to my tranſlation.

" That Charles was a hero, his exploits bear evidence. The ſubjugation of the Lombards, protected as they were by the Alps, by fortreſſes and fortified towns, by numerous armies, and by a great name; of the Saxons, ſecured by their ſavage reſoluteneſs, by an untameable love of freedom, by their deſert plains and enormous foreſts, and by their own poverty; the humbling of the Dukes of Bavaria, Aquitania, Bretagne, and Gaſcony; proud of their anceſtry as well as of their ample domains; the almoſt entire extirpation of the Avars, ſo long the terror of Europe; are aſſuredly works which demanded a courage and a firmneſs of mind ſuch as Charles only poſſeſſed.

" How great his reputation was, and this too beyond the limits of Europe, is proved by the embaſſies ſent to him out of Perſia, Paleſtine, Mauritania, and even from the Khalifs of Bagdad. If at the preſent day an embaſſy from the Black or Caſpian Sea comes to a prince on the Baltic, it is not to be wondered at, ſince ſuch are now the political relations of the four quarters of the world, that a blow which is given to any one of them is felt more or leſs by all the others. Whereas in the times of Charlemagne, the inhabitants in one of the known parts of the world scarcely knew what was going on in the rest. Nothing but the extraordinary, all-piercing, report of Charles's exploits could bring this to pass. His greatness, which set the world in astonishment, was likewise, without doubt, that which begot in the Pope and the Romans the first idea of the re-establishment of their empire.

"It is true, that a number of things united to make Charles a great man—favourable circumstances of time, a nation already disciplined to warlike habits, a long life, and the consequent acquisition of experience, such as no one possessed in his whole realm. Still, however, the principal means of his greatness Charles found in himself. His great mind was capable of extending its attention to the greatest multiplicity of affairs. In the middle of Saxony he thought on Italy and Spain, and at Rome he made provisions for Saxony, Bavaria, and Pannonia. He gave audience to the ambassadors of the Greek emperor and other potentates, and himself audited the accounts of his own farms, where every thing was entered even to the number of the eggs. Busy as his mind was, his body was not less in one continued state of motion. Charles would see into every thing himself, and do every thing himself, as far as his powers extended: and even this it was, too, which gave to his undertakings such force and energy.

"But with all this the government of Charles was the government of a conqueror, that is splendid abroad and fearfully oppressive at home. What a grievance must it not have been for the people, that Charles for forty years together dragged them now to the Elbe, then to the Ebro, after this to the Po, and from thence back again to the Elbe, and this not to check an invading enemy, but to make conquests which little profited the French nation! This must prove too much, at length, for a hired soldier: how much more for conscripts, who did not live only to fight, but who were fathers of families, citizens, and proprietors? But above all, it is to be wondered at, that a nation, like the French, should suffer themselves to be used as Charles used them. But the people no longer possessed any considerable share of influence. All depended on the great chieftains, who gave their willing suffrage for endless wars, by which they were always sure to win. They found the best opportunity, under such circumstances, to make themselves great and mighty at the expense of the freemen resident within the circle of their baronial courts; and when conquests were made, it was far more for their advantage than that of the monarchy. In the conquered provinces there was a necessity for dukes, vassal kings, and different high offices: all this fell to their share.

"I would not say this if we did not possess incontrovertible original documents of those times, which prove clearly to us that Charles's government was an unhappy one for the people, and that this great man, by his actions, laboured to the direct subversion of his first principles. It was his first pretext to establish a greater equality among the members of his vast community, and to make all free and equal subjects under a common sovereign. And from the necessity occasioned by continual war, the exact contrary took place. Nothing gives us a better notion of the interior state of the French monarchy, than the third capitular of the year 811.* All is full of complaint, the bishops and earls clamouring against the freeholders, and these in their turn against the bishops and earls. And in truth the freeholders had no small reason to be discontented and to resist, as far as they dared, even the imperial levies. A dependant must be content to follow his lord without further questioning: for he was paid for it. But a free citizen, who lived wholly on his own property, might reasonably object to suffer himself to be dragged about in all quarters of the world, at the fancies of his lord: especially as there was so much injustice intermixed. Those who gave up their properties entirely, or in part, of their own accord, were left undisturbed at home, while those, who refused to do this, were forced so often into service, that at length, becoming impoverished, they were compelled by want to give up, or dispose of, their free tenures to the bishops or earls.†

---

* Compare with this the four or five quarto volumes of the French Conscript Code.

† It would require no great ingenuity to discover parallels, or at least, equivalent hardships to these, in the treatment of, and regulations concerning, the reluctant conscripts.

"It almost surpasses belief to what a height, at length, the aversion to war rose in the French nation, from the multitude of the campaigns and the grievances connected with them. The national vanity was now satiated by the frequency of victories: and the plunder which fell to the lot of individuals, made but a poor compensation for the losses and burthens sustained by their families at home. Some, in order to become exempt from military service, sought for menial employments in the establishments of the bishops, abbots, abbesses, and earls. Others made over their free property to become tenants at will of such lords, as from their age or other circumstances, they thought would be called to no further military services. Others even privately took away the life of their mothers, aunts, or other of their relatives, in order that no family residents might remain through whom their names might be known, and themselves traced; others voluntarily made slaves of themselves, in order thus to render themselves incapable of the military rank."

When this extract was first published, namely, September 7, 1809, I prefixed the following sentence. "This passage contains so much matter for political anticipation and well-grounded hope, that I feel no apprehension of the reader's being dissatisfied with its length." I trust, that I may now derive the same confidence from his genial exultation, as a Christian, and from his honest pride as a Briton, in the retrospect of its completion. In this belief I venture to conclude the essay with the following extract from a "Comparison of the French republic, under Buonaparte, with the Roman empire under the first Cæsars," published by me in the Morning Post, 21 Sept. 1802.

If, then, there be no counterpoise of dissimilar circumstances, the prospect is gloomy indeed. The commencement of the public slavery in Rome was in the most splendid æra of human genius. Any unusually flourishing period of the arts and sciences in any country, is, even to this day, called the Augustan age of that country. The Roman poets, the Roman historians, the Roman orators, rivalled those of Greece; in military tactics, in machinery, in all the conveniences of private life, the Romans greatly surpassed the Greeks. With few exceptions, all the emperors, even the worst of them, were, like Buonaparte,* the liberal encouragers of

---

* Imitators succeed better in copying the vices than the excellences of their archetypes. Where shall we find in the First Consul of France a counterpart to the generous and dreadless clemency of the first Cæsar? *Acerbe loquentibus satis habuit pro concione denunciare, ne perseverarent. Aulique Cæcinæ criminosissimo libro, et Pitholai carminibus maledicentissimis laceratam existimationem suam civili animo tulit.*—(Sueton. I. 75.—*Ed.*)

It deserves translation for English readers. "To those who spoke bitterly against him, he held it sufficient to signify publicly, that they should not persevere in the use of such language. His character had been mangled in a most libellous work of Aulus Cæcina, and he had been grossly lampooned in some verses by Pitholaus; but he bore both with the temper of a good citizen."

For this part of the First Consul's character, if common report speaks the truth, we must seek a parallel in the dif-

all great public works, and of every species of public merit not connected with the assertion of political freedom:

> ―― *O juvenes, circumspicit atque agitat vos,*
> *Materiamque sibi Ducis indulgentia quærit.**

It is even so, at this present moment in France. Yet, both in France and in Rome, we have learned, that the most abject dispositions to slavery rapidly trod on the heels of the most outrageous fanaticism for an almost anarchical liberty. *Ruere in servitium consules, patres, eques: quanto quis illustrior, tanto magis falsi ac festinantes.†* Peace and the coadunation of all the civilized provinces of the earth were the grand and plausible pretexts of Roman despotism: the degeneracy of the human species itself, in all the nations so blended, was the melancholy effect. To-morrow, therefore, we shall endeavour to detect all those points and circumstances of dissimilarity, which, though they cannot impeach the rectitude of the parallel, for the present, may yet render it probable, that as the same constitution of government has been built up in France with incomparably greater rapidity, so it may have an incomparably shorter

---

positions of the third Cæsar, who dreaded the pen of a paragraph writer, hinting aught against his morals and measures, with as great anxiety, and with as vindictive feelings, as if it had been the dagger of an assassin lifted up against his life. From the third Cæsar, too, he adopted the abrogation of all popular elections.

* Juvenal. Sat. vii. 20.—*Ed.*
† Tacit. Ann. i. 7.—*Ed.*

duration. We are not confcious of any feelings of bitternefs towards the Firft Conful; or, if any, only that venial prejudice, which naturally refults from the having hoped proudly of an individual, and the having been miferably difappointed. But we will not voluntarily ceafe to think freely and fpeak openly. We owe grateful hearts, and uplifted hands of thankfgiving to the Divine Providence, that there is yet one European country— and that country our own— in which the actions of public men may be boldly analyzed, and the refult publicly ftated. And let the Chief Conful, who profeffes in all things to follow his fate, learn to fubmit to it, if he finds that it is ftill his fate to ftruggle with the fpirit of Englifh freedom, and the virtues which are the offspring of that fpirit;— if he finds, that the genius of Great Britain, which blew up his Egyptian navy into the air, and blighted his Syrian laurels, ftill follows him with a calm and dreadful eye; and in peace, equally as in war, ftill watches for that liberty, in which alone the genius of our ifle lives, and moves, and has its being; and which being loft, all our commercial and naval greatnefs would inftantly languifh, like a flower, the root of which had been filently eaten away by a worm; and without which, in any country, the public feftivals, and pompous merriments of a nation prefent no other fpectacle to the eye of reafon, than a mob of maniacs dancing in their fetters.

ESSAY XIII.

Must there be still some discord mix'd among
The harmony of men, whose mood accords
Best with contention tun'd to notes of wrong?
That when war fails, peace must make war with words,
*With words unto destruction arm'd more strong
Than ever were our foreign foemen's swords;*
Making as deep, tho' not yet bleeding wounds?
What war left scarless, calumny confounds.

Truth lies entrapp'd where cunning finds no bar:
Since no proportion can there be betwixt
Our actions which in endless motions are,
And ordinances which are always fixt.
Ten thousand laws more cannot reach so far,
But malice goes beyond, or lives commixt
So close with goodness, that it ever will
Corrupt, disguise, or counterfeit it still.

And therefore *would our glorious Alfred,* who
Join'd with the king's the good man's majesty,
Not leave law's labyrinth without a clue—
Gave to deep skill its just authority,—

* * * * * *

But the last judgment—this his jury's plan—
Left to the natural sense of work-day man.*

---

* Daniel. Epistle to Sir Thomas Egerton. The lines in italics are substituted by the author for the original, and there are a few other verbal alterations.—*Ed.*

VOL. I.   I

I RECUR to the dilemma stated in the eighth essay. How shall we solve this problem? Its solution is to be found in that spirit which, like the universal *menstruum* sought for by the old alchemists, can blend and harmonize the most discordant elements;—it is to be found in the spirit of a rational freedom diffused and become national, in the consequent influence and controul of public opinion, and in its most precious organ, the jury. It is to be found, wherever juries are sufficiently enlightened to perceive the difference, and to comprehend the origin and necessity of the difference, between libels and other criminal over-acts, and are sufficiently independent to act upon the conviction, that in a charge of libel, the degree, the circumstances, and the intention, constitute—not merely modify—the offence, give it its being, and determine its legal name. The words maliciously and advisedly, must here have a force of their own, and a proof of their own. They will consequently consider the law as a blank power provided for the punishment of the offender, not as a light by which they are to determine and discriminate the offence. The understanding and conscience of the jury are the judges, *in toto:* the law a blank *congé d'élire.* The law is the clay and those the potter's wheel. Shame fall on that man, who shall labour to confound what reason and nature have put asunder, and who at once, as far as in him lies, would render the press ineffectual and the law odious: who would lock up the main river, the Thames, of our intellectual commerce; would throw a bar across the stream, that must render its navigation dangerous or partial, using as his materials the very banks, which were intended to deepen its channel and guard against its inundations! Shame fall on him, and a participation of the infamy of those, who misled an English jury to the murder of Algernon Sidney.

But though the virtuous intention of the writer must be allowed a certain influence in facilitating his acquittal, the degree of his moral guilt is not the true index or mete-wand of his condemnation. For juries do not sit in a court of conscience, but of law; they are not the representatives of religion, but the guardians of external tranquillity. The leading principle, the pole star, of the judgment in its decision concerning the libellous nature of a published writing, is its more or less remote connection with after overt-acts, as the cause or occasion of the same. Thus the publication of actual facts may be, and most often will be, criminal and libellous, when directed against private characters: not only because the charge will reach the minds of many who cannot be competent judges of the truth or falsehood of facts to which themselves were not witnesses, against a man whom they do not know, or at best know imperfectly; but because such a publication is of itself a very serious overt-act, by which the author without authority and without trial, has inflicted punishment on a fellow subject, himself being witness and jury, judge and executioner. Of such publications there can be no legal justification, though the wrong may be palliated by the circumstance that the injurious charges are not only true but wholly out of the reach of the law. But in libels on the government there are two things to be balanced against each other: first, the incomparably greater mischief of the overt-acts, if we suppose them actually occasioned by the libel —(as for instance, the subversion of government and property, if the principles taught by Thomas Paine had been realized, or if even an attempt had been made to realize them, by the many thousands of his readers); and second, the very great improbability that such effects will be produced by such writings. Government concerns all generally, and no one in particular. The facts are commonly as well known to the readers, as to the writer: and falsehood therefore easily detected. It is proved, likewise, by experience, that the frequency of open political discussion, with all its blameable indiscretions, indisposes a nation to overt-acts of practical sedition or conspiracy. They talk ill, said Charles V. of his Belgian provinces, but they suffer so much the better for it. His successor thought differently: he determined to be master of their words and opinions, as well as of their actions, and in consequence lost one half of those provinces, and retained the other half at an expense of strength and treasure greater than the original worth of the whole. An enlightened jury, therefore, will require proofs of more than ordinary malignity of intention, as furnished by the style, price, mode of circulation, and so forth; or of punishable indiscretion arising out of the state of the times, as of dearth, for instance, or of whatever other calamity is likely to render the lower classes turbulent, and apt to be alienated from the government of their country. For the absence of a right disposition of mind must be considered both in law and in morals, as nearly equivalent to the presence of a wrong disposition. Under such circumstances the legal paradox, that a libel may be the more a libel for being true, becomes strictly just, and as such ought to be acted upon.

Concerning the right of punishing by law the authors of heretical or deistical writings, I reserve my remarks for a future essay, in which I hope to state the grounds and limits of toleration more accurately than they seem to me to have been hitherto traced. There is one maxim, however, which I am tempted to seize as it passes across me. If I may trust my own memory, it is indeed a very old truth: and yet if the fashion of acting in apparent ignorance thereof be any presumption of its novelty, it ought to be new, or at least have become so by courtesy of oblivion. It is this: that as far as human practice can realize the sharp limits and exclusive proprieties of science, law and religion should be kept distinct. There is, in strictness, no proper opposition but between the two polar forces of one and the same power.* If I say then, that law and religion are natural opposites, and that the latter is the requisite counterpoise of the former, let it not be interpreted, as if I had declared them to be contraries. The law has rightfully invested the creditor with the power of arresting and imprisoning an insolvent debtor, the farmer with the power of transporting, mediately at least, the pillagers of his hedges and copses; but the law does not compel him to exercise that power, while it will often happen that religion commands him to forego it. Nay, so well was this understood by our grandfathers, that a man who squares his conscience by the law was a common paraphrase or synonyme of

---

* Every power in nature and in spirit must evolve an opposite as the sole means and condition of its manifestation: and all opposition is a tendency to re-union. This is the universal law of polarity or essential dualism, first promulgated by Heraclitus, 2000 years afterwards re-published, and made the foundation both of logic, of physics, and of metaphysics by Giordano Bruno. The principle may be thus expressed. The identity of *thesis* and *antithesis* is the substance of all being; their opposition the condition of all existence or being manifested; and every thing or *phænomenon* is the exponent of a *synthesis* as long as the opposite energies are retained in that *synthesis*. Thus water is neither oxygen nor hydrogen, nor yet is it a commixture of both; but the *synthesis* or indifference of the two: and as long as the *copula* endures, by which it becomes water, or rather which alone is water, it is not less a simple body than either of the imaginary elements, improperly called its ingredients or components. It is the object of the mechanical atomistic pfilosophy to confound *synthesis* with *synartesis*, or rather with mere juxta-position of corpuscules separated by invisible interspaces. I find it difficult to determine, whether this theory contradicts the reason or the senses most: for it is alike inconceivable and unimaginable.

a wretch without any conscience at all. We have all of us learnt from history, that there was a long and dark period, during which the powers and the aims of law were usurped in the name of religion by the clergy and the courts spiritual: and we all know the result. Law and religion thus interpenetrating neutralized each other; and the baleful product, or *tertium aliquid*, of this union retarded the civilization of Europe for centuries. Law splintered into the *minutiæ* of religion, the awful function and prerogative of which it is to take account of every *idle word*, became a busy and inquisitorial tyranny: and religion substituting legal terrors for the ennobling influences of conscience remained religion in name only. The present age appears to me approaching fast to a similar usurpation of the functions of religion by law: and if it were required, I should not want strong presumptive proofs in favour of this opinion, whether I sought for them in the charges from the bench concerning wrongs, to which religion denounces the fearful penalties of guilt, but for which the law of the land assigns damages only: or in sundry statutes—and all praise to the late Mr. Wyndham, *Romanorum ultimo*—in a still greater number of attempts towards new statutes, the authors of which displayed the most pitiable ignorance, not merely of the distinction between perfect and imperfect obligations, but even of that still more sacred distinction between things and persons. What the son of Sirach advises concerning the soul, every senator should apply to his legislative capacity:—reverence it in meekness, knowing how feeble and how mighty a thing it is!*

From this hint concerning toleration, we may pass by an easy transition to the, perhaps, still more interesting subject of tolerance. And here I fully coincide with Frederic H. Jacobi, that the only true spirit of tolerance consists in our conscientious toleration of each other's intolerance. Whatever pretends to be more than this, is either the unthinking cant of fashion, or the soul-palsying narcotic of moral and religious indifference. All of us without exception, in the same mode though not in the same degree, are necessarily subjected to the risk of mistaking positive opinions for certainty and clear insight. From this yoke we cannot free ourselves, but by ceasing to be men; and this too not in order to transcend, but to sink below, our human nature. For if in one point of view it be the mulct of our fall, and of the corruption of our will; it is equally true, that contemplated from another point, it is the price and consequence of our progressiveness. To him who is compelled to pace to and fro within the high walls and in the narrow court-yard of a prison, all objects may appear clear and distinct. It is the traveller journeying onward, full of heart and hope, with an ever-varying horizon, on the boundless plain, who

---

* The reference, probably, is to Ecclus. x. 28. *My son, glorify thy soul in meekness, and give it honour according to the dignity thereof.*—Ed.

is liable to mistake clouds for mountains, and the *mirage* of drouth for an expanse of refreshing waters.

But notwithstanding this deep conviction of our general fallibility, and the most vivid recollection of my own, I dare avow with the German philosopher, that as far as opinions, and not motives, principles, and not men,—are concerned; I neither am tolerant, nor wish to be regarded as such. According to my judgment, it is mere ostentation, or a poor trick that hypocrisy plays with the cards of nonsense, when a man makes protestation of being perfectly tolerant in respect of all principles, opinions, and persuasions, those alone excepted which render the holders intolerant. For he either means to say by this, that he is utterly indifferent towards all truth, and finds nothing so insufferable as the persuasion of there being any such mighty value or importance attached to the possession of the truth as should give a marked preference to any one conviction above any other; or else he means nothing, and amuses himself with articulating the pulses of the air instead of inhaling it in the more healthful and profitable exercise of yawning. That which doth not withstand, hath itself no standing place. To fill a station is to exclude or repel others,—and this is not less the definition of moral, than of material, solidity. We live by continued acts of defence, that involve a sort of offensive warfare. But a man's principles, on which he grounds his hope and his faith, are the life of his life. *We live by faith*, says the philosophic Apostle; and faith without principles is but a flattering phrase for wilful positiveness, or fanatical bodily sensation. Well, and of good right therefore, do we maintain with more zeal, than we should defend body or estate, a deep and inward conviction, which is as the moon to us; and like the moon with all its massy shadows and deceptive gleams, it yet lights us on our way, poor travellers as we are, and benighted pilgrims. With all its spots and changes and temporary eclipses, with all its vain halos and bedimming vapours, it yet reflects the light that is to rise on us, which even now is rising, though intercepted from our immediate view by the mountains that inclose and frown over the vale of our mortal life.

This again is the mystery and the dignity of our human nature, that we cannot give up our reason, without giving up at the same time our individual personality. For that must appear to each man to be his reason which produces in him the highest sense of certainty; and yet it is not reason, except so far as it is of universal validity and obligatory on all mankind. There is a one heart for the whole mighty mass of humanity, and every pulse in each particular vessel strives to beat in concert with it. He who asserts that truth is of no importance except in the signification of sincerity, confounds sense with madness, and the word of God with a dream. If the power of reasoning be the gift of the supreme Reason, that we be sedulous, yea, and militant in the endeavour to reason aright, is his implied command. But what is of permanent and essential interest to one man must needs be so to all, in proportion to the means and opportunities of each. Woe to him by whom these are neglected, and double woe to him by whom they are withholden; for he robs at once himself and his neighbour. That man's soul is not dear to himself, to whom the souls of his brethren are not dear. As far as they can be influenced by him, they are parts and properties of his own soul, their faith his faith, their errors his burthen, their righteousness and bliss his righteousness and his reward—and of their guilt and misery his own will be the echo. As much as I love my fellow-men, so much and no more will I be intolerant of their heresies and unbelief—and I will honour and hold forth the right hand of fellowship to every individual who is equally intolerant of that which he conceives such in me.—We will both exclaim—'I know not what antidotes among the complex views, impulses and circumstances, that form your moral being, God's gracious providence may have vouchsafed to you against the serpent fang of this error,—but it is a viper, and its poison deadly, although through higher influences some men may take the reptile to their bosom, and remain unstung.'

In one of those poisonous journals, which deal out profaneness, hate, fury, and sedition through the land, I read the following paragraph. " The

Brahmin believes that every man will be saved in his own persuasion, and that all religions are equally pleasing to the God of all. The Christian confines salvation to the believer in his own Vedas and Shasters. Which is the more humane and philosophic creed of the two?" Let question answer question. Self-complacent scoffer! Whom meanest thou by God? The God of truth?—and can He be pleased with falsehood, and the debasement or utter suspension of the reason which he gave to man that he might receive from him the sacrifice of truth? Or the God of love and mercy?—and can He be pleased with the blood of thousands poured out under the wheels of Jaggernaut, or with the shrieks of children offered up as fire offerings to Baal or to Moloch?—Or dost thou mean the God of holiness and infinite purity?—and can He be pleased with abominations unutterable and more than brutal defilements,—and equally pleased too as with that religion, which commands us that we have no fellowship with the unfruitful works of darkness but to reprove them; —with that religion, which strikes the fear of the Most High so deeply, and the sense of the exceeding sinfulness of sin so inwardly, that the believer anxiously inquires: *Shall I give my first-born for my transgression, the fruit of my body for the sin of my soul?*—and which makes answer to him,—*He hath showed thee, O man, what is good; and what doth the Lord require of thee, but to do justly, and to love mercy, and to walk humbly with thy God?** But I check myself. It is at once folly and profanation of truth, to reason with the man who can place before his eyes a minister of the Gospel directing the eye of the widow from the corpse of her husband upward to his and her Redeemer,—(the God of the living and not of the dead)—and then the remorseless Brahmin goading on the disconsolate victim to the flames of her husband's funeral pile, abandoned by, and abandoning, the helpless pledges of their love—and yet dare ask, which is the more humane and philosophic creed of the two?—No! No! when such opinions are in question I neither am, nor will be, nor wish to be regarded as, tolerant.

---

* Micah vi. 7, 8.—*Ed.*

ESSAY XIV.

> Knowing the heart of man is set to be
> The centre of this world, about the which
> These revolutions of disturbances
> Still roll; where all the aspects of misery
> Predominate; whose strong effects are such,
> As he must bear, being powerless to redress:
> And that unless above himself he can
> Erect himself, how poor a thing is man!
>   DANIEL.*

I HAVE thus endeavoured, with an anxiety which may perhaps have misled me into prolixity, to detail and ground the conditions under which the communication of truth is commanded or forbidden to us as individuals, by our conscience; and those too, under which it is permissible by the law which controuls our conduct as members of the state. But is the subject of sufficient importance to deserve so minute an examination? O that my readers would look round the world, as it now is, and make to themselves a faithful catalogue of its many miseries! From what do these proceed,

---

* Epistle to the Countess of Cumberland.—*Ed.*

and on what do they depend for their continuance? Assuredly, for the greater part, on the actions of men, and those again on the want of a vital principle of action. *We live by faith.* The essence of virtue consists in the principle. And the reality of this, as well as its importance, is believed by all men in fact, few as there may be who bring the truth forward into the light of distinct consciousness. Yet all men feel, and at times acknowledge to themselves, the true cause of their misery. There is no man so base, but that at some time or other, and in some way or other, he admits that he is not what he ought to be, though by a curious art of self-delusion, by an effort to keep at peace with himself as long and as much as possible, he will throw off the blame from the amenable part of his nature, his moral principle, to that which is independent of his will, namely, the degree of his intellectual faculties. Hence, for once that a man exclaims, how dishonest I am! on what base and unworthy motives I act! we may hear a hundred times, what a fool I am! curse on my folly! and the like.*

Yet even this implies an obscure sentiment, that with clearer conceptions in the understanding, the

---

* I do not consider as exceptions the thousands that abuse themselves by rote with lip-penitence, or the wild ravings of fanaticism: for these persons at the very time they speak so vehemently of the wickedness and rottenness of their hearts, are then commonly the warmest in their own good opinion, covered round and comfortable in the wrap-rascal of self-hypocrisy.

principle of action would become purer in the will. Thanks to the image of our Maker not wholly obliterated from any human soul, we dare not purchase an exemption from guilt by an excuse, which would place our melioration out of our own power. Thus the very man, who will abuse himself for a fool but not for a villain, would rather, spite of the usual professions to the contrary, be condemned as a rogue by other men, than be acquitted as a blockhead. But be this as it may, in and out of himself, however, he sees plainly the true cause of our common complaints. Doubtless, there seem many physical causes of distress, of disease, of poverty and of desolation— tempests, earthquakes, volcanos, wild or venomous animals, barren soils, uncertain or tyrannous climates, pestilential swamps, and death in the very air we breathe. Yet when do we hear the general wretchedness of mankind attributed to these? Even in the most awful of the Icelandic and Sicilian eruptions, when the earth has opened and sent forth vast rivers of fire, and the smoke and vapour have dimmed the light of heaven for months, how small has been the comparative injury to the human race;— and how much even of this injury might be fairly attributed to combined imprudence and superstition! Natural calamities that do indeed spread devastation wide, (for instance, the marsh fever,) are almost without exception, voices of nature in her all-intelligible language— do this! or cease to do that! By the mere absence of one superstition, and of the sloth engendered by it, the plague would probably cease to exist throughout Asia and Africa. Pronounce meditatively the name of Jenner, and ask what might we not hope, what need we deem unattainable, if all the time, the effort, the skill, which we waste in making ourselves miserable through vice, and vicious through misery, were embodied and marshalled to a systematic war against the existing evils of nature! No, It is a wicked world! This is so generally the solution, that this very wickedness is assigned by selfish men, as their excuse for doing nothing to render it better, and for opposing those who would make the attempt. What have not Clarkson, Granville Sharp, Wilberforce, and the Society of the Friends, effected for the honour, and if we believe in a retributive Providence, for the continuance of the prosperity, of the English nation, imperfectly as the intellectual and moral faculties of the people at large are developed at present! What may not be effected, if the recent discovery of the means of educating nations (freed, however, from the vile sophistications and mutilations of ignorant mountebanks,) shall have been applied to its full extent! Would I frame to myself the most inspiriting representation of future bliss, which my mind is capable of comprehending, it would be embodied to me in the idea of Bell receiving, at some distant period, the appropriate reward of his earthly labours, when thousands and ten thousands of glorified spirits, whose reason and conscience

had, through his efforts, been unfolded, shall sing the song of their own redemption, and pouring forth praises to God and to their Saviour, shall repeat his *new name* in heaven, give thanks for his earthly virtues, as the chosen instruments of divine mercy to themselves, and not seldom perhaps turn their eyes toward him, as from the sun to its image in the fountain, with secondary gratitude and the permitted utterance of a human love! Were but a hundred men to combine a deep conviction that virtuous habits may be formed by the very means by which knowledge is communicated, that men may be made better, not only in consequence, but by the mode, and in the process, of instruction;—were but a hundred men to combine that clear conviction of this, which I myself at this moment feel, even as I feel the certainty of my being, with the perseverance of a Clarkson or a Bell, the promises of ancient prophecy would disclose themselves to our faith, even as when a noble castle hidden from us by an intervening mist, discovers itself by its reflection in the tranquil lake, on the opposite shore of which we stand gazing.*
What an awful duty, what a nurse of all other, the fairest virtues, does not hope become! We are bad ourselves, because we despair of the goodness of others.

If then it be a truth, attested alike by common

---

* This is, I fear, too complex, too accidental an image to be conveyed by words to those, who have not seen it themselves in nature. 1830.

feeling and common sense, that the greater part of human misery depends directly on human vices and the remainder indirectly, by what means can we act on men so as to remove or preclude these vices and purify their principle of moral election? The question is not by what means each man is to alter his own character—in order to this, all the means prescribed and all the aidances given by religion, may be necessary for him. Vain, of themselves, may be

>   ———— the sayings of the wise
> In ancient and in modern books inrolled
> . . . .
> Unless he feel within
> Some source of consolation from above,
> Secret refreshings, that repair his strength
> And fainting spirits uphold.*

This is not the question. Virtue would not be virtue, could it be given by one fellow-creature to another. To make use of all the means and appliances in our power to the actual attainment of rectitude, is the abstract of the duty which we owe to ourselves: to supply those means as far as we can, comprizes our duty to others. The question then is, what are these means? Can they be any other than the communication of knowledge, and the removal of those evils and impediments which prevent its reception? It may not be in our power to combine both, but it is in the power of every man to contribute to the former, who is sufficiently informed to feel that it is his duty. If it

---

* Samson Agonistes.

be said, that we should endeavour not so much to remove ignorance, as to make the ignorant religious;—religion herself, through her sacred oracles, answers for me, that all effective faith pre-supposes knowledge and individual conviction. If the mere acquiescence in truth, uncomprehended and unfathomed, were sufficient, few indeed would be the vicious and the miserable, in this country at least, where speculative infidelity is, God be praised! confined to a small number. Like bodily deformity, there is one instance here and another there; but three in one place are already an undue proportion. It is highly worthy of observation, that the inspired writings received by Christians are distinguishable from all other books pretending to inspiration, from the scriptures of the Brahmins, and even from the Koran, in their strong and frequent recommendations of truth. I do not here mean veracity, which cannot but be enforced in every code which appeals to the religious principle of man; but knowledge. This is not only extolled as the crown and honour of a man, but to seek after it is again and again commanded us as one of our most sacred duties. Yea, the very perfection and final bliss of the glorified spirit is represented by the Apostle as a plain aspect, or intuitive beholding, of truth in its eternal and immutable source. Not that knowledge can of itself do all! The light of religion is not that of the moon, light without heat; but neither is its warmth that of the stove, warmth without light. Religion is the sun, the warmth of which indeed swells, and stirs, and actuates the life of nature, but who at the same time beholds all the growth of life with a master-eye, makes all objects glorious on which he looks, and by that glory visible to all others.

But though knowledge be not the only, yet that it is an indispensable and most effectual, agent in the direction of our actions, one consideration will convince us. It is an undoubted fact of human nature, that the sense of impossibility quenches all will. Sense of utter inaptitude does the same. The man shuns the beautiful flame, which is eagerly grasped at by the infant. The sense of a disproportion of certain after-harm to present gratification produces effects almost equally uniform: though almost perishing with thirst, we should dash to the earth a goblet of wine in which we had seen a poison infused, though the poison were without taste or odour, or even added to the pleasures of both. Are not all our vices equally inapt to the universal end of human actions, the satisfaction of the agent? Are not their pleasures equally disproportionate to the after-harm? Yet many a maiden, who will not grasp at the fire, will yet purchase a wreath of diamonds at the price of her health, her honour, nay, and she herself knows it at the moment of her choice,—at the sacrifice of her peace and happiness. The sot would reject the poisoned cup, yet the trembling hand with which he raises his daily or hourly draught to his lips, has not left him ignorant that this too is altogether a poison. I know it will be objected, that the consequences foreseen are less immediate; that they are diffused over a larger space of time; and that the slave of vice hopes where no hope is. This, however, only removes the question one step further: for why should the distance or diffusion of known consequences produce so great a difference? Why are men the dupes of the present moment? Evidently because the conceptions are indistinct in the one case, and vivid in the other; because all confused conceptions render us restless; and because restlessness can drive us to vices that promise no enjoyment, no not even the cessation of that restlessness. This is indeed the dread punishment attached by nature to habitual vice, that its impulses wax as its motives wane. No object, not even the light of a solitary taper in the far distance, tempts the benighted mind from before; but its own restlessness dogs it from behind, as with the iron goad of destiny. What then is or can be the preventive, the remedy, the counteraction, but the habituation of the intellect to clear, distinct, and adequate conceptions concerning all things that are the possible objects of clear conception, and thus to reserve the deep feelings which belong, as by a natural right to those obscure ideas *

---

* I have not expressed myself as clearly as I could wish. But the truth of the assertion, that deep feeling has a tendency to combine with obscure ideas, in preference to distinct and clear notions, may be proved by the history of fanatics and fanaticism in all ages and countries. The *odium theologicum* is even proverbial: and it is the common complaint of philosophers and philosophic historians, that the

that are necessary to the moral perfection of the human being, notwithstanding, yea, even in consequence, of their obscurity—to reserve these feelings, I repeat, for objects, which their very sublimity renders indefinite, no less than their indefiniteness renders them sublime,—namely, to the ideas of being, form, life, the reason, the law of conscience, freedom, immortality, God? To connect with the objects of our senses the obscure notions and consequent vivid feelings, which are due only to immaterial and permanent things, is profanation relatively to the heart, and superstition in the understanding. It is in this sense, that the philosophic Apostle calls covetousness idolatry. Could we emancipate ourselves from the bedimming influences of custom, and the transforming witchcraft of early associations, we should see as numerous tribes of *fetisch*-worshippers in the streets of London and Paris, as we hear of on the coasts of Africa.

---

passions of the disputants are commonly violent in proportion to the subtlety and obscurity of the questions in dispute. Nor is this fact confined to professional theologians: for whole nations have displayed the same agitations, and have sacrificed national policy to the more powerful interest of a controverted obscurity.

ESSAY XV.

A palace when 'tis that which it should be
Leaves growing, and stands such, or else decays;
With him who dwells there, 'tis not so: for he
Should still urge upward, and his fortune raise.

Our bodies had their morning, have *their* noon,
And shall not better—*the* next change is night;
But *their* far larger guest, t' whom sun and moon
Are sparks and short-lived, claims another right.

The noble soul by age grows lustier,
Her appetite and her digestion mend;
We must not starve nor hope to pamper her
With woman's milk and pap unto the end.

Provide you manlier diet!   DONNE.*

I AM fully aware, that what I am writing and have written (in these latter essays at least) will expose me to the censure of some, as bewildering myself and readers with metaphysics; to the ridicule of others as a school-boy declaimer on old and worn-out truisms or exploded fancies; and to the objection of most as obscure. The last real or supposed defect has already received an answer both in the preceding essays, and in the appendix to my first

---

* Letter to Sir Henry Goodere. The words in italics are substituted for the original.—*Ed.*

Lay-Sermon, entitled The Statesman's Manual. Of the former two, I shall take the present opportunity of declaring my sentiments; especially as I have already received a hint that my idol, Milton, has represented metaphysics as the subject which the bad spirits in hell delight in discussing. And truly, if I had exerted my subtlety and invention in persuading myself and others that we are but living machines, and that, as one of the late followers of Hobbes and Hartley has expressed the system, the assassin and his dagger are equally fit objects of moral esteem and abhorrence; or if with a writer of wider influence and higher authority, I had reduced all virtue to a selfish prudence eked out by superstition,*—for, assuredly, a creed which takes its central point in conscious selfishness, whatever be the forms or names that act on the selfish passion, a ghost or a constable, can have but a distant relationship to that religion, which places its essence in our loving our neighbour as ourselves, and God above all,—I know not, by what arguments I could repel the sarcasm. But what are my metaphysics?—Merely the referring of the

---

* " And from this account of obligation it follows, that we are obliged to nothing but what we ourselves are to gain or lose something by; for nothing else can be a violent motive to us. As we should not be obliged to obey the laws, or the magistrate, unless rewards or punishments, pleasure or pain, somehow or other, depended upon our obedience; so neither should we, without the same reason, be obliged to do what is right, to practise virtue, or to obey the commands of God." Paley, Moral and Political Philosophy, B. II. c. 2, *et passim.*—*Ed.*

mind to its own consciousness for truths indispensable to its own happiness! To what purpose do I, or am I about to, employ them? To perplex our clearest notions and living moral instincts? To deaden the feelings of will and free power, to extinguish the light of love and of conscience, to make myself and others worthless, soulless, God-less? No! to expose the folly and the legerdemain of those who have thus abused the blessed machine of language; to support all old and venerable truths; and by them to support, to kindle, to project the spirit; to make the reason spread light over our feelings, to make our feelings, with their vital warmth, actualize our reason:—these are my objects, these are my subjects; and are these the metaphysics which the bad spirits in hell delight in?

But how shall I avert the scorn of those critics who laugh at the oldness of my topics, evil and good, necessity and arbitrement, immortality and the ultimate aim? By what shall I regain their favour? My themes must be new, a French constitution; a balloon; a change of ministry; a fresh batch of kings on the Continent, or of peers in our happier island; or who had the best of it of two parliamentary gladiators, and whose speech, on the subject of Europe bleeding at a thousand wounds, or our own country struggling for herself and all human nature, was cheered by the greatest number of "laughs," "loud laughs," and "very loud laughs:"—(which, carefully marked by italics, form most conspicuous and strange parentheses in the newspaper reports.) Or if I must be philosophical, the last chemical discoveries,—provided I do not trouble my reader with the principle which gives them their highest interest, and the character of intellectual grandeur to the discoverer; or the last shower of stones, and that they were supposed, by certain philosophers, to have been projected from some volcano in the moon,—care being taken not to add any of the cramp reasons for this opinion! Something new, however, it must be, quite new and quite out of themselves! for whatever is within them, whatever is deep within them, must be as old as the first dawn of human reason. But to find no contradiction in the union of old and new, to contemplate the Ancient of days with feelings as fresh, as if they then sprang forth at his own *fiat*—this characterizes the minds that feel the riddle of the world, and may help to unravel it! To carry on the feelings of childhood into the powers of manhood, to combine the child's sense of wonder and novelty with the appearances which every day for perhaps forty years has rendered familiar,

> With sun and moon and stars throughout the year,
> And man and woman ———

this is the character and privilege of genius, and one of the marks which distinguish genius from talent. And so to represent familiar objects as to awaken the minds of others to a like freshness of sensation concerning them—that constant accompaniment of mental, no less than of bodily, health

—to the same modest questioning of a self-discovered and intelligent ignorance, which, like the deep and massy foundations of a Roman bridge, forms half of the whole structure—(*prudens interrogatio dimidium scientiæ*, says Lord Bacon)—this is the prime merit of genius, and its most unequivocal mode of manifestation. Who has not, a thousand times, seen it snow upon water? Who has not seen it with a new feeling, since he has read Burns's comparison of sensual pleasure,

> To snow that falls upon a river,
> A moment white—then gone for ever! *

In philosophy equally, as in poetry, genius produces the strongest impressions of novelty, while it rescues the stalest and most admitted truths from the impotence caused by the very circumstance of their universal admission. Extremes meet;—a proverb, by the by, to collect and explain all the instances and exemplifications of which, would constitute and exhaust all philosophy. Truths, of all others the most awful and mysterious, yet being at the same time of universal interest, are too often considered as so true that they lose all the powers of truth, and lie bed-ridden in the dormitory of the soul, side by side with the most despised and exploded errors.

But as the class of critics, whose contempt I have anticipated, commonly consider themselves as men of the world, instead of hazarding additional

---

* Tam O'Shanter.—*Ed.*

sneers by appealing to the authorities of recluse philosophers,—for such, in spite of all history, the men who have distinguished themselves by profound thought, are generally deemed, from Plato and Aristotle to Cicero, and from Bacon to Berkeley—I will refer them to the darling of the polished court of Augustus, to the man, whose works have been in all ages deemed the models of good sense, and are still the pocket-companion of those who pride themselves on uniting the scholar with the gentleman. This accomplished man of the world has given us an account of the subjects of conversation between himself and the illustrious statesmen who governed, and the brightest luminaries who then adorned, the empire of the civilized world:

Sermo oritur non de villis domibusve alienis,
Nec male, necne, lepus saltet. Sed quod magis ad nos
Pertinet, et nescire malum est, agitamus: utrumne
Divitiis homines, an sint virtute beati?
Quidve ad amicitias, usus rectumne, trahat nos;
Et quæ sit natura boni, summumque quid ejus.—Hor.*

Berkeley indeed asserts, and is supported in his assertion by Lord Bacon and Sir Walter Raleigh, that without an habitual interest in these subjects,

---

* Serm. II. vi. 71. Conversation arises not concerning the country seats or families of strangers, nor whether the dancing hare performed well or ill. But we discuss what more nearly concerns us, and which it is an evil not to know: whether men are made happy by riches or by virtue: whether interest or a love of virtue should lead us to friendship; and in what consists the nature of good, and what is the ultimate or supreme good—*the summum bonum.*

a man may be a dexterous intriguer, but never can be a statesman. Would to Heaven that the verdict to be passed on my labours depended on those who least needed them! The water lily in the midst of waters lifts up its broad leaves, and expands its petals at the first pattering of the shower, and rejoices in the rain with a quicker sympathy, than the parched shrub in the sandy desert.

God created man in his own image. To be the image of his own eternity created he man! Of eternity and self-existence what other likeness is possible, but immortality and moral self-determination? In addition to sensation, perception, and practical judgment—instinctive or acquirable—concerning the notices furnished by the organs of perception, all which in kind at least, the dog possesses in common with his master; in addition to these, God gave us reason, and with reason he gave us reflective self-consciousness; gave us principles, distinguished from the maxims and generalizations of outward experience by their absolute and essential universality and necessity; and above all, by superadding to reason the mysterious faculty of free-will and consequent personal amenability, he gave us conscience — that law of conscience, which in the power, and as the indwelling word, of a holy and omnipotent legislator commands us—from among the numerous ideas mathematical and philosophical, which the reason by the necessity of its own excellence creates for itself,—unconditionally commands us to attribute reality, and actual existence, to those ideas and to those only, without which the conscience itself would be baseless and contradictory, to the ideas of soul, of free-will, of immortality, and of God. To God, as the reality of the conscience and the source of all obligation; to free-will, as the power of the human being to maintain the obedience, which God through the conscience has commanded, against all the might of nature; and to the immortality of the soul, as a state in which the weal and woe of man shall be proportioned to his moral worth. With this faith all nature,

> ———— all the mighty world
> Of eye and ear ———— *

presents itself to us, now as the aggregated material of duty, and now as a vision of the Most High revealing to us the mode, and time, and particular instance of applying and realizing that universal rule, pre-established in the heart of our reason.

"The displeasure of some readers," to use Berkeley's words, † " may, perhaps, be incurred by my *having surprized* them into certain reflections and inquiries, for which they have no curiosity. But perhaps some others may be pleased to find *themselves* carried into ancient times, *even though they should consider* the hoary maxims, *defended* in these essays, barely as hints to awaken and exercise the

---

* Wordsworth. Lines near Tintern Abbey.—*Ed.*
† Siris, 350. The words in italics are substituted for the original.—*Ed.*

inquisitive reader, on points not beneath the attention of the ablest men. Those great men, Pythagoras, Plato, and Aristotle, men the most consummate in politics, who founded states, or instructed princes, or wrote most accurately on public government, were at the same time the most acute at all abstracted and sublime speculations;—the clearest light being ever necessary to guide the most important actions. And whatever the world *may opine*, he who hath not much meditated upon God, the human mind, and the *summum bonum*, may possibly make a thriving earth-worm, but will most indubitably make a *blundering* patriot and a sorry statesman."

ESSAY XVI.

Blind is that soul which from this truth can swerve,
No state stands sure, but on the grounds of right,
Of virtue, knowledge; judgment to preserve,
And all the pow'rs of learning requisite:
Though other shifts a present turn may serve,
Yet in the trial they will weigh too light.
DANIEL.*

I EARNESTLY entreat the reader not to be dissatisfied either with himself or with the author, if he should not at once understand every part of the preceding essay; but rather to consider it as a mere annunciation of a magnificent theme, the different parts of which are to be demonstrated and developed, explained, illustrated, and exemplified in the progress of the work. I likewise entreat him to peruse with attention and with candour, the weighty extract from the judicious Hooker, prefixed as the motto to a following essay.† In works of reasoning, as distinguished from narrations of events or statements of facts; but

---

* *Musophilus.* The line in italics is substituted.—*Ed.*
† Essay IV. Sect. On the Principles of Political Knowledge. See Eccl. Pol. I. c. I. 2.—*Ed.*

more particularly in works, the object of which is to make us better acquainted with our own nature, a writer, whose meaning is everywhere comprehended as quickly as his sentences can be read, may indeed have produced an amusing composition, nay, by awakening and re-enlivening our recollections, a useful one; but most assuredly he will not have added either to the stock of our knowledge, or to the vigour of our intellect. For how can we gather strength, but by exercise? How can a truth, new to us, be made our own without examination and self-questioning — any new truth, I mean, that relates to the properties of the mind, and its various faculties and affections? But whatever demands effort, requires time. Ignorance seldom vaults into knowledge, but passes into it through an intermediate state of obscurity, even as night into day through twilight. All speculative truths begin with a postulate, even the truths of geometry. They all suppose an act of the will; for in the moral being lies the source of the intellectual. The first step to knowledge, or rather the previous condition of all insight into truth, is to dare commune with our very and permanent self. It is Warburton's remark, not the Friend's, that of all literary exercitations, whether designed for the use or entertainment of the world, there are none of so much importance, or so immediately our concern, as those which let us into the knowledge of our own nature. Others may exercise the understanding or amuse the imagination; but these only can improve the heart and form the human mind to wisdom.

> *The* recluse hermit ofttimes *more doth* know
> *Of the world's inmost wheels,* than worldlings can.
> As man is of the world, the heart of man
> Is an epitome of God's great book
> Of creatures, and men need no farther look.
> DONNE.*

The higher a man's station, the more arduous and full of peril his duties, the more comprehensive should his foresight be, the more rooted his tranquillity concerning life and death. But these are gifts which no experience can bestow, but the experience from within: and there is a nobleness of the whole personal being, to which the contemplation of all events and *phænomena* in the light of the three master ideas, announced in the foregoing pages, can alone elevate the spirit. *Anima sapiens,* says Giordano Bruno,—and let the sublime piety of the passage excuse some intermixture of error, or rather let the words, as they well may, be interpreted in a safe sense—*anima sapiens non timet mortem, immo interdum illam ultro appetit, illi ultro occurrit. Manet quippe substantiam omnem pro duratione eternitas, pro loco immensitas, pro actu omniformitas. Non levem igitur ac futilem, atqui gravissimam perfectoque homine dignissimam contemplationis partem persequimur, ubi divinitatis, naturæque splendorem, fusionem, et communicationem, non in cibo, potu, et ignobiliore quadam materia cum*

---

* Eclogue. The words in italics are substituted.—*Ed.*

*attonitorum seculo perquirimus; sed in augusta Omnipotentis regia, immenso ætheris spatio, in infinita naturæ geminæ omnis fientis et omnia facientis potentia, unde tot astrorum, mundorum, inquam, et numinum, uni altissimo concinentium atque saltantium absque numero atque fine juxta propositos ubique fines atque ordines contemplamur. Sic ex visibilium æterno, immenso et innumerabili effectu sempiterna immensa illa majestas atque bonitas intellecta conspicitur, proque sua dignitate innumerabilium deorum (mundorum dico) adsistentia, concinentia, et gloriæ ipsius enarratione, immo ad oculos expressa concione glorificatur. Cui immenso mensum non quadrabit domicilium atque templum;—ad cujus majestatis plenitudinem agnoscendam atque percolendam, numerabilium ministrorum nullus esset ordo. Eia igitur ad omniformis Dei omniformem imaginem conjectemus oculos, vivum et magnum illius admiremur simulacrum!—Hinc miraculum magnum a Trismegisto appellabatur homo, qui in Deum transeat quasi ipse sit Deus, qui conatur omnia fieri sicut Deus est omnia; ad objectum sine fine, ubique tamen finiendo, contendit, sicut infinitus est Deus, immensus, ubique totus.**

---

* *De monade, &c.* A wise spirit does not fear death, nay, sometimes—as in cases of voluntary martyrdom—seeks and goes forth to meet it, of its own accord. For there awaits all actual beings, for duration eternity, for place immensity, for action omniformity. We pursue, therefore, a species of contemplation not light or futile, but the weightiest and most worthy of an accomplished man, while we examine and seek for the splendour, the interfusion, and communication of the Divinity and of nature, not in meats

ESSAY XVI.

If this be regarded as the fancies of an enthusiast, by such as

> deem themselves most free,
> When they within this gross and visible sphere
> Chain down the winged soul, scoffing ascent,
> Proud in their meanness, ———*

by such as pronounce every man out of his senses who has not lost his reason; even such men may find some weight in the historical fact that from persons, who had previously strengthened their intellects and feelings by the contemplation of principles — principles, the actions correspondent to which involve one half of their consequences, by their ennobling influence on the agent's own soul, and have omnipotence, as the pledge for the re-

---

or drink, or any yet ignoble matter, with the race of the thunder-stricken; but in the august palace of the Omnipotent, in the illimitable etherial space, in the infinite power, that creates all things, and is the abiding being of all things.

There we may contemplate the host of stars, of worlds and their guardian deities, numbers without number, each in its appointed sphere, singing together, and dancing in adoration of the One Most High. Thus from the perpetual, immense, and innumerable goings on of the visible world, that sempiternal and absolutely infinite Majesty is intellectually beheld, and is glorified according to his glory, by the attendance and choral symphonies of innumerable gods, who utter forth the glory of their ineffable Creator in the expressive language of vision! To him illimitable, a limited temple will not correspond — to the acknowledgment and due worship of the plenitude of his majesty there would be no proportion in any numerable army of minis-

---

* Poetical Works, I. p. 99.—*Ed.*

mainder — we have derived the surest and most general maxims of prudence. Of high value are they all. Yet there is one among them worth all the rest, which in the fullest and primary sense of the word is, indeed, the maxim, that is, *maximum*, of human prudence; and of which history itself in all that makes it most worth studying, is one continued comment and exemplification. It is this: that there is a wisdom higher than prudence, to which prudence stands in the same relation as the mason and carpenter to the genial and scientific architect; and it is from the habits of thinking and feeling, which in this wisdom had

---

trant spirits. Let us then cast our eyes upon the omniform image of the attributes of the all-creating Supreme, nor admit any representation of his excellency but the living universe, which he has created!—Thence was man entitled by Trismegistus, the great miracle, inasmuch as he has been made capable of entering into union with God, as if he were himself a divine nature; tries to become all things, even as in God all things are; and in limitless progression of limited states of being, urges onward to the ultimate aim, even as God is simultaneously infinite, and every where all!

Giordano Bruno, the friend of Sir Philip Sidney and Fulk Greville, was burnt under pretence of atheism, at Rome, on the 17th of February, 1599-1600. (Scioppio ends his narrative in these words: *Sic ustulatus misere periit, renunciaturus, credo, in reliquis illis, quos finxit, mundis, quonam pacto homines blasphemi et impii a Romanis tractari solent. Hic itaque modus in Roma est, quo contra homines impios et monstra hujusmodi procedi a nobis solet.*—Ed.) His works are perhaps the scarcest books ever printed. They are singularly interesting as portraits of a vigorous mind struggling after truth, amid many prejudices, which from the state of the Romish Church, in which he was born,

their first formation, that our Nelsons and Wellingtons inherit that glorious hardihood, which completes the undertaking, ere the contemptuous calculator, who has left nothing omitted in his scheme of probabilities, except the might of the human mind, has finished his pretended proof of its impossibility. You look to facts, and profess to take experience for your guide. Well! I too appeal to experience: and let facts be the ordeal of my position! Therefore, although I have in this and the preceding essays quoted more frequently and copiously than I shall permit myself to do in future, I owe it to the cause I am plead-

---

have a claim to much indulgence. One of them (entitled Ember Week) is curious for its lively accounts of the rude state of London, at that time, both as to the streets and the manners of the citizens. (*La cena de le ceneri.* See particularly the second dialogue.—*Ed.*) The most industrious historians of speculative philosophy, have not been able to procure more than a few of his works. Accidentally I have been more fortunate in this respect, than those who have written hitherto on the unhappy philosopher of Nola; as out of eleven works, the titles of which are preserved to us, I have had an opportunity of perusing six. I was told, when in Germany, that there is a complete collection of them in the royal library at Copenhagen. If so, it is unique.

(Wagner has collected and published seven of the Italian works of Bruno: Leipzig, 1830. These are, *Il Candelajo*; *La cena de le ceneri*; *De la causa, principio etuno*; *De l'infinito, universo e mondi*; *Spaccio de la bestia trionfante*; *Cabala del caballo Pegaseo*; and *De gli eroici furori.* Two others are mentioned by Bruno, himself in the *Cena*, &c.; namely, *L'arca di Noè*, and *Purgatorio dell' inferno.* Wagner could not discover these. The titles of twenty-three works in Latin are given by Wagner.—*Ed.*)

ing, not to deny myself the gratification of supporting this connection of practical heroism with previous habits of philosophic thought, by a singularly appropriate passage from an author whose works can be called rare only from their being, I fear, rarely read, however commonly talked of. It is the instance of Xenophon as stated by Lord Bacon, who would himself furnish an equal instance, if there could be found an equal commentator.

"It is of Xenophon the philosopher, who went from Socrates's school into Asia, in the expedition of Cyrus the younger, against King Artaxerxes. This Xenophon, at that time, was very young, and never had seen the wars before; neither had any command in the army, but only followed the war as a volunteer, for the love and conversation of Proxenus, his friend. He was present when Falinus came in message from the great King to the Grecians, after that Cyrus was slain in the field, and they, a handful of men, left to themselves in the midst of the King's territories, cut off from their country by many navigable rivers, and many hundred miles. The message imported, that they should deliver up their arms and submit themselves to the King's mercy. To which message, before answer was made, divers of the army conferred familiarly with Falinus, and amongst the rest Xenophon happened to say: 'Why, Falinus! we have now but these two things left, our arms and our virtue; and if we yield up our arms, how shall we make use of our virtue?' Whereto Falinus, smiling on him, said, 'If I be not deceived, young gentleman, you are an Athenian, and I believe, you study philosophy, and it is pretty that you say; but you are much abused, if you think your virtue can withstand the King's power.' Here was the scorn: the wonder followed;—which was, that this young scholar or philosopher, after all the captains were murdered in parley, by treason, conducted those ten thousand foot through the heart of all the King's high countries from Babylon to Græcia, in safety, in despite of all the King's forces, to the astonishment of the world, and the encouragement of the Grecians, in time succeeding, to make invasion upon the kings of Persia; as was after purposed by Jason the Thessalian, attempted by Agesilaus the Spartan, and achieved by Alexander the Macedonian, all upon the ground of the act of that young scholar."*

Often have I reflected with awe on the great and disproportionate power, which an individual of no extraordinary talents or attainments may exert, by merely throwing off all restraint of conscience. What then must not be the power, where an individual, of consummate wickedness, can organize into the unity and rapidity of an individual will all the natural and artificial forces of a populous and wicked nation? And could we bring within the field of imagination, the devastation effected in the

---

* Advancement of Learning. B. I.—*Ed.*

moral world, by the violent removal of old customs, familiar sympathies, willing reverences, and habits of subordination almost naturalized into instinct; of the mild influences of reputation, and the other ordinary props and aidances of our infirm virtue, or at least, if virtue be too high a name, of our well-doing; and above all, if we could give form and body to all the effects produced on the principles and dispositions of nations by the infectious feelings of insecurity, and the soul-sickening sense of unsteadiness in the whole edifice of civil society; the horrors of battle, though the miseries of a whole war were brought together before our eyes in one disastrous field, would present but a tame tragedy in comparison. Nay it would even present a sight of comfort and of elevation, if this field of carnage were the sign and result of a national resolve, of a general will, so to die, that neither deluge nor fire should take away the name of country from their graves, rather than to tread the same clods of earth, no longer a country, and themselves alive in nature, but dead in infamy. What is Greece at this present moment? It is the country of the heroes from Codrus to Philopæmen; and so it would be, though all the sands of Africa should cover its corn-fields and olive gardens, and not a flower were left on Hymettus for a bee to murmur in.

If then the power with which wickedness can invest the human being be thus tremendous, greatly does it behove us to inquire into its source and causes. So doing we shall quickly discover that it is not vice, as vice, which is thus mighty; but systematic vice. Vice self-consistent and entire; crime corresponding to crime; villany entrenched and barricadoed by villany; this is the condition and main constituent of its power. The abandonment of all principle of right enables the soul to choose and act upon a principle of wrong, and to subordinate to this one principle all the various vices of human nature. For it is a mournful truth, that as devastation is incomparably an easier work than production, so may all its means and instruments be more easily arranged into a scheme and system: even as in a siege every building and garden, which the faithful governor must destroy, as impeding the defensive means of the garrison, or furnishing means of offence to the besieger, occasions a wound in feelings which virtue herself has fostered: and virtue, because it is virtue, loses perforce part of her energy in the reluctance with which she proceeds to a business so repugnant to her wishes, as a choice of evils. But he, who has once said with his whole heart, Evil, be thou my good! has removed a world of obstacles by the very decision, that he will have no obstacles but those of force and brute matter. The road of justice

> Curves round the corn-field and the hill of vines,
> Honouring the holy bounds of property;—*

---

* Poetical Works, III. p. 24.—*Ed.*

but the path of the lightning is ftraight; and ftraight the fearful path

Of the cannon-ball. Direct it flies and rapid,
Shatt'ring that it may reach, and fhatt'ring what it reaches.*

Happily for mankind, however, the obftacles which a confiftently evil mind no longer finds in itfelf, it finds in its own unfuitablenefs to human nature. A limit is fixed to its power: but within that limit, both as to the extent and duration of its influence, there is little hope of checking its career, if giant and united vices are oppofed only by mixed and fcattered virtues; and thofe too, probably, from the want of fome combining principle, which affigns to each its due place and rank, at civil war with themfelves, or at beft perplexing and counteracting each other. In our late agony of glory and of peril, did we not too often hear even good men declaiming on the horrors and crimes of war, and foftening or ftaggering the minds of their brethren by details of individual wretchednefs? Thus under pretence of avoiding blood, they were withdrawing the will from the defence of the very fource of thofe bleffings without which the blood would flow idly in our veins! Thus left a few fhould fall on the bulwarks in glory, they were preparing us to give up the whole ftate to bafenefs, and the children of free anceftors to become flaves, and the fathers of flaves!

Machiavelli has well obferved, *Sono di tre gene-*

---

* Poetical Works, III. p. 23.—*Ed.*

razioni cervelli: l'uno intende per sè; l'altro intende quanto da altri gli è mostro; e il terzo non intende nè per sè stesso, nè per dimostrazione di altri.* " There are brains of three races. The one understands of itself; the second understands as much as is shewn it by others; the third neither understands of itself nor what is shewn it by others."† I should have no hesitation in placing that man in the third class of brains, for whom the history of the last twenty years has not supplied a copious comment on the preceding text. The widest maxims of prudence are like arms without hearts, disjoined from those feelings which flow forth from principle as from a fountain. So little are even the genuine maxims of expedience likely to be perceived or acted upon by those who have been habituated to admit nothing higher than expedience, that I dare hazard the assertion, that in the whole chapter of contents of European ruin, every article might be unanswerably deduced from the neglect of some maxim which has been repeatedly laid down, demonstrated, and enforced with a host of illustrations, in some one or other

---

* *Il Principe,* c. xxii.—*Ed.*

† Οὗτος μὲν πανάριστος, ὃς αὐτῷ πάντα νοήσῃ,
Φρασσάμενος τά κ' ἔπειτα καὶ ἐς τέλος ᾖσιν ἀμείνω·
Ἐσθλὸς δ' αὖ κἀκεῖνος, ὃς εὖ εἰπόντι πίθηται.
Ὃς δέ κε μήτ' αὐτὸς νοέῃ, μήτ' ἄλλου ἀκούων
Ἐν θυμῷ βάλληται, ὁ δ' αὖτ' ἀχρήϊος ἀνήρ.

Op. et Dies. 293, &c.

Cic. p. Cluent. c. 31. Liv. xxii. 29. Diog. Laer. vii. 1. 21.—*Ed.*

of the works of Machiavelli, Bacon, or Harrington. Indeed I can remember no one event of importance which was not distinctly foretold, and this not by a lucky prize drawn among a thousand blanks out of the lottery wheel of conjecture, but legitimately deduced as certain consequences from established premisses. It would be a melancholy, but a very profitable employment, for some vigorous mind, intimately acquainted with the recent history of Europe, to collect the weightiest aphorisms of Machiavelli alone, and illustrating by appropriate facts the breach or observation of each, to render less mysterious the present triumph of lawless violence. The apt motto to such a work would be,—*The children of darkness are wiser in their generation than the children of light.*

So grievously, indeed, have men been deceived by the showy theories of unlearned mock thinkers, that there seems a tendency in the public mind to shun all thought, and to expect help from any quarter rather than from seriousness and reflection; as if some invisible power would think for us, when we gave up the pretence of thinking for ourselves. But in the first place, did those, who opposed the theories of innovators, conduct their untheoretic opposition with more wisdom or to a happier result? And secondly, are societies now constructed on principles so few and so simple, that we could, if even we wished it, act as it were by instinct, like our distant forefathers in the infancy of states? Doubtless, to act is nobler than to think: but as the old man doth not become a child by means of his second childishness, as little can a nation exempt itself from the necessity of thinking which has once learnt to think. Miserable was the delusion of the late mad realizer of mad dreams, in his belief that he should ultimately succeed in transforming the nations of Europe into the unreasoning hordes of a Babylonian or Tartar empire, or even in reducing the age to the simplicity — so desirable for tyrants — of those times, when the sword and the plough were the sole implements of human skill. Those are epochs in the history of a people which having been can never more recur. Extirpate all civilization and all its arts by the sword, trample down all ancient institutions, rights, distinctions, and privileges, drag us backward to our old barbarism, as beasts to the den of Cacus—deem you that thus you could re-create the unexamining and boisterous youth of the world, when the sole questions were—" What is to be conquered? and who is the most famous leader?"

In an age in which artificial knowledge is received almost at the birth, intellect and thought alone can be our upholder and judge. Let the importance of this truth procure pardon for its repetition. Only by means of seriousness and meditation and the free infliction of censure in the spirit of love, can the true philanthropist of the present time, curb-in himself and his contemporaries; only by these can he aid in preventing the evils which threaten us, not from the terrors of an enemy so much as from our own fear of, and aversion to, the toils of reflection. For all must now be taught in sport—science, morality, yea, religion itself. And yet few now sport from the actual impulse of a believing fancy and in a happy delusion. Of the most influential class, at least, of our literary guides—the anonymous authors of our periodical publications—the most part assume this character from cowardice or malice, till having begun with studied ignorance and a premeditated levity, they at length realize the lie, and end indeed in a pitiable destitution of all intellectual power.

To many I shall appear to speak insolently, because the public,—(for that is the phrase which has succeeded to The Town, of the wits of the reign of Charles II.)—the public is at present accustomed to find itself appealed to as the infallible judge, and each reader complimented with excellencies, which if he really possessed, to what purpose is he a reader, unless, perhaps, to remind himself of his own superiority! I confess that I think very differently. I have not a deeper conviction on earth, than that the principles of taste, morals, and religion, which are taught in the commonest books of recent composition, are false, injurious, and debasing. If these sentiments should be just, the consequences must be so important, that every well-educated man, who professes them in sincerity, deserves a patient hearing. He may fairly appeal even to those whose perfuasions are most opposed to his own, in the words of the philosopher of Nola:—*Ad isthæc quæso vos, qualiacunque prima videantur aspectu, adtendite, ut qui vobis forsan insanire videar, saltem quibus insaniam rationibus cognoscatis.* What I feel deeply, freely will I utter. Truth is not detraction; and assuredly we do not hate him to whom we tell the truth. But with whomsoever we play the deceiver and flatterer, him at the bottom we despise. We are, indeed, under a necessity to conceive a vileness in him, in order to diminish the sense of the wrong we have committed, by the worthlessness of the object.

Through no excess of confidence in the strength of my talents, but with the deepest assurance of the justice of my cause, I bid defiance to all the flatterers of the folly and foolish self-opinion of the half-instructed many;—to all who fill the air with festal explosions and false fires sent up against the lightnings of heaven, in order that the people may neither distinguish the warning flash nor hear the threatening thunder! How recently did we stand alone in the world? And though the one storm has blown over, another may even now be gathering: or haply the hollow murmur of the earthquake within the bowels of our own commonweal may strike a direr terror than ever did the tempest of foreign warfare. Therefore, though the first quatrain is no longer applicable, yet the moral truth and the sublime exhortation of the following sonnet can never be superannuated. With it I conclude this essay, thanking God that I have communed with, honoured, and loved its wise and high-minded author. To know that such men are among us, is of itself an antidote against despondence.—

> Another year!—another deadly blow!
> Another mighty empire overthrown!
> And we are left, or shall be left, alone;
> The last that dares to struggle with the foe.
> 'Tis well! from this day forward we shall know
> That in ourselves our safety must be sought;
> That by our own right hands it must be wrought;
> That we must stand unpropt or be laid low.
> O dastard! whom such foretaste doth not cheer!
> We shall exult, if they, who rule the land,
> Be men who hold its many blessings dear,
> Wise, upright, valiant; not a venal band,
> Who are to judge of danger which they fear,
> And honour, which they do not understand.
> WORDSWORTH.

THE LANDING-PLACE:

Or Essays interposed for Amusement, Retrospect, and Preparation.

MISCELLANY THE FIRST.

Etiam a Musis si quando animum paulisper abducamus, apud Musas nihilominus feriamur: at reclines quidem, at otiosas, at de his et illis inter se libere colloquentes.

THE LANDING-PLACE.

ESSAY I.

> O blessed letters! that combine in one
> All ages past, and make one live with all:
> By you we do confer with who are gone,
> And the dead-living unto council call!
> By you the unborn shall have communion
> Of what we feel and what doth us befall.
>
> Since writings are the veins, the arteries,
> And undecaying life-strings of those hearts,
> That still shall pant and still shall exercise
> Their mightiest powers when nature none imparts:
> And the strong constitution of their praise
> Wear out the infection of distemper'd days.
>
> DANIEL's MUSOPHILUS.

THE intelligence, which produces or controuls human actions and occurrences, is often represented by the Mystics under the name and notion of the supreme harmonist. I do not myself approve of these metaphors: they seem to imply a restlessness to understand that which is not among the appointed objects of our comprehension or discursive faculty. But certainly there is one excellence in good music, to which, without mysticism, we may find or make an analogy in the records of history. I allude to that sense of recognition, which accompanies our sense of novelty in the most original passages of a great composer. If we listen to a symphony of Cimarosa, the present strain still seems not only to recall, but almost to renew, some past movement, another and yet the same! Each present movement bringing back as it were, and embodying the spirit of some melody that had gone before, anticipates and seems trying to overtake something that is to come: and the musician has reached the summit of his art, when having thus modified the present by the past, he at the same time weds the past in the present to some prepared and corresponsive future. The auditor's thoughts and feelings move under the same influence: retrospection blends with anticipation, and hope and memory, a female Janus, become one power with a double aspect. A similar effect the reader may produce for himself in the pages of history, if he will be content to substitute an intellectual complacency for pleasurable sensation. The events and characters of one age, like the strains in music, recall those of another, and the variety by which each is individualized, not only gives a charm and poignancy to the resemblance, but likewise renders the whole more intelligible. Meantime ample room is afforded for the exercise both of the judgment and the fancy, in distinguishing cases of real resemblance from those of intentional imitation, the analogies of nature, revolving upon herself, from the masquerade figures of cunning and vanity.

It is not from identity of opinions, or from similarity of events and outward actions, that a real resemblance in the radical character can be deduced. On the contrary, men of great and stirring powers, who are destined to mould the age in which they are born, must first mould themselves upon it. Mohammed born twelve centuries later, and in the heart of Europe, would not have been a false prophet; nor would a false prophet of the present generation have been a Mohammed in the seventh century. I have myself, therefore, derived the deepest interest from the comparison of men, whose characters at first view appear widely dissimilar, who yet have produced similar effects on their different ages, and this by the exertion of powers which on examination will be found far more alike, than the altered drapery and costume would have led us to suspect. Of the heirs of fame, few are more respected by me, though for very different qualities, than Erasmus and Luther; scarcely any one has a larger share of my aversion than Voltaire; and even of the better-hearted Rousseau I was never more than a very lukewarm admirer. I should perhaps too rudely affront the general opinion, if I avowed my whole creed concerning the proportions of real talent between the two purifiers of revealed religion, now neglected as obsolete, and the two modern conspirators against its authority, who are still the Alpha and Omega of continental genius. Yet when I abstract the questions of evil and good, and measure only the effects produced and the mode of producing them, I have repeatedly found the names of Voltaire, Rousseau, and Robespierre, recall in a similar cluster and connection those of Erasmus, Luther, and Muncer.

Those who are familiar with the works of Erasmus, and who know the influence of his wit, as the pioneer of the Reformation; and who likewise know, that by his wit, added to the vast variety of knowledge communicated in his works, he had won over by anticipation so large a part of the polite and lettered world to the Protestant party; will be at no loss in discovering the intended counterpart in the life and writings of the veteran Frenchman. They will see, indeed, that the knowledge of the one was solid through its whole extent, and that of the other extensive at a cheap rate, by its superficiality; that the wit of the one is always bottomed on sound sense, peoples and enriches the mind of the reader with an endless variety of distinct images and living interests; and that his broadest laughter is every where translatable into grave and weighty truth: while the wit of the Frenchman, without imagery, without character, and without that pathos which gives the magic charm to genuine humour, consists, when it is most perfect, in happy turns of phrase, but far too often in fantastic incidents, outrages of the pure imagination, and the poor low trick of combining the ridiculous with the venerable, where he, who does not laugh, abhors. Neither will they have forgotten, that the object of the one was to drive the thieves and mummers out of the temple, while the other was propelling a worse banditti, first to profane and pillage, and ultimately to raze it. Yet not the less will they perceive, that the effects remain parallel, the circumstances analogous, and the instruments the same. In each case the effects extended over Europe, were attested and augmented by the praise and patronage of thrones and dignities, and are not to be explained but by extraordinary industry and a life of literature; in both instances the circumstances were supplied by an age of hopes and promises—the age of Erasmus restless from the first vernal influences of real knowledge, that of Voltaire from the hectic of imagined superiority. In the voluminous works of both, the instruments employed are chiefly those of wit and amusing erudition, and alike in both the errors and evils, real or imputed, in religion and politics are the objects of the battery. And here we must stop. The two men were essentially different. Exchange mutually their dates and spheres of action, yet Voltaire, had he been ten-fold a Voltaire, could not have made up an Erasmus; and Erasmus must have emptied himself of half his greatness and all his goodness, to have become a Voltaire.

Shall I succeed better or worse with the next pair, in this our new dance of death, or rather of the shadows which I have brought forth—two by two—from the historic ark? In our first couple I have at least secured an honourable retreat, and though I failed as to the agents, I have maintained a fair analogy in the actions and the objects. But the heroic Luther, a giant awaking in his strength, and the crazy Rousseau, the dreamer of love-sick tales, and the spinner of speculative cob-webs; shy of light as the mole, but as quick-eared too for every whisper of the public opinion; the teacher of stoic pride in his principles, yet the victim of morbid vanity in his feelings and conduct! From what point of likeness can we commence the comparison between a Luther and a Rousseau? And truly had I been seeking for characters that, taken as they really existed, closely resemble each other, and this too to our first apprehensions, and according to the common rules of biographical comparison, I could scarcely have made a more unlucky choice: unless I had desired that my parallel of the German *son of thunder* and the visionary of Geneva, should sit on the same bench with honest Fluellen's of Alexander the Great and Harry of Monmouth. Still, however, the same analogy would hold as in my former instance: the effects produced on their several ages by Luther and Rousseau, were commensurate with each other, and were produced in both cases by what their contemporaries felt as serious and vehement eloquence, and an elevated tone of moral feeling: and Luther, not less than Rousseau, was actuated by an almoſt ſuperſtitious hatred of ſuperſtition, and a turbulent prejudice againſt prejudices. In the relation too which their writings ſeverally bore to thoſe of Eraſmus and Voltaire, and the way in which the latter co-operated with them to the ſame general end, each finding its own claſs of admirers and proſelytes, the parallel is complete.

I cannot, however, reſt here. Spite of the apparent incongruities, I am diſpoſed to plead for a reſemblance in the men themſelves, for that ſimilarity in their radical natures, which I abandoned all pretence and deſire of ſhewing in the inſtances of Voltaire and Eraſmus. But then my readers muſt think of Luther not as he really was, but as he might have been, if he had been born in the age and under the circumſtances of the Swiſs philoſopher. For this purpoſe I muſt ſtrip him of many advantages which he derived from his own times, and muſt contemplate him in his natural weakneſſes as well as in his original ſtrength. Each referred all things to his own ideal. The ideal was indeed widely different in the one and in the other: and this was not the leaſt of Luther's many advantages, or, to uſe a favourite phraſe of his own, not one of his leaſt favours of preventing grace. Happily for him he had derived his ſtandard from a common meaſure already received by the good and wiſe; I mean the inſpired writings, the ſtudy of which Eraſmus had previouſly reſtored among the learned. To know that we are in ſympathy with others, moderates our feelings as well as strengthens our convictions: and for the mind, which opposes itself to the faith of the multitude, it is more especially desirable, that there should exist an object out of itself, on which it may fix its attention, and thus balance its own energies.

Rousseau, on the contrary, in the inauspicious spirit of his age and birth-place,* had slipped the cable of his faith, and steered by the compass of unaided reason, ignorant of the hidden currents that were bearing him out of his course, and too proud to consult the faithful charts prized and held sacred by his forefathers. But the strange influences of his bodily temperament on his understanding; his constitutional melancholy pampered into a morbid excess by solitude; his wild dreams of suspicion; his hypochondriacal fancies of hosts of conspirators all leagued against him and his cause, and headed by some arch-enemy, to whose machinations he attributed every trifling mishap—all as much the creatures of his imagination, as if instead of men he had conceived them to be infernal spirits and beings preternatural—these, or at least the predisposition to them, existed in the

---

* Infidelity was so common in Geneva about that time, that Voltaire in one of his letters exults, that in this, Calvin's own city, some half dozen only of the most ignorant believed in Christianity under any form. This was, no doubt, one of Voltaire's usual lies of exaggeration: it is not however to be denied, that here, and throughout Switzerland, he and the dark master in whose service he employed himself, had ample grounds of triumph.

ground-work of his nature: they were parts of Rousseau himself. And what corresponding in kind to these, not to speak of degree, can we detect in the character of his supposed parallel? This difficulty will suggest itself at the first thought, to those who derive all their knowledge of Luther from the meagre biography met with in the Lives of eminent Reformers, or even from the ecclesiastical histories of Mosheim or Milner: for a life of Luther, in extent and style of execution proportioned to the grandeur and interest of the subject, a life of the man Luther, as well as of Luther the theologian, is still a *desideratum* in English literature, though perhaps there is no subject for which so many unused materials are extant, both printed and in manuscript.*

---

* The affectionate respect in which I hold the name of Dr. Jortin — one of the many illustrious nurslings of the college to which I deem it no small honour to have belonged — Jesus, Cambridge — renders it painful to me to assert, that the above remark holds almost equally true of a life of Erasmus. But every scholar well read in the writings of Erasmus and his illustrious contemporaries, must have discovered, that Jortin had neither collected sufficient, nor the best, materials for his work: and — perhaps from that very cause — he grew weary of his task, before he had made a full use of the scanty materials which he had collected.

ESSAY II.

Is it, I ask, most important to the best interests of mankind, temporal as well as spiritual, that certain works, the names and number of which are fixed and unalterable, should be distinguished from all other works, not in degree only but even in kind?* And that these, collectively, should form THE BOOK, to which in all the concerns of faith and morality the last recourse is to be had, and from the admitted decisions of which no man dare appeal?—If the mere existence of a book so called and charactered be, as the Koran itself suffices to evince, a mighty bond of union, among nations whom all other causes tend to separate; if moreover the book revered by us and our forefathers has been the foster-nurse of learning in the darkest, and of civilization in the rudest, times; and lastly, if this so vast and wide a blessing is not to be founded in a delusion, and doomed therefore to the impermanence and scorn

---

* This is one of the hinges on which the gate of egress from the spiritual Rome turns. Historically, the affirmative to the question has been the constant and close companion of Protestantism:—but whether it be likewise its indispensable support, remains yet to be discussed, at the tribunal of sound philosophy. Hitherto both the ay and the no have been, as it appears to me, but very weakly and superficially argued. But I confess that Chillingworth makes me half a Roman Catholic on this point; lest in acceding to the grounds of his arguments against the Romanists, I should become less than half a Christian, and lose the substantive in my earnestness to tear off its parasitical and suffocating epithet:—that is, cease to be a Catholic in aversion to the Papal *bull* of Roman Catholic. 1830.

in which sooner or later all delusions must end; how, I pray you, is it conceivable that this should be brought about and secured, otherwise than by God's special vouchsafement to this one book, exclusively, of that divine MEAN, that uniform and perfect middle way, which in all points is at safe and equal distance from all errors whether of excess or defect? But again, if this be true—and what Protestant Christian worthy of his baptismal dedication will deny its truth?—if in the one book we are entitled, or even permitted, to expect the golden mean throughout;—surely we ought not to be hard and over-stern in our censures of the mistakes and infirmities of those, who pretending to no warrant of extraordinary inspiration have yet been raised up by God's providence to be of highest power and eminence in the reformation of his Church. Far rather does it behove us to consider, in how many instances the peccant humour native to the man had been wrought upon by the faithful study of that only faultless model, and corrected into an unsinning, or at least a venial, predominance in the writer or preacher. Yea, that not seldom the infirmity of a zealous soldier in the warfare of Christ has been made the very mould and ground-work of that man's peculiar gifts and virtues. Grateful too we should be, that the very faults of famous men have been fitted to the age, on which they were to act: and that thus the folly of man has proved the wisdom of God, and been made the instrument of his mercy to mankind.

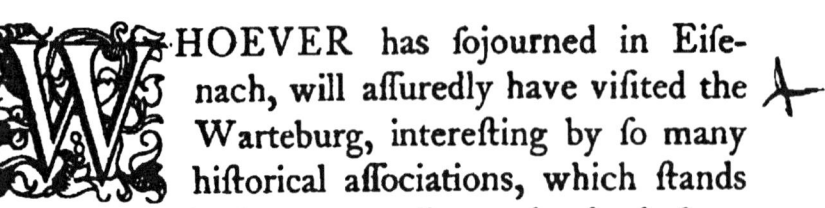

WHOEVER has sojourned in Eisenach, will assuredly have visited the Warteburg, interesting by so many historical associations, which stands on a high rock, about two miles to the south from the city gate. To this castle Luther was taken on his return from the imperial Diet, where Charles V. had pronounced the ban upon him, and limited his safe convoy to one and twenty days. On the last but one of these days, as he was on his way to Waltershausen, a town in the duchy of Saxe Gotha, a few leagues to the south-east of Eisenach, he was stopped in a hollow behind the castle Altenstein, and carried to the Warteburg. The Elector of Saxony, who could not have refused to deliver up Luther, as one put in the ban by the Emperor and the Diet, had ordered John of Berleptsch, the governor of the Warteburg, and Burckhardt von Hundt, the governor of Altenstein, to take Luther to one or the other of these castles, without acquainting him which; in order that he might be able, with safe conscience, to declare, that he did not know where Luther was. Accordingly they took him to the Warteburg, under the name of the Chevalier (*Ritter*) George.

To this friendly imprisonment the Reformation owes many of Luther's most important labours. In this place he wrote his works against auricular confession, against Jacob *Latronum*, the tract on the abuse of masses, that against clerical and monastic vows, composed his exposition of the 22, 27, and 68 Psalms, finished his declaration of the *Magnificat*, began to write his Church homilies, and translated the New Testament. Here too, and during this time, he is said to have hurled his inkstand at the devil, the black spot from which yet remains on the stone wall of the room he studied in; which, surely, no one will have visited the Warteburg without having had pointed out to him by the good catholic who is, or at least some few years ago was, the warden of the castle. He must have been either a very fupercilious or a very incurious traveller if he did not, for the gratification of his guide at leaft, inform himfelf by means of his pen-knife, that the faid marvellous blot bids defiance to all the toils of the fcrubbing brufh, and is to remain a fign for ever; and with this advantage over moft of its kindred, that being capable of a double interpretation, it is equally flattering to the Proteftant and the Papift, and is regarded by the wonder-loving zealots of both parties, with equal faith.

Whether the great man ever did throw his inkftand at his Satanic Majefty, whether he ever boafted of the exploit, and himfelf declared the dark blotch on his ftudy wall in the Warteburg, to be the refult and relict of this author-like hand-grenado,—(happily for mankind he ufed his inkftand at other times to better purpofe, and with more effective hoftility againft the arch-fiend)—I leave to my reader's own judgment; on condition, however, that he has previoufly perufed Luther's Table Talk, and other writings of the fame ftamp, of fome of his moft illuftrious contemporaries, which contain facts ftill more ftrange and whimfical, related by themfelves and of themfelves, and accompanied with folemn proteftations of the truth of their ftatements. Luther's Table Talk, which to a truly philofophic mind, will not be lefs interefting than Rouffeau's Confeffions, I have not myfelf the means of confulting at prefent, and cannot therefore say, whether this ink-pot adventure is, or is not, told or referred to, in it;* but many considerations incline me to give credit to the story.

Luther's unremitting literary labour and his sedentary mode of life, during his confinement in the Warteburg, where he was treated with the greatest kindness, and enjoyed every liberty consistent with his own safety, had begun to undermine his former unusually strong health. He suffered many and most distressing effects of indigestion and a deranged state of the digestive organs. Melancthon, whom he had desired to consult the physicians at Erfurth, sent him some de-obstruent medicines, and the advice to take regular and severe exercise. At first he followed the advice, sate and laboured less, and spent whole days in the chase; but like the younger Pliny, he strove in vain to form a taste for this favourite amusement of the gods of the earth, as appears from a passage in his letter to George Spalatin, which I translate for an additional reason;—to prove to the admirers of Rousseau, who perhaps will not be less affronted by this biographical parallel, than the zealous Lutherans will be offended, that if my comparison should turn out groundless on the whole, the failure will not have arisen either from the want of sensibility in our great reformer, or of angry aversion to those in high places, whom he re-

---

* It is not.—*Ed.*

garded as the oppreffors of their rightful equals. "I have been," he writes, "employed for two days in the fports of the field, and was willing myfelf to tafte this bitter-fweet amufement of the great heroes: we have caught two hares, and one brace of poor little partridges. An employment this which does not ill fuit quiet leifurely folks: for even in the midft of the ferrets and dogs, I have had theological fancies. But as much pleafure as the general appearance of the fcene and the mere looking-on occafioned me, even fo much it pitied me to think of the myftery and emblem which lies beneath it. For what does this fymbol fignify, but that the devil, through his godlefs huntfmen and dogs, the bifhops and theologians to wit, doth privily chafe and catch the innocent poor little beafts? Ah! the fimple and credulous fouls came thereby far too plain before my eyes. Thereto comes a yet more frightful myftery: as at my earneft entreaty we had faved alive one poor little hare, and I had concealed it in the fleeve of my great coat, and had ftrolled off a fhort diftance from it, the dogs in the mean time found the poor hare. Such, too, is the fury of the Pope with Satan, that he deftroys even the fouls that had been faved, and troubles himfelf little about my pains and entreaties. Of fuch hunting then I have had enough." In another paffage he tells his correfpondent, "You know it is hard to be a prince, and not in fome degree a robber, and the greater a prince the more a robber." Of our Henry VIII. he fays, "I muft answer the grim lion that passes himself off for king of England. The ignorance in the book is such as one naturally expects from a king; but the bitterness and impudent falsehood is quite leonine." And in his circular letter to the princes, on occasion of the peasants' war, he uses a language so inflammatory, and holds forth a doctrine which borders so near on the holy right of insurrection, that it may as well remain untranslated.

Had Luther been himself a prince he could not have desired better treatment than he received during his eight months stay in the Warteburg; and in consequence of a more luxurious diet than he had been accustomed to, he was plagued with temptations both from the flesh and the devil. It is evident from his letters* that he suffered under great irritability of his nervous system, the common effect of deranged digestion in men of sedentary habits, who are at the same time intense thinkers; and this irritability added to, and revivifying, the impressions made upon him in early life, and fostered by the theological systems of his manhood, is abundantly sufficient to explain all his apparitions and all his nightly combats with

---

* I can scarcely conceive a more delightful volume than might be made from Luther's letters, especially from those that were written from the Warteburg, if they were translated in the simple, sinewy, idiomatic, hearty, mother-tongue of the original. A difficult task I admit—and scarcely possible for any man, however great his talents in other respects, whose favourite reading has not lain among the English writers from Edward VI. to Charles I.

evil spirits. I see nothing improbable in the supposition, that in one of those unconscious half-sleeps, or rather those rapid alternations of the sleeping with the half-waking state, which is the true witching time,

——————————————— the season
Wherein the spirits hold their wont to walk.

the fruitful *matrix* of ghosts — I see nothing improbable, that in some one of those momentary slumbers, into which the suspension of all thought in the perplexity of intense thinking so often passes, Luther should have had a full view of the room in which he was sitting, of his writing table and all the implements of study, as they really existed, and at the same time a brain-image of the devil, vivid enough to have acquired apparent outness, and a distance regulated by the proportion of its distinctness to that of the objects really impressed on the outward senses.

If this Christian Hercules, this heroic cleanser of the Augean stable of apostasy, had been born and educated in the present or the preceding generation, he would, doubtless, have holden himself for a man of genius and original power. But with this faith alone he would scarcely have removed the mountains which he did remove. The darkness and superstition of the age, which required such a reformer, had moulded his mind for the reception of impressions concerning himself, better suited to inspire the strength and enthusiasm necessary for the task of reformation, impressions more in sympathy with the spirits whom he was to influence. He deemed himself gifted with supernatural influxes, an especial servant of heaven, a chosen warrior, fighting as the general of a small but faithful troop, against an army of evil beings headed by the prince of the air. These were no metaphorical beings in his apprehension. He was a poet indeed, as great a poet as ever lived in any age or country; but his poetic images were so vivid, that they mastered the poet's own mind! He was possessed with them, as with substances distinct from himself: Luther did not write, he acted poems. The Bible was a spiritual, indeed, but not a figurative armoury in his belief: it was the magazine of his warlike stores, and from thence he was to arm himself, and supply both shield and sword, and javelin, to the elect. Methinks I see him sitting, the heroic student, in his chamber in the Warteburg, with his midnight lamp before him, seen by the late traveller in the distant plain of Bischofsroda, as a star on the mountain! Below it lies the Hebrew Bible open, on which he gazes, his brow pressing on his palm, brooding over some obscure text, which he desires to make plain to the simple boor and to the humble artizan, and to transfer its whole force into their own natural and living tongue. And he himself does not understand it! Thick darkness lies on the original text: he counts the letters, he calls up the roots of each separate word, and questions them as the familiar spirits of an oracle. In vain; thick darkness continues to cover it; not a ray of meaning dawns through it. With sullen and angry hope he reaches for the Vulgate, his old and sworn enemy, the treacherous confederate of the Roman anti-Christ, which he so gladly, when he can, rebukes for idolatrous falsehoods, that had dared place

> Within the sanctuary itself their shrines,
> Abominations! ———————

Now—O thought of humiliation—he must entreat its aid. See! there has the sly spirit of apostasy worked-in a phrase, which favours the doctrine of purgatory, the intercession of saints, or the efficacy of prayers for the dead; and what is worst of all, the interpretation is plausible. The original Hebrew might be forced into this meaning: and no other meaning seems to lie in it, none to hover above it in the heights of allegory, none to lurk beneath it even in the depths of cabala! This is the work of the tempter; it is a cloud of darkness conjured up between the truth of the sacred letters and the eyes of his understanding, by the malice of the evil one, and for a trial of his faith! Must he then at length confess, must he subscribe the name of Luther to an exposition which consecrates a weapon for the hand of the idolatrous hierarchy? Never! never!

There still remains one auxiliary in reserve, the translation of the Seventy. The Alexandrine Greeks, anterior to the Church itself, could intend no support to its corruptions—the Septuagint will have profaned the altar of truth with no incense for the nostrils of the universal bishop to snuff up. And here again his hopes are baffled! Exactly at this perplexed passage had the Greek translator given his understanding a holiday, and made his pen supply its place. O honoured Luther! as easily mightest thou convert the whole city of Rome, with the Pope and the conclave of Cardinals inclusively, as strike a spark of light from the words, and nothing but words, of the Alexandrine version. Disappointed, despondent, enraged, ceasing to think, yet continuing his brain on the stretch in solicitation of a thought; and gradually giving himself up to angry fancies, to recollections of past persecutions, to uneasy fears and inward defiances and floating images of the evil being, their supposed personal author; he sinks, without perceiving it, into a trance of slumber; during which his brain retains its waking energies, excepting that what would have been mere thoughts before, now — the action and counterweight of his senses and of their impressions being withdrawn — shape and condense themselves into things, into realities. Repeatedly half-wakening, and his eye-lids as often reclosing, the objects which really surround him form the place and scenery of his dream. All at once he sees the arch-fiend coming forth on the wall of the room, from the very spot, perhaps, on which his eyes had been fixed vacantly during the perplexed moments of his former meditation: the ink-stand which he had at the same time been using, becomes associated with it: and in that struggle of rage, which in these distempered dreams almost constantly precedes the helpless terror by the pain of which we are finally awakened, he imagines that he hurls it at the intruder, or not improbably in the first instant of awakening, while yet both his imagination and his eyes are possessed by the dream, he actually hurls it. Some weeks after, perhaps, during which interval he had often mused on the incident, undetermined whether to deem it a visitation of Satan to him in the body or out of the body, he discovers for the first time the dark spot on his wall, and receives it as a sign and pledge vouchsafed to him of the event having actually taken place.

Such was Luther under the influences of the age and country in and for which he was born. Conceive him a citizen of Geneva, and a contemporary of Voltaire: suppose the French language his mother-tongue, and the political and moral philosophy of English free-thinkers re-modelled by Parisian *fort esprits*, to have been the objects of his study;—conceive this change of circumstances, and Luther will no longer dream of fiends or of anti-Christ—but will he have no dreams in their place? His melancholy will have changed its drapery; but will it find no new costume wherewith to clothe itself? His impetuous temperament, his deep working mind, his busy and vivid imaginations—would they not have been a trouble to him in a world, where nothing was to be altered, where nothing was to obey his power, to cease to be that which it had been, in order to realize his pre-conceptions of what it ought to be? His sensibility, which found objects for itself, and shadows of human suffering in the harmless brute, and even in the flowers which he trod upon — might it not naturally, in an unspiritualized age, have wept, and trembled, and dissolved, over scenes of earthly passion, and the struggles of love with duty? His pity, that so easily passed into rage, would it not have found in the inequalities of mankind, in the oppressions of governments and the miseries of the governed, an entire instead of a divided object? And might not a perfect constitution, a government of pure reason, a renovation of the social contract, have easily supplied the place of the reign of Christ in the new Jerusalem, of the restoration of the visible Church, and the union of all men by one faith in one charity? Henceforward then, we will conceive his reason employed in building up anew the edifice of earthly society, and his imagination as pledging itself for the possible realization of the structure. We will lose the great reformer, who was born in an age which needed him, in the philosopher of Geneva, who was doomed to misapply his energies to materials the properties of which he misunderstood, and happy only that he did not live to witness the direful effects of his own system.

ESSAY III.

Pectora cui credam? quis me lenire docebit
Mordaces curas, quis longas fallere noctes,
Ex quo summa dies tulerit Damona sub umbras?

Omnia paulatim consumit longior ætas,
Vivendoque simul morimur, rapimurque manendo.

Ite tamen, lacrymæ! purum colis æthera, Damon!
Nec mihi conveniunt lacrymæ. Non omnia terræ
Obruta! vivit amor, vivit dolor! ora negatur
Dulcia conspicere: flere et meminisse relictum est.

MILTON: PETRARCH: MILTON.

THE two following essays I devote to elucidation, the first of the theory of Luther's apparitions stated perhaps too briefly in the preceding essay; the second for the purpose of removing the only obstacle, which I can discover in the next section of the Friend, to the reader's ready comprehension of the principles, on which the arguments are grounded. First, I will endeavour to make my ghost theory more clear to those of my readers, who are fortunate enough to find it obscure in consequence of their own good health and unshattered nerves. The window of my library at Keswick is opposite to the fire-place, and looks out on the very large garden that occupies the whole slope of the hill on which the houfe ftands. Confequently, the rays of light tranfmitted through the glafs, that is, the rays from the garden, the oppofite mountains, and the bridge, river, lake, and vale interjacent, and the rays reflected from it, of the fire-place, &c., enter the eye at the fame moment. At the coming on of evening, it was my frequent amufement to watch the image or reflection of the fire, that feemed burning in the bufhes or between the trees in different parts of the garden or the fields beyond it, according as there was more or lefs light; and which ftill arranged itfelf among the real objects of vifion, with a diftance and magnitude proportioned to its greater or leffer faintnefs. For ftill as the darknefs increafed, the image of the fire leffened and grew nearer and more diftinct; till the twilight had deepened into perfect night, when all outward objects being excluded, the window became a perfect looking-glafs: fave only that my books on the fide fhelves of the room were lettered, as it were, on their backs with ftars, more or fewer as the fky was lefs or more clouded, the rays of the ftars being at that time the only ones tranfmitted. Now fubftitute the phantom from Luther's brain for the images of reflected light, the fire for inftance, and the forms of his room and its furniture for the tranfmitted rays, and you have a fair refemblance of an apparition, and a juft conception of the manner in which it is feen together with real objects. I have long wifhed to devote an entire work to the fubject of dreams, vifions, ghofts, and witchcraft, in which I might firſt give, and then endeavour to explain, the moſt intereſting and beſt atteſted fact of each, which has come within my knowledge, either from books or from perſonal teſtimony. I might then explain in a more ſatisfactory way the mode in which our thoughts, in ſtates of morbid ſlumber, become at times perfectly dramatic,—for in certain ſorts of dreams the dulleſt wight becomes a Shakeſpeare,— and by what law the form of the viſion appears to talk to us its own thoughts in a voice as audible as the ſhape is viſible; and this too oftentimes in connected trains, and not ſeldom even with a concentration of power which may eaſily impoſe on the ſoundeſt judgments, uninſtructed in the optics and acouſtics of the inner ſenſe, for revelations and gifts of preſcience. In aid of the preſent caſe, I will only remark, that it would appear incredible to perſons not accuſtomed to theſe ſubtle notices of ſelf-obſervation, what ſmall and remote reſemblances, what mere hints of likeneſs from ſome real external object, eſpecially if the ſhape be aided by colour, will ſuffice to make a vivid thought conſubſtantiate with the real object, and derive from it an outward perceptibility. Even when we are broad awake, if we are in anxious expectation, how often will not the moſt confuſed ſounds of nature be heard by us as articulate ſounds? For inſtance, the babbling of a brook will appear for a moment the voice of a friend, for whom we are waiting, calling out our own names. A ſhort meditation, therefore, on the great law of the imagination, that a likeneſs in part tends to become a likeness of the whole, will make it not only conceivable but probable, that the inkstand itself, and the dark-coloured stone on the wall, which Luther perhaps had never till then noticed, might have a considerable influence in the production of the fiend, and of the hostile act by which his obtrusive visit was repelled.

A lady once asked me if I believed in ghosts and apparitions. I answered with truth and simplicity: No, madam! I have seen far too many myself. I have indeed a whole memorandum book filled with records of these *phænomena*, many of them interesting as facts and *data* for psychology, and affording some valuable materials for a theory of perception and its dependence on the memory and imagination. *In omnem actum perceptionis imaginatio influit efficienter;* says Wolfe. But he[*] is no more, who would have realized this idea: who had already established the foundations and the law of the theory; and for whom I had so often found a pleasure and a comfort, even during the wretched and restless nights of sickness, in watching and instantly recording these experiences of the world within us, of the *gemina natura, quæ fit et facit, et creat et creatur!* He is gone, my friend; my munificent co-patron, and not less the benefactor of my intellect!—He who, beyond all other men known to me, added a fine and ever-wakeful sense of beauty to the most patient accuracy in experimental philosophy and the

---

[*] Thomas Wedgwood.

profounder researches of metaphysical science; he who united all the play and spring of fancy with the subtlest discrimination and an inexorable judgment; and who controlled an almost painful exquisiteness of taste by a warmth of heart, which in the practical relations of life made allowances for faults as quickly as the moral taste detected them; a warmth of heart, which was indeed noble and pre-eminent, for alas! the genial feelings of health contributed no spark toward it. Of these qualities I may speak, for they belonged to all mankind.— The higher virtues, that were blessings to his friends, and the still higher that resided in and for his own soul, are themes for the energies of solitude, for the awfulness of prayer!—virtues exercised in the barrenness and desolation of his animal being; while he thirsted with the full stream at his lips, and yet with unwearied goodness poured out to all around him, like the master of a feast among his kindred in the day of his own gladness! Were it but for the remembrance of him alone and of his lot here below, the disbelief of a future state would sadden the earth around me, and blight the very grass in the field.

ESSAY IV.

Χαλεπὸν, ὦ δαιμόνιε, μὴ παραδείγμασι χρώμενον, ἱκανῶς ἐνδείκνυσθαί τι τῶν μειζόνων. κινδυνεύει γὰρ ἡμῶν ἕκαςος, οἷον ὄναρ, εἰδὼς ἅπαντα, πάντ' αὖ πάλιν ὥσπερ ὕπαρ ἀγνοεῖν. PLATO, Politicus.

It is difficult, excellent friend! to make any comprehensive truth completely intelligible, unless we avail ourselves of an example. Otherwise we may, as in a dream, seem to know all, and then, as it were awaking, find that we know nothing.

AMONG my earliest impressions I still distinctly remember that of my first entrance into the mansion of a neighbouring baronet, awfully known to me by the name of the great house,* its exterior having been long connected in my childish imagination with the feelings and fancies stirred up in me by the perusal of the Arabian Nights' Entertainments.† Beyond all other objects, I was

---

* Escot, near Ottery St. Mary, Devon, then the seat of Sir George Young, and since burnt down in 1808. ED.

† As I had read one volume of these tales over and over again before my fifth birth-day, it may be readily conjectured of what sort these fancies and feelings must have been. The book, I well remember, used to lie in a corner of the parlour window at my dear father's vicarage-house: and I can never forget with what a strange mixture of obscure

most struck with the magnificent staircase, relieved at well proportioned intervals by spacious landing-places, this adorned with grand or shewy plants, the next looking out on an extensive prospect through the stately window with its side panes of rich blues and saturated amber or orange tints: while from the last and highest the eye commanded the whole spiral ascent with the marble pavement of the great hall, from which it seemed to spring up as if it merely used the ground on which it rested. My readers will find no difficulty in translating these forms of the outward senses into their intellectual analogies, so as to understand the purport of The Friend's landing-places, and the objects I proposed to myself, in the small groups of essays interposed under this title between the main divisions of the work.

My best powers would have sunk within me, had I not soothed my solitary toils with the anticipation of many readers—(whether during my life, or when my grave shall have shamed my detractors into a sympathy with its own silence, formed no part in this self-flattery—) who would submit to any reasonable trouble rather than read, ' as in a dream seeming to know all, to find on awaking that they know nothing.' Having, therefore, in

---

dread and intense desire I used to look at the volume and watch it, till the morning sunshine had reached and nearly covered it, when, and not before, I felt the courage given me to seize the precious treasure and hurry off with it to some funny corner in our play-ground.

the three preceding essays selected from my conservatory a few plants, of somewhat gayer petals and a livelier green, though like the geranium tribe of a sober character in the whole physiognomy and odour, I shall first devote a few sentences to a catalogue of my introductory lucubrations, and the remainder of the essay to the prospect, as far as it can be seen distinctly from our present site. Within a short distance, several ways meet: and at that point only does it appear to me that the reader will be in danger of mistaking the road. Dropping the metaphor, I would say that there is one term, reason, the meaning of which has become unsettled. To different persons it conveys a different notion, and not seldom to the same person at different times; while the force, and to a certain extent, the intelligibility of the following sections depend on its being interpreted in one sense exclusively.

Essays I. to IV. inclusively convey the design and contents of the work; my judgment respecting the style, and my defence of myself from the charges of arrogance and presumption. Say rather, that such are the personal threads of the discourse: for it will not have escaped the reader's observation, that even in these prefatory pages principles and truths of general interest form the true contents, and that amid all the usual compliments and courtesies of a first presentation to the reader's acquaintance the substantial object is still to assert the practicability, without disguising the difficulties, of improving the morals of mankind by a direct appeal to their understandings; to show the distinction between attention and thought, and the necessity of the former as a habit or discipline without which the very word, thinking, must remain a thoughtless substitute for dreaming with our eyes open; and lastly, the tendency of a certain fashionable style with all its accommodations to paralyze the very faculties of manly intellect by a series of petty stimulants. After this preparation, I proceed at once to lay the foundations common to the whole work by an inquiry into the duty of communicating truth, and the conditions under which it may be communicated with safety, from essay V. to XVI. inclusively. Each essay will, I believe, be found complete in itself, yet an organic part of the whole considered as one disquisition. First, the inexpediency of pious frauds is proved from history, the shameless assertion of the indifference of truth and falsehood exposed to its deserved infamy, and an answer given to the objection derived from the impossibility of conveying an adequate notion of the truths, we may attempt to communicate. The conditions are then detailed, under which, right though inadequate notions may be taught without danger, and proofs given, both from facts and from reason, that he, who fulfils the conditions required by conscience, takes the surest way of answering the purposes of prudence. This is, indeed, the main characteristic of the moral system taught by The Friend throughout, that the diftinct forefight of confequences belongs exclufively to the infinite Wifdom which is one with that Almighty Will, on which all confequences depend; but that for man—to obey the fimple unconditional commandment of efchewing every act that implies a felf-contradiction, or, in other words, to produce and maintain the greateft poffible harmony in the component impulfes and faculties of his nature, involves the effects of prudence. It is, as it were, prudence in fhort-hand or cypher. A pure confcience, that inward fomething, that θεὸς οἰκειος, which being abfolutely unique no man can defcribe, becaufe every man is bound to know, and even in the eye of the law is held to be a perfon no longer than he may be fuppofed to know it —the confcience, I fay, bears the fame relation to God, as an accurate time-piece bears to the fun. The time-piece merely indicates the relative path of the fun, yet we can regulate our plans and proceedings by it with the fame confidence as if it was itfelf the efficient caufe of light, heat, and the revolving feafons: on the felf-evident axiom, that in whatever fenfe two things—for inftance, A. and C. D. E.,—are both equal to a third thing, B., they are in the fame fenfe equal to each other. Cunning is circuitous folly. In plain Englifh, to act the knave is but a round about way of playing the fool; and the man, who will not permit himfelf to call an action by its proper name without a previous calculation of all its probable confequences, may be indeed only a coxcomb, who is looking at his fingers through an opera glafs; but he runs no fmall rifk of becoming a knave. The chances are againft him. Though he fhould begin by calculating the confequences with regard to others, yet by the mere habit of never contemplating an action in its own proportions and immediate relations to his moral being, it is fcarcely poffible but that he muft end in felfifhnefs: for the 'you,' and the 'they' will ftand on different occafions for a thoufand different perfons, while the 'I' is one only, and recurs in every calculation. Or grant that the principle of expediency fhould prompt to the fame outward deeds as are commanded by the law of reafon; yet the doer himfelf is debafed. But if it be replied, that the re-action on the agent's own mind is to form a part of the calculation, then it is a rule that deftroys itfelf in the very propounding, as will be more fully demonftrated in the fecond or ethical divifion of The Friend, when I shall have detected and expofed the equivoque between an action and a feries of motions, by which the determinations of the will are to be realized in the world of the fenfes. What modification of the latter correfponds to the former, and is entitled to be called by the fame name, will often depend on time, place, perfons and circumftances, the confideration of which requires an exertion of the judgment; but the action itfelf remains the fame, and like all other ideas pre-exifts in the reafon, or, in the more expreffive and perhaps more precife and philofophical language of St. Paul, in the spirit, unalterable because unconditional, or with no other than that most awful condition, *as sure as God liveth, it is so!*

These remarks are inserted in this place, because the principle admits of easiest illustration in the instance of veracity and the actions connected with the same, and may then be intelligibly applied to other departments of morality, all of which Woollston indeed considers as only so many different forms of truth and falsehood. So far I treated of oral communication of the truth. The applicability of the same principle is then tried and affirmed in publications by the press, first as between the individual and his own conscience, and then between the publisher and the state: and under this head I have considered at large the questions of a free press and the law of libel, the anomalies and peculiar difficulties of the latter, and the only possible solution compatible with the continuance of the former: a solution rising out of and justified by the necessarily anomalous and unique nature of the law itself. I confess that I look back on this discussion concerning the press and its limits with a satisfaction unusual to me in the review of my own labours: and if the date of their first publication (September, 1809) be remembered, it will not perhaps be denied on an impartial comparison, that I have treated this most important subject, so especially interesting in the present time, more fully and more systematically than it had up to that time been. *Interim tum recti conscientia, tum illo me consolor, quod optimis quibusque certe non improbamur, fortassis omnibus placituri, simul atque livor ab obitu conquieverit.*

Lastly, the subject is concluded even as it commenced, and as beseemed a disquisition placed as the steps and vestibule of the whole work, with an enforcement of the absolute necessity of principles grounded in reason as the basis or rather as the living root of all genuine expedience. Where these are despised or at best regarded as aliens from the actual business of life, and consigned to the ideal world of speculative philosophy and Utopian politics, instead of state wisdom we shall have state-craft, and for the talent of the governor the cleverness of an embarrassed spendthrift—which consists in tricks to shift off difficulties and dangers when they are close upon us, and to keep them at arm's length, not in solid and grounded courses to preclude or subdue them. We must content ourselves with expedient-makers — with fire-engines against fires, life-boats against inundations; but no houses built fire-proof, no dams that rise above the water-mark. The reader will have observed that already has the term, reason, been frequently contradistinguished from the understanding and the judgment. If I could succeed in fully explaining the sense in which the word reason is employed by me, and in satisfying the reader's mind concerning the grounds and importance of the distinction, I should feel little or no apprehension concerning the intelligibility of these essays from first to last. The following section is in part founded on this distinction: the which remaining obscure, all else will be so as a system, however clear the component paragraphs may be, taken separately. In the appendix* to my first Lay Sermon, I have, indeed, treated the question at considerable length, but chiefly in relation to the heights of theology and metaphysics. In the next number I attempt to explain myself more popularly, and trust that with no great expenditure of attention the reader will satisfy his mind, that our remote ancestors spoke as men acquainted with the constituent parts of their own moral and intellectual being, when they described one man as 'being out of his senses,' another as 'out of his wits,' or 'deranged in his understanding,' and a third as having 'lost his reason.' Observe, the understanding may be deranged, weakened, or perverted; but the reason is either lost or not lost, that is, wholly present or wholly absent.

---

* The third essay, erroneously lettered B.—*Ed.*

ESSAY V.

Man may rather be defined a religious than a rational creature, in regard that in other creatures there may be something of reason, but there is nothing of religion.
HARRINGTON.

IF the reader will substitute the word "understanding" for "reason," and the word "reason" for "religion," Harrington has here completely expressed the truth for which I am contending. Man may rather be defined a rational than an intelligent creature, in regard that in other creatures there may be something of understanding, but there is nothing of reason. But that this was Harrington's meaning is evident. Otherwise, instead of comparing two faculties with each other, he would contrast a faculty with one of its own objects, which would involve the same absurdity as if he had said, that man might rather be defined an astronomical than a seeing animal, because other animals possessed the sense of sight, but were incapable of beholding the satellites of Saturn, or the *nebulæ* of fixed stars. If further confirmation be necessary, it may be supplied by the following reflections, the leading thought of which I remember to have read in the works of a continental philosopher. It should seem easy to give the definite distinction of the reason from the understanding, because we constantly imply it when we speak of the difference between ourselves and the brute creation. No one, except as a figure of speech, ever speaks of an animal reason;* but that many animals possess a share of understanding, perfectly distinguishable from mere instinct, we all allow. Few persons have a favourite dog without making instances of its intelligence an occasional topic of conversation. They call for our admiration of the individual animal, and not with exclusive reference to the wisdom in nature, as in the case of the στοργὴ, or maternal instinct of beasts; or of the hexangular cells of the bees, and the wonder-

---

* I have this moment looked over a translation of Blumenbach's Physiology by Dr. Elliotson, which forms a glaring exception, p. 45. I do not know Dr. Elliotson, but I do know Professor Blumenbach, and was an assiduous attendant on the lectures, of which this classical work was the text-book: and I know that that good and great man would start back with surprise and indignation at the gross materialism mortised on to his work: the more so because during the whole period, in which the identification of man with the brute in kind was the fashion of naturalists, Blumenbach remained ardent and instant in controverting the opinion, and exposing its fallacy and falsehood, both as a man of sense and as a naturalist. I may truly say, that it was uppermost in his heart and foremost in his speech. Therefore, and from no hostile feeling to Dr. Elliotson, (whom I hear spoken of with great regard and respect, and to whom I myself give credit for his manly openness in the avowal of his opinions,) I have felt the present animadversion a duty of justice as well as gratitude.   April 8, 1817.

ful coincidence of this form with the geometrical demonstration of the largest possible number of rooms in a given space. Likewise, we distinguish various degrees of understanding there, and even discover from inductions supplied by the zoologists, that the understanding appears, as a general rule, in an inverse proportion to the instinct. We hear little or nothing of the instincts of the " half-reasoning elephant," and as little of the understanding of caterpillars and butterflies.* But reason is wholly denied, equally to the highest as to the lowest of the brutes; otherwise it must be wholly attributed to them, and with it therefore self-consciousness, and personality, or moral being.

I should have no objection to define reason with Jacobi, and with his friend Hemsterhuis, as an organ bearing the same relation to spiritual objects, the universal, the eternal, and the necessary, as the eye bears to material and contingent *phænomena*. But then it must be added, that it is an organ identical with its appropriate objects. Thus, God, the soul, eternal truth, &c. are the objects of reason; but they are themselves reason. We name God the Supreme Reason; and Milton says,—

—whence the soul
Reason receives, and reason is her being.†

---

* Note, that though " reasoning " does not in our language, in the lax use of words natural in conversation or popular writings, imply scientific conclusion, yet the phrase " half-reasoning " is evidently used by Pope as a poetic hyperbole.
† P. L. v. 486.—*Ed.*

Whatever is conscious self-knowledge is reason: and in this sense it may be safely defined the organ of the supersensuous; even as the understanding wherever it does not possess or use the reason, as its inward eye, may be defined the conception of the sensuous, or the faculty by which we generalize and arrange the *phænomena* of perception; that faculty, the functions of which contain the rules and constitute the possibility of outward experience. In short, the understanding supposes something that is understood. This may be merely its own acts or forms, that is, formal logic; but real objects, the materials of substantial knowledge, must be furnished, I might safely say revealed, to it by organs of sense. The understanding of the higher brutes has only organs of outward sense, and consequently material objects only; but man's understanding has likewise an organ of inward sense, and therefore the power of acquainting itself with invisible realities or spiritual objects. This organ is his reason.

Again, the understanding and experience may exist[*] without reason. But reason cannot exist without understanding; nor does it or can it manifest itself but in and through the understanding,

---

[*] Of this no one would feel inclined to doubt, who had seen the poodle dog, whom the celebrated BLUMENBACH,— a name so dear to science, as a physiologist and comparative anatomist, and not less dear as a man to all Englishmen who have ever resided at Göttingen in the course of their education,—trained up, not only to hatch the eggs of the hen with all the mother's care and patience, but to attend

which in our elder writers is often called discourse, or the discursive faculty, as by Hooker, Lord Bacon, and Hobbes: and an understanding enlightened by reason Shakespeare gives as the contradistinguishing character of man, under the name 'discourse of reason.' In short, the human understanding possesses two distinct organs, the outward sense, and the mind's eye, which is reason: wherever we use that phrase, the 'mind's eye,' in its proper sense, and not as a mere synonyme of the memory or the fancy. In this way we reconcile the promise of revelation, that the blessed will see God, with the declaration of St. John, *No man hath seen God at any time.*[*]

I will add one other illustration to prevent any misconception, as if I were dividing the human soul into different essences, or ideal persons. In this piece of steel I acknowledge the properties of hardness, brittleness, high polish, and the capability of forming a mirror. I find all these likewise in the plate glass of a friend's carriage; but in addition to all these I find the quality of transparency, or the power of transmitting, as well as of reflecting, the rays of light. The application is obvious.

If the reader therefore will take the trouble of

---

the chickens afterwards, and find the food for them. I have myself known a Newfoundland dog, who watched and guarded a family of young children with all the intelligence of a nurse, during their walks.

[*] 1 *Ep.* iv. 12.—*Ed.*

bearing in mind these and the following explanations, he will have removed before hand every possible difficulty from The Friend's political section. For there is another use of the word, reason, arising out of the former indeed, but less definite, and more exposed to misconception. In this latter use it means the understanding considered as using the reason, so far as by the organ of reason only we possess the ideas of the necessary and the universal; and this is the more common use of the word, when it is applied with any attempt at clear and distinct conceptions. In this narrower and derivative sense the best definition of reason, which I can give, will be found in the third member of the following sentence, in which the understanding is described in its three-fold operation, and from each receives an appropriate name. The sense,—*vis sensitiva vel intuitiva*—perceives: *vis regulatrix*—the understanding, in its own peculiar operation—conceives: *vis rationalis*—the reason or rationalized understanding—comprehends. The first is impressed through the organs of sense; the second combines these multifarious impressions into individual notions, and by reducing these notions to rules, according to the analogy of all its former notices, constitutes experience: the third subordinates both of them, the notions, namely, and the rules of experience, to absolute principles or necessary laws: and thus concerning objects, which our experience has proved to have real existence, it demonstrates, moreover, in what way they are possible, and in doing this constitutes science. Reason therefore, in this secondary sense, and used, not as a spiritual organ, but as a faculty, namely, the understanding or soul enlightened by that organ,—reason, I say, or the scientific faculty, is the intellection of the possibility or essential properties of things by means of the laws that constitute them. Thus the rational idea of a circle is that of a figure constituted by the circumvolution of a straight line with its one end fixed.

Every man must feel, that though he may not be exerting different faculties, he is exerting his faculties in a different way, when in one instance he begins with some one self-evident truth,—that the *radii* of a circle, for instance, are all equal,—and in consequence of this being true sees at once, without any actual experience, that some other thing must be true likewise, and that, this being true, some third thing must be equally true, and so on till he comes, we will say, to the properties of the lever, considered as the spoke of a circle; which is capable of having all its marvellous powers demonstrated even to a savage who had never seen a lever, and without supposing any other previous knowledge in his mind, but this one, that there is a conceivable figure, all possible lines from the middle to the circumference of which are of the same length: or when, in another instance, he brings together the facts of experience, each of which has its own separate value, neither increased nor diminished by the truth of any other fact which may have preceded it; and making these several facts bear upon some particular project, and finding some in favour of it, and some against it, determines for or against the project, according as one or the other class of facts preponderate: as, for example, whether it would be better to plant a particular spot of ground with larch, or with Scotch fir, or with oak in preference to either. Surely every man will acknowledge, that his mind was very differently employed in the first case from what it was in the second; and all men have agreed to call the results of the first class the truths of science, such as not only are true, but which it is impossible to conceive otherwise: while the results of the second class are called facts, or things of experience: and as to these latter we must often content ourselves with the greater probability, that they are so or so, rather than otherwise—nay, even when we have no doubt that they are so in the particular case, we never presume to assert that they must continue so always, and under all circumstances. On the contrary, our conclusions depend altogether on contingent circumstances. Now when the mind is employed, as in the case first mentioned, I call it reasoning, or the use of the pure reason; but, in the second case, the understanding or prudence.

This reason applied to the motives of our conduct, and combined with the sense of our moral responsibility, is the conditional cause of conscience, which is a spiritual sense or testifying state of the coincidence or discordance of the free will with the reason. But as the reasoning consists wholly in a man's power of seeing, whether any two conceptions which happen to be in his mind, are, or are not in contradiction to each other, it follows of necessity, not only that all men have reason, but that every man has it in the same degree. For reasoning, or reason, in this its secondary sense, does not consist in the conceptions themselves or in their clearness, but simply, when they are in the mind, in seeing whether they contradict each other or no.

And again, as in the determinations of conscience the only knowledge required is that of my own intention—whether in doing such a thing, instead of leaving it undone, I did what I should think right if any other person had done it; it follows that in the mere question of guilt or innocence, all men have not only reason equally, but likewise all the materials on which the reason, considered as conscience, is to work. But when we pass out of ourselves, and speak, not exclusively of the agent as meaning well or ill, but of the action in its consequences, then of course experience is required, judgment in making use of it, and all those other qualities of the mind which are so differently dispensed to different persons, both by nature and education. And though the reason itself is the same in all men, yet the means of exercising it, and the materials,—that is, the facts and conceptions—on which it is exercised, being possessed in very different degrees by different persons, the practical result is, of course, equally different—and the whole ground work of Rousseau's philosophy ends in a mere nothingism.—Even in that branch of knowledge, where the conceptions, on the congruity of which with each other, the reason is to decide, are all possessed alike by all men, namely in geometry;—for all men in their senses possess all the component images, namely simple curves and straight lines; yet the power of attention required for the perception of linked truths, even of such truths, is so very different in A and in B, that Sir Isaac Newton professed that it was in this power only that he was superior to ordinary men. In short, the sophism is as gross as if I should say,—the souls of all men have the faculty of sight in an equal degree—forgetting to add, that this faculty cannot be exercised without eyes, and that some men are blind and others short-sighted,—and should then take advantage of this my omission to conclude against the use or necessity of spectacles, and microscopes,—or of choosing the sharpest sighted men for our guides.

Having exposed this gross sophism, I must warn against an opposite error—namely, that if reason, as distinguished from prudence, consists merely in knowing that black cannot be white—or when a man has a clear conception of an inclosed figure, and another equally clear conception of a straight line, his reason teaches him that these two conceptions are incompatible in the same object, that is,

that two ſtraight lines cannot include a ſpace— —
the reaſon muſt therefore be a very inſignificant
faculty. For a moment's ſteady ſelf-reflection will
ſhew us, that in the ſimple determination 'black
is not white'—or, 'that two ſtraight lines cannot
include a ſpace'—all the powers are implied, that
diſtinguiſh man from animals;—firſt, the power
of reflection—2d, of compariſon—3d, and therefore of ſuſpenſion of the mind—4th, therefore of
a controlling will, and the power of acting from
notions, inſtead of mere images exciting appetites;
from motives, and not from mere dark inſtincts.
Was it an inſignificant thing to weigh the planets,
to determine all their courſes, and propheſy every
poſſible relation of the heavens a thouſand years
hence? Yet all this mighty chain of ſcience is
nothing but a linking together of truths of the ſame
kind, as, the whole is greater than its part;—or,
if A and B=C., then A=B : or 3+4=7, therefore 7+5=12, and ſo forth. X is to be found
either in A or B, or C or D : it is not found in
A, B, or C; therefore it is to be found in D.—
What can be ſimpler? Apply this to a brute animal.
A dog miſſes his maſter where four roads meet;—
he has come up one, ſmells to two of the others,
and then with his head aloft darts forward to the
fourth road without any examination. If this were
done by a concluſion, the dog would have reaſon;
—how comes it then, that he never ſhews it in
his ordinary habits? Why does this ſtory excite
either wonder or incredulity?—If the ſtory be a

fact, and not a fiction, I should say—the breeze brought his master's scent down the fourth road to the dog's nose, and that therefore he did not put it down to the road, as in the two former instances. So awful and almost miraculous does the simple act of concluding, that 'take three from four, there remains one,' appear to us, when attributed to one of the most sagacious of all brute animals.

THE FRIEND.

SECTION THE FIRST.

On the Principles of Political Knowledge.

Hoc potissimum pacto felicem ac magnum regem se fore judicans, non si quam plurimis sed si quam optimis imperet. Proinde parum esse putat justis præsidiis regnum suum muniisse, nisi idem viris eruditione juxta ac vitæ integritate præcellentibus ditet atque honestet. Nimirum intelligit hæc demum esse vera regni decora, has veras opes.
　　　　ERASMUS: EPIST. AD EPISC. PARIS.

THE FRIEND.

ESSAY I.

Dum politici sæpiuscule hominibus magis insidiantur quam consulunt, potius callidi quam sapientes; theoretici e contrario se rem divinam facere et sapientiæ culmen attingere credunt, quando humanam naturam, quæ nullibi est, multis modis laudare, et eam, quæ re vera est, dictis lacessere norunt. Unde factum est, ut nunquam politicam conceperint quæ possit ad usum revocari; sed quæ in Utopia vel in illo poetarum aureo sæculo, ubi scilicet minime necesse erat, institui potuisset. At mihi plane persuadeo, experientiam omnia civitatum genera, quæ concipi possunt ut homines concorditer vivant, et simul media, quibus multitudo dirigi, seu quibus intra certos limites contineri debeat, ostendisse: ita ut non credam, nos posse aliquid, quod ab experientia sive praxi non abhorreat, cogitatione de hac re assequi, quod nondum expertum compertumque sit.

Cum igitur animum ad politicam applicuerim, nihil quod novum vel inauditum est; sed tantum ea quæ cum praxi optime conveniunt, certa et indubitata ratione demonstrare aut ex ipsa humanæ naturæ conditione deducere, intendi. Et ut ea quæ ad hanc scientiam spectant, eadem animi libertate, qua res mathematicas solemus, inquirerem, sedulo curavi humanas actiones non ridere, non lugere, neque detestari; sed intelligere. Nec ad imperii securitatem refert quo animo homines inducantur ad res recte administrandas, modo res recte administrentur. Animi enim libertas, seu fortitudo, privata virtus est; at imperii virtus securitas.

SPINOSA Op. Post. p. 267.

While the mere practical statesman too often rather plots against mankind, than consults their interest, crafty, not wife; the mere theorists, on the other hand, imagine that they are employed in a glorious work, and believe themselves at the very summit of earthly wisdom, when they are able, in set and varied language, to extol that human nature, which exists no where, except indeed in their own fancy, and to accuse and vilify our nature as it really is. Hence it has happened, that these men have never conceived a practicable scheme of civil policy, but, at best, such forms of government only, as might have been instituted in Utopia, or during the golden age of the poets: that is to say, forms of government excellently adapted for those who need no government at all. But I am fully persuaded, that experience has already brought to light all conceivable sorts of political institutions under which human society can be maintained in concord, and likewise the chief means of directing the multitude, or retaining them within given boundaries: so that I can hardly believe, that on this subject the deepest research would arrive at any result, not abhorrent from experience and practice, which has not been already tried and proved.

When, therefore, I applied my thoughts to the study of political philosophy, I proposed to myself nothing original or strange as the fruits of my reflections; but simply to demonstrate from plain and undoubted principles, or to deduce from the very condition and necessities of human nature, those plans and maxims which square the best with practice. And that in all things which relate to this province, I might conduct my investigations with the same freedom of intellect with which we proceed in questions of pure science, I sedulously disciplined my mind neither to laugh at, nor bewail, nor detest, the actions of men; but to understand them. For to the safety of the state it is not of necessary importance, what motives induce men to administer public affairs rightly, provided only that public affairs be rightly administered.* For moral strength, or freedom from the selfish passions, is the virtue of individuals; but security is the virtue of a state.

---

* I regret, that I should have given, by thus selecting it for my motto, an implied consent to this very plausible, but false and dangerous position. 1830.

ESSAY I.

On the Principles of Political Philosophy.

ALL the different philosophical systems of political justice, all the theories on the rightful origin of government, are reducible in the end to three classes, correspondent to the three different points of view, in which the human being itself may be contemplated. The first denies all truth and distinct meaning to the words, right and duty; and affirming that the human mind consists of nothing but manifold modifications of passive sensation, considers men as the highest sort of animals indeed, but at the same time the most wretched; inasmuch as their defenceless nature forces them into society: while such is the multiplicity of wants engendered by the social state, that the wishes of one are sure to be in contradiction to those of some other. The assertors of this system consequently ascribe the origin and continuance of government to fear, or the power of the stronger, aided by the force of custom. This is the system of Hobbes. Its statement is its confutation. It is, indeed, in the literal sense of the word preposterous: for fear pre-supposes conquest, and conquest a previous union and agreement between the conquerors. A vast empire may perhaps be governed by fear; at least the supposition is not absolutely inconceivable, under circumstances which prevent the consciousness of a common strength. A million of men united by mutual confidence and free intercourse of thoughts form one power, and this is as much a real thing as a steam engine; but a million of insulated individuals is only an abstraction of the mind, and but one told so many times over without addition, as an idiot would tell the clock at noon—one, one, one. But when, in the first instances, the descendants of one family joined together to attack those of another family, it is impossible that their chief or leader should have appeared to them stronger than all the rest together; they must therefore have chosen him, and this as for particular purposes, so doubtless under particular conditions, expressed or understood. Such we know to be the case with the North American tribes at present; such, we are informed by history, was the case with our own remote ancestors. Therefore, even on the system of those who, in contempt of the oldest and most authentic records, consider the savage as the first and natural state of man, government must have originated in choice and an agreement. The apparent exceptions in Africa and Asia are, if possible, still more subversive of this system: for they will be found to have originated in religious imposture, and the first chiefs to have secured a willing and enthusiastic obedience to themselves as delegates of the Deity.

But the whole theory is baseless. We are told by history, we learn from our experience, we know from our own hearts, that fear, of itself, is utterly incapable of producing any regular, continuous, and calculable effect, even on an individual; and that the fear, which does act systematically upon the mind, always presupposes a sense of duty, as its cause. The most cowardly of the European nations, the Neapolitans and Sicilians, those among whom the fear of death exercises the most tyrannous influence relatively to their own persons, are the very men who least fear to take away the life of a fellow-citizen by poison or assassination; while in Great Britain, a tyrant, who has abused the power, which a vast property has given him, to oppress a whole neighbourhood, can walk in safety unarmed and unattended, amid a hundred men, each of whom feels his heart burn with rage and indignation at the sight of him. It was this man who broke my father's heart; or, it is through him that my children are clad in rags, and cry for the food which I am no longer able to provide for them. And yet they dare not touch a hair of his head! Whence does this arise? Is it from a cowardice of sensibility that makes the injured man shudder at the thought of shedding blood? Or from a cowardice of selfishness which makes him afraid of hazarding his own life? Neither the one nor the other! The field of Waterloo, as the most recent of a hundred equal proofs, has borne witness that,—

> ———bring a *Briton* frae his hill,
> . . . .
> Say, such is royal George's will,
>   An' there's the foe,

>   He has nae thought but how to kill
>   Twa at a blow.
>   Nae cauld, faint-hearted doubtings teafe him;
>   Death comes, wi' fearlefs eye he fees him;
>   Wi' bluidy hand, a welcome gies him;
>   And when he fa's,
>   His lateft draught o' breathin leaves him
>   In faint huzzas.*

Whence then arifes the difference of feeling in the former cafe? To what does the oppreffor owe his fafety? To the fpirit-quelling thought;—the laws of God and of my country have made his life facred! I dare not touch a hair of his head!—'Tis confcience that makes cowards of us all,—but oh! it is confcience too which makes heroes of us all.

---

* Burns.—*Ed*.

ESSAY II.

Le plus fort n'est jamais assez fort pour être toujours le maître, s'il ne transforme sa force en droit et l'obeissance en devoir.
ROUSSEAU.

Viribus parantur provinciæ, jure retinentur. Igitur breve id gaudium, quippe Germani victi magis, quam domiti.
FLORUS, iv. 12.*

The strongest is never strong enough to be always the master, unless he transforms his power into right, and obedience into duty.

Provinces are taken by force, but they are kept by right. This exultation therefore was of brief continuance, inasmuch as the Germans had been overcome, but not subdued.

A TRULY great man,† the best and greatest public character that I had ever the opportunity of making myself acquainted with, — on assuming the command of a man of war, found a mutinous crew, more than one half of them uneducated Irishmen, and of the remainder no small portion had become sailors by compromise of punishment. What terror could effect by severity and frequency of acts of discipline, had been already effected.

---

* Slightly altered.—*Ed.*
† Sir Alexander Ball.—*Ed.*

And what was this effect? Something like that of a polar winter on a flask of brandy. The furious spirit concentered itself with tenfold strength at the heart; open violence was changed into secret plots and conspiracies; and the consequent orderliness of the crew, as far as they were orderly, was but the brooding of a tempest. The new commander instantly commenced a system of discipline as near as possible to that of ordinary law;—as much as possible, he avoided, in his own person, the appearance of any will or arbitrary power to vary, or to remit, punishment. The rules to be observed were affixed to a conspicuous part of the ship, with the particular penalties for the breach of each particular rule; and care was taken that every individual of the ship should know and understand this code. With a single exception in the case of mutinous behaviour, a space of twenty-four hours was appointed between the first charge and the second hearing of the cause, at which time the accused person was permitted and required to bring forward whatever he thought conducive to his defence or palliation. If, as was commonly the case — for the officers well knew that the commander would seriously resent in them all caprice of will, and by no means permit to others what he denied to himself,—no answer could be returned to the three questions — Did you not commit the act? Did you not know that it was in contempt of such a rule, and in defiance of such a punishment? And was it not wholly in your own power to have obeyed the one and avoided the other?—the sentence was then passed with the greatest solemnity, and another, but shorter, space of time was again interposed between it and its actual execution. During this space the feelings of the commander, as a man, were so well blended with his inflexibility, as the organ of the law; and how much he suffered previously to and during the execution of the sentence was so well known to the crew, that it became a common saying with them when a sailor was about to be punished, the captain takes it more to heart than the fellow himself. But whenever the commander perceived any trait of pride in the offender, or the germs of any noble feeling, he lost no opportunity of saying, "It is not the pain that you are about to suffer which grieves me! You are none of you, I trust, such cowards as to turn faint-hearted at the thought of that! but that, being a man, and one who is to fight for his king and country, you should have made it necessary to treat you as a vicious beast,—it is this that grieves me."

I have been assured, both by a gentleman who was a lieutenant on board that ship at the time when the heroism of its captain, aided by his characteristic calmness and foresight, greatly influenced the decision of the most glorious battle recorded in the annals of our naval history; and very recently by a grey-headed sailor, who did not even know my name, or could have suspected that I was previously acquainted with the circumstances—I have been assured, I say, that the success of this plan was such as astonished the oldest officers, and convinced the most incredulous. Ruffians, who, like the old Buccaneers, had been used to inflict torture on themselves for sport, or in order to harden themselves beforehand, were tamed and overpowered, how or why they themselves knew not. From the fiercest spirits were heard the most earnest entreaties for the forgiveness of their commander: not before the punishment, for it was too well known that then they would have been to no purpose, but days after it, when the bodily pain was remembered but as a dream. An invisible power it was, that quelled them, a power, which was therefore irresistible, because it took away the very will of resisting. It was the awful power of law, acting on natures pre-configured to its influences. A faculty was appealed to in the offender's own being; a faculty and a presence, of which he had not been previously made aware,—but it answered to the appeal; its real existence therefore could not be doubted, or its reply rendered inaudible; and the very struggle of the wilder passions to keep uppermost counteracted their own purpose, by wasting in internal contest that energy which before had acted in its entireness on external resistance or provocation. Strength may be met with strength; the power of inflicting pain may be baffled by the pride of endurance; the eye of rage may be answered by the stare of defiance, or the downcast look of dark and revengeful resolve; and with all this there is an outward and determined object to which the mind can attach its paffions and purpofes, and bury its own difquietudes in the full occupation of the fenfes. But who dares ftruggle with an invifible combatant,—with an enemy which exifts and makes us know its exiftence—but where it is, we afk in vain?—No fpace contains it—time promifes no control over it—it has no ear for my threats—it has no fubftance, that my hands can grafp, or my weapons find vulnerable—it commands and cannot be commanded—it acts and is infufceptible of my re-action—the more I ftrive to fubdue it, the more am I compelled to think of it—and the more I think of it, the more do I find it to poffefs a reality out of myfelf, and not to be a phantom of my own imagination; that all, but the moft abandoned men, acknowledge its authority, and that the whole ftrength and majefty of my country are pledged to fupport it; and yet that for me its power is the fame with that of my own permanent felf, and that all the choice, which is permitted to me, confifts in having it for my guardian angel or my avenging fiend! This is the fpirit of law! the lute of Amphion, the harp of Orpheus! This is the true neceffity, which compels man into the focial ftate, now and always, by a ftill-beginning, never-ceafing, force of moral cohefion.

Thus is man to be governed, and thus only can he be governed. For from his creation the objects of his fenfes were to become his fubjects, and the tafk allotted to him was to fubdue the vifible world within the sphere of action circumscribed by those senses, as far as they could act in concert. What the eye beholds, the hand strives to reach; what it reaches, it conquers, and makes the instrument of further conquest. We can be subdued by that alone which is analagous in kind to that by which we subdue: therefore by the invisible powers of our nature, whose immediate presence is disclosed to our inner sense, and only as the symbols and language of which all shapes and modifications of matter become formidable to us.

A machine continues to move by the force which first set it in motion. If only the smallest number in any state, properly so called, hold together through the influence of any fear that does not itself pre-suppose the sense of duty, it is evident that the state itself could not have commenced through animal fear. We hear, indeed, of conquests; but how does history represent these? Almost without exception as the substitution of one set of governors for another: and so far is the conqueror from relying on fear alone to secure the obedience of the conquered, that his first step is to demand an oath of fealty from them, by which he would impose upon them the belief, that they become subjects: for who would think of administering an oath to a gang of slaves? But what can make the difference between slave and subject, if not the existence of an implied contract in the one case, and not in the other? And to what purpose would a contract serve, if, however it might be entered into through fear, it were deemed binding only in confequence of fear? To repeat my former illuftration—where fear alone is relied on, as in a flave fhip, the chains that bind the poor victims muft be material chains: for thefe only can act upon feelings which have their fource wholly in the material organization. Hobbes has faid, that laws without the fword are but bits of parchment. How far this is true, every honeft man's heart will beft tell him, if he will content himfelf with afking his own heart, and not falfify the anfwer by his notions concerning the hearts of other men. But were it true, ftill the fair anfwer would be—Well! but without the laws the fword is but a piece of iron. The wretched tyrant, who difgraces the prefent age and human nature itfelf, had exhaufted the whole magazine of animal terror, in order to confolidate his truly Satanic government. But look at the new French catechifm, and in it read the mifgivings of his mind, as to the fufficiency of terror alone! The fyftem, which I have been confuting, is indeed fo inconfiftent with the facts revealed to us by our own mind, and fo utterly unfupported by any facts of hiftory, that I fhould be cenfurable in wafting my own time and my reader's patience by the expofure of its falfehood, but that the arguments adduced have a value of themfelves independently of their prefent application. Elfe it would have been an ample and fatisfactory reply to an affertor of this beftial theory: —Government is a thing which relates to men, and what you fay applies only to beafts.

Before I proceed to the second of these systems, let me remove a possible misunderstanding that may have arisen from the use of the word contract: as if I had asserted, that the whole duty of obedience to governors is derived from, and dependent on, the fact of an original contract. I freely admit, that to make this the cause and origin of political obligation, is not only a dangerous but an absurd theory; for what could give moral force to the contract? The same sense of duty which binds us to keep it, must have pre-existed as impelling us to make it. For what man in his senses would regard the faithful observation of a contract entered into to plunder a neighbour's house, but as a treble crime? First the act, which is a crime of itself; secondly, the entering into a contract which it is a crime to observe, and yet a weakening of one of the main pillars of human confidence not to observe, and thus voluntarily placing ourselves under the necessity of choosing between two evils;—and thirdly, the crime of choosing the greater of the two evils, by the unlawful observance of an unlawful promise. But in my sense, the word contract is merely synonymous with the sense of duty acting in a specific direction, that is, determining our moral relations, as members of a body politic. If I have referred to a supposed origin of government, it has been in courtesy to a common notion: for I myself regard the supposition as no more than a means of simplifying to our apprehension the ever-continuing causes of social union, even as the converſation of the world may be repreſented as an act of continued creation. For, what if an original contract had really been entered into, and formally recorded? Still it could do no more than bind the contracting parties to act for the general good in the beſt manner, that the exiſting relations among themſelves, (ſtate of property, religion, and ſo forth) on the one hand, and the external circumſtances on the other (ambitious or barbarous neighbours, and the like,) required or permitted. In after times it could be appealed to only for the general principle, and no more, than the ideal contract, could it affect a queſtion of ways and means. As each particular age brings with it its own exigencies, ſo muſt it rely on its own prudence for the ſpecific meaſures by which they are to be encountered.

Nevertheleſs, it aſſuredly cannot be denied, that an original,—more accurately, an ever-originating,—contract is a very natural and ſignificant mode of expreſſing the reciprocal duties of ſubject and ſovereign. We need only conſider the utility of a real and formal ſtate contract, — the Bill of Rights for inſtance,—as a ſort of *eſt demonſtratum* in politics; and the contempt laviſhed on this notion, though ſufficiently compatible with the tenets of a Hume, will ſeem ſtrange to us in the writings of a Proteſtant clergyman,* who ſurely owed ſome reſpect to a mode of thinking which God himſelf

---

* See Paley's Moral and Political Philoſophy. B. vi. c. 3.—*Ed.*

had authorised by his own example, in the establishment of the Jewish constitution. In this instance there was no necessity for deducing the will of God from the tendency of the laws to the general happiness: his will was expressly declared. Nevertheless, it seemed good to the divine wisdom, that there should be a covenant, an original contract, between himself as sovereign, and the Hebrew nation as subjects. This I admit was a written and formal contract; but the relations of mankind, as members of a body spiritual, or religious commonwealth, to the Saviour, as its head or regent;—is not this, too, styled a covenant, though it would be absurd to ask for the material instrument that contained it, or the time when it was signed or voted by the members of the church collectively.*

With this explanation, the assertion of an original or a perpetual contract is rescued from all rational objection; and however speciously it may be urged, that history can scarcely produce a single example of a state dating its primary establishment from a free and mutual covenant, the answer is ready: if there be any difference between a government and a band of robbers, an act of consent must be supposed on the part of the people governed.

---

* It is perhaps to be regretted, that the words, Old and New Testament,—they having lost the sense intended by the translators of the Bible,—have not been changed into the Old and New Covenant. We cannot too carefully keep in sight a notion, which appeared to the Primitive Church the fittest and most scriptural mode of representing the sum of the contents of the sacred writings.

ESSAY III.

Human institutions cannot be wholly constructed on principles of science, which is proper to immutable objects. In the government of the visible world the Supreme Wisdom itself submits to be the author of the better; not of the best, but of the best possible in the subsisting relations. Much more must all human legislators give way to many evils rather than encourage the discontent that would lead to worse remedies. If it is not in the power of man to construct even the arch of a bridge that shall exactly correspond in its strength to the calculations of geometry, how much less can human science construct a constitution except by rendering itself flexible to experience and expediency: where so many things must fall out accidentally, and come not into any compliance with the preconceived ends: but men are forced to comply subsequently, and to strike in with things as they fall out, by after applications of them to their purposes, or by framing their purposes to them.   SOUTH.

THE second system corresponds to the second point of view under which the human being may be considered, namely, as an animal gifted with understanding, or the faculty of suiting measures to circumstances. According to this theory, every institution of national origin needs no other justification than a proof, that under the particular circumstances it is expedient. Having in my former essays expressed myself,—so at least I am conscious I shall have appeared to do to many persons;—with comparative slight of the understanding considered as the sole guide of human conduct, and even with something like contempt and reprobation of the maxims of expedience, when represented as the only steady light of the conscience, and the absolute foundation of all morality; I shall perhaps seem guilty of an inconsistency, in declaring myself an adherent of this second system, a zealous advocate for deriving the various forms and modes of government from human prudence, and of deeming that to be just which experience has proved to be expedient. From this charge of inconsistency* I shall best exculpate myself by the full statement of the third system, and by the exposition of its grounds and consequences.

---

* Distinct notions do not suppose different things. When I make a threefold distinction in human nature, I am fully aware, that it is a distinction, not a division, and that in every act of mind the man unites the properties of sense, understanding, and reason. Nevertheless it is of great practical importance, that these distinctions should be made and understood, the ignorance or perversion of them being alike injurious; as the first French constitution has most lamentably proved. It was the fashion in the profligate times of Charles II. to laugh at the Presbyterians, for distinguishing between the person and the king; while in fact they were ridiculing the most venerable maxims of English law;—the king never dies—the king can do no wrong,—and subverting the principles of genuine loyalty, in order to prepare the minds of the people for despotism.

Under the term " sense," I comprise whatever is passive in our being, without any reference to the question of materialism or immaterialism; all that man is in common with animals, in kind at least—his sensations, and impressions, whether of his outward senses, or the inner sense of imagination. This, in the language of the schools, was called

The third and last system, then, denies all rightful origin to government, except as far as it is derivable from principles contained in the reason of man, and judges all the relations of man in society by the laws of moral necessity, according to ideas.—I here use the word in its highest and primitive sense, and as nearly synonymous with the modern word ideal,—according to archetypal ideas co-essential with the reason, the consciousness of these ideas being indeed the sign and necessary product of the full development of the reason. The following then is the fundamental principle of this theory: Nothing is to be deemed rightful in civil society, or to be tolerated as such, but what is capable of being demonstrated out of the original

---

the *vis receptiva*, or recipient property of the soul, from the original constitution of which we perceive and imagine all things under the forms of space and time. By the "understanding," I mean the faculty of thinking and forming judgments on the notices furnished by the sense, according to certain rules existing in itself, which rules constitute its distinct nature. By the pure "reason," I mean the power by which we become possessed of principles,—the eternal verities of Plato and Descartes, and of ideas, not images—as the ideas of a point, a line, a circle, in mathematics;* and of justice, holiness, free-will, and the like, in morals. Hence in works of pure science the definitions of necessity precede the reasoning, in other works they more aptly form the conclusion.

To many of my readers it will, I trust, be some recommendation of these distinctions, that they are more than once expressed, and every where supposed, in the writings of St. Paul. I have no hesitation in undertaking to prove,

---

* In the severity of logic, the geometrical point, line, surface, circle, and so forth, are theorems, not ideas.

laws of the pure reason. Of course, as there is but one system of geometry, so according to this theory there can be but one constitution and one system of legislation, and this consists in the freedom, which is the common right of all men, under the controul of that moral necessity, which is the common duty of all men. Whatever is not every where necessary, is no where right. On this assumption the whole theory is built. To state it nakedly is to confute it satisfactorily. So at least it should seem. But in how winning and specious a manner this system may be represented even to minds of the loftiest order, if undisciplined and unhumbled by practical experience, has been proved by the general impassioned admiration and momen-

---

that every heresy which has disquieted the Christian Church, from Tritheism to Socinianism, has originated in and supported itself by, arguments rendered plausible only by the confusion of these faculties, and thus demanding for the objects of one, a sort of evidence appropriated to those of another faculty.—These disquisitions have the misfortune of being in ill-report, as dry and unsatisfactory; but I hope, in the course of the work, to gain them a better character—and if elucidations of their practical importance from the most momentous events of history, can render them interesting, to give them that interest at least. Besides, there is surely some good in the knowledge of truth, as truth—*we were not made to live by bread alone*—and in the strengthening of the intellect. It is an excellent remark of Scaliger's—*Harum indagatio subtilitatum, etsi non est utilis ad machinas farinarias conficiendas, exuit animum tamen inscitiæ rubigine, acuitque ad alia.*—Exerc. 307. §§ 3. The investigation of these subtleties, though of no use to the construction of machines for grinding corn, yet clears the mind from the rust of ignorance, and sharpens it or other things.

tous effects of Rousseau's *Du Contrat Social*, and the writings of the French economists, or, as they more appropriately entitled themselves, physiocratic philosophers: and in how tempting and dangerous a manner it may be represented to the populace, has been made too evident in our own country by the temporary effects of Paine's Rights of Man. Relatively, however, to this latter work it should be observed, that it is not a legitimate offspring of any one theory, but a confusion of the immorality of the first system with the misapplied universal principles of the last: and in this union, or rather lawless alternation, consists the essence of Jacobinism, as far as Jacobinism is any thing but a term of abuse, or has any meaning of its own distinct from democracy and sedition.

A constitution equally suited to China and America, or to Russia and Great Britain, must surely be equally unfit for both, and deserve as little respect in political, as a quack's panacea in medical, practice. Yet there are three weighty motives for a distinct exposition of this theory,* and of the

---

* As metaphysics are the science which determines what can, and what can not, be known of being and the laws of being, *a priori*,—that is, from those necessities of the mind or forms of thinking, which, though first revealed to us by experience, must yet have pre-existed in order to make experience itself possible, even as the eye must exist previously to any particular act of seeing, though by sight only can we know that we have eyes—so might the philosophy of Rousseau and his followers not inaptly be entitled, metapolitics, and the doctors of this school metapoliticians.

ground on which its pretensions are bottomed: and I dare affirm, that for the same reasons there are few subjects which in the present state of the world have a fairer claim to the attention of every serious Englishman, who is likely, directly or indirectly, as partizan or as opponent, to interest himself in schemes of reform.

The first motive is derived from the propensity of mankind to mistake the abhorrence occasioned by the unhappy effects or accompaniments of a particular system for an insight into the falsehood of its principles. And it is the latter only, a clear insight, not any vehement emotion, that can secure its permanent rejection. For by a wise ordinance of nature our feelings have no abiding-place in our memory; nay, the more vivid they are in the moment of their existence, the more dim and difficult to be remembered do they make the thoughts which accompanied them. Those of my readers, who at any time of their life have been in the habit of reading novels, may easily convince themselves of this truth, by comparing their recollections of those stories which most excited their curiosity, and even painfully affected their feelings, with their recollections of the calm and meditative pathos of Shakespeare and Milton. Hence it is that human experience, like the stern lights of a ship at sea, illumines only the path which we have passed over. The horrors of the Peasants' War in Germany, and the direful effects of the Anabaptist tenets, which were only nominally different from those of Jacobinism by the substitution of religious for philosophical jargon, struck all Europe for a time with affright. Yet little more than a century was sufficient to obliterate all effective memory of those events: the same principles budded forth anew, and produced the same fruits from the imprisonment of Charles I. to the restoration of his son. In the succeeding generations, to the follies and vices of the European courts, and to the oppressive privileges of the nobility, were again transferred those feelings of disgust and hatred, which for a brief while the multitude had attached to the crimes and extravagances of political and religious fanaticism: and the same principles, aided by circumstances and dressed out in the ostentatious garb of a fashionable philosophy, once more rose triumphant, and effected the French revolution. That man has reflected little on human nature who does not perceive that the detestable maxims and correspondent crimes of the existing French despotism, have already dimmed the recollections of the democratic phrenzy in the minds of men; by little and little, have drawn off to other objects the electric force of the feelings, which had massed and upholden those recollections; and that a favourable concurrence of occasions is alone wanting to awaken the thunder and precipitate the lightning from the opposite quarter of the political heaven. The true origin of human events is so little susceptible of that kind of evidence which can compel our belief even against our will; and so many are the disturbing forces which modify the motion given by the first projection; and every age has, or imagines it has, its own circumstances which render past experience no longer applicable to the present case; that there will never be wanting answers and explanations, and specious flatteries of hope. I well remember, that when the examples of former Jacobins, Julius Cæsar, Cromwell, &c. were adduced in France and England at the commencement of the French Consulate, it was ridiculed as pedantry and pedants' ignorance, to fear a repetition of such usurpation at the close of the enlightened eighteenth century. Those who possess the *Moniteurs* of that date will find set proofs, that such results were little less than impossible, and that it was an insult to so philosophical an age, and so enlightened a nation, to dare direct the public eye towards them as lights of admonition and warning.

It is a common weakness with official statesmen, and with those who deem themselves honoured by their acquaintance, to attribute great national events to the influence of particular persons, to the errors of one man and to the intrigues of another, to any possible spark of a particular occasion, rather than to the true cause, the predominant state of public opinion. I have known men who, with most significant nods, and the civil contempt of pitying half smiles, have declared the natural explanation of the French revolution, to be the mere fancies of garretteers, and then, with the solemnity of cabinet ministers, have proceeded to explain the whole by anecdotes. It is so stimulant to the pride of a vulgar mind, to be persuaded that it knows what few others know, and that it is the important depository of a sort of state secret, by communicating which it confers an obligation on others! But I have likewise met with men of intelligence, who at the commencement of the revolution were travelling on foot through the French provinces, and they bear witness, that in the remotest villages every tongue was employed in echoing and enforcing the doctrines of the Parisian journalists; that the public highways were crowded with enthusiasts, some shouting the watchwords of the revolution, others disputing on the most abstract principles of the universal constitution, which they fully believed, that all the nations of the earth were shortly to adopt; the most ignorant among them confident of his fitness for the highest duties of a legislator; and all prepared to shed their blood in the defence of the inalienable sovereignty of the self-governed people. The more abstract the notions were, with the closer affinity did they combine with the most fervent feelings, and all the immediate impulses to action. The Lord Chancellor Bacon lived in an age of court intrigues, and was familiarly acquainted with all the secrets of personal influence. He, if any man, was qualified to take the gauge and measurement of their comparative power; and he has told us, that there is one, and but one infallible source of political prophecy, the knowledge of the predominant opinions and the speculative principles of men in general, between the age of twenty and thirty. Sir Philip Sidney,—the favourite of Queen Elizabeth, the paramount gentleman of Europe, the nephew, and —as far as a good man could be—the confidant of the intriguing and dark-minded Earl of Leicester, —was so deeply convinced that the principles diffused through the majority of a nation are the true oracles from whence statesmen are to learn wisdom, and that when the people speak loudly it is from their being strongly possessed either by the godhead or the dæmon, that in the revolution of the Netherlands he considered the universal adoption of one set of principles, as a proof of the divine presence. 'If Her Majesty,' says he, ' were the fountain, I would fear, considering what I daily find, that we should wax dry. But she is but a means which God useth.' But if my readers wish to see the question of the efficacy of principles and popular opinions for evil and for good proved and illustrated with an eloquence worthy of the subject, I can refer them with the hardiest anticipation of their thanks, to the late work concerning the relations of Great Britain, Spain, and Portugal, by my honoured friend, William Wordsworth, *quem quoties lego, non verba mihi videor audire, sed tonitrua.* *

---

* I consider this reference to, and strong recommendation of, the work above mentioned, not as a voluntary tribute of admiration, but as an act of mere justice both to myself and

ESSAY III.

That erroneous political notions—they having become general and a part of the popular creed—

to the readers of The Friend. My own heart bears me witness, that I am actuated by the deepest sense of the truth of the principles, which it has been and still more will be my endeavour to enforce, and of their paramount importance to the well-being of society at the present juncture: and that the duty of making the attempt, and the hope of not wholly failing in it, are, far more than the wish for the doubtful good of literary reputation, or any yet meaner object, my great and ruling motives. Mr. Wordsworth I deem a fellow-labourer in the same vineyard, actuated by the same motives and teaching the same principles, but with far greater powers of mind, and an eloquence more adequate to the importance and majesty of the cause. I am strengthened too by the knowledge, that I am not unauthorized by the sympathy of many wise and good men, and men acknowledged as such by the public, in my admiration of his pamphlet.—*Neque enim debet operibus ejus obesse, quod vivit. An si inter eos, quos numquam vidimus, floruisset, non solum libros ejus, verum etiam imagines conquireremus, ejusdem nunc honor præsentis, et gratia quasi satietate languescet? At hoc pravum, malignumque est, non admirari hominem admiratione dignissimum, quia videre, alloqui, audire, complecti, nec laudare tantum, verum etiam amare, contingit.* PLIN. Epis. Lib. I. 16.

It is hardly possible for a man of ingenuous mind to act under the fear that he shall be suspected by honest men of the vileness of praising a work to the public, merely because he happens to be personally acquainted with the author. That this is so commonly done in reviews, furnishes only an additional proof of the morbid hardness produced in the moral sense by the habit of writing anonymous criticisms, especially under the further disguise of a pretended board or association of critics, each man expressing himself, to use the words of Andrew Marvel, as a synodical *individuum*. With regard, however, to the probability of being warped by partiality, I can only say that I judge of all works indifferently by certain fixed rules previously formed in my mind with all the power and vigilance of my judgment; and that I should certainly of the two apply them with greater

have practical consequences, and these, of course, of a most fearful nature, is a truth as certain as historic evidence can make it: and that when the feelings excited by these calamities have passed away, and the interest in them has been displaced by more recent events, the same errors are likely to be started afresh, pregnant with the same calamities, is an evil rooted in human nature in the present state of general information, for which we have hitherto found no adequate remedy. It may, perhaps in the scheme of Providence, be proper and conducive to its ends, that no adequate remedy should exist: for the folly of men is the wisdom of God. But if there be any means, if not of preventing, yet of palliating, the disease, and, in the more favoured nations, of checking its progress at the first symptoms; and if these means are to be at all compatible with the civil and intellectual free-

---

rigour to the production of a friend than to that of a person indifferent to me. But wherever I find in any work all the conditions of excellence in its kind, it is not the accident of the author's being my contemporary or even my friend, or the sneers of bad-hearted men, that shall prevent me from speaking of it, as in my inmost convictions I deem it deserves.

—————————————— no, friend!
Though it be now the fashion to commend,
As men of strong minds, those alone who can
Censure with judgment, no such piece of man
Makes up my spirit: where desert does live,
There will I plant my wonder, and there give
My best endeavours to build up his glory,
That truly merits!

Recommendatory Verses to one of the old plays.

dom of mankind; they are to be found only in an intelligible and thorough expofure of the error, and, through that difcovery, of the fource, from which it derives its fpecioufnefs and powers of influence on the human mind. This therefore is my firft motive for undertaking the difquifition.

The fecond is, that though the French code of revolutionary principles is now generally rejected as a fyftem, yet every where in the fpeeches and writings of the Englifh reformers, nay, not feldom in thofe of their opponents, I find certain maxims afferted or appealed to, which are not tenable, except as conftituent parts of that fyftem. Many of the moft fpecious arguments in proof of the imperfection and injuftice of the prefent conftitution of our legiflature will be found, on clofer examination, to pre-fuppofe the truth of certain principles, from which the adducers of thefe arguments loudly profefs their diffent. But in political changes no permanence can be hoped for in the edifice, without confiftency in the foundation.

The third motive is, that by detecting the true fource of the influence of thefe principles, we fhall at the fame time difcover their natural place and object: and that in themfelves they are not only truths, but moft important and fublime truths; and that their falfehood and their danger confift altogether in their mifapplication. Thus the dignity of human nature will be fecured, and at the fame time a leffon of humility taught to each individual, when we are made to fee that the univerfal neceffary laws, and pure ideas of reason, were given us, not for the purpose of flattering our pride and enabling us to become national legislators; but that, by an energy of continued self-conquest, we might establish a free and yet absolute government in our own spirits.

ESSAY IV.

Albeit therefore, much of that we are to speak in this present cause, may seem to a number perhaps tedious, perhaps obscure, dark and intricate, (for many talk of the truth, which never sounded the depth from whence it springeth: and therefore, when they are led thereunto, they are soon weary, as men drawn from those beaten paths, wherewith they have been inured;) yet this may not so far prevail, as to cut off that which the matter itself requireth, howsoever the nice humour of some be therewith pleased or no. They unto whom we shall seem tedious, are in no wise injured by us, because it is in their own hands to spare that labour which they are not willing to endure. And if any complain of obscurity, they must consider, that in these matters it cometh no otherwise to pass, than in sundry the works both of art, and also of nature, where that which hath greatest force in the very things we see, is, notwithstanding, itself oftentimes not seen. The stateliness of houses, the goodliness of trees, when we behold them, delighteth the eye: but that foundation which beareth up the one, that root which ministereth unto the other nourishment and life, is in the bosom of the earth concealed; and if there be at any time occasion to search into it, such labour is then more necessary than pleasant, both to them which undertake it and for the lookers-on. In like manner, the use and benefit of good laws, all that live under them, may enjoy with delight and comfort, albeit the grounds and first original causes from whence they have sprung, be unknown, as to the greatest part of men they are: But when they who withdraw their obedience, pretend that the laws which they should obey are corrupt and vicious; for better examination of their quality, it behoveth the very foundation and root, the highest wellspring and fountain of them to be discovered. Which, because we are not oftentimes accustomed to do, when we do it, the pains we take are more needful a great deal than acceptable, and the matters which we handle, seem by reason of newness, (till the mind grow better acquainted with them) dark, intricate, and unfamiliar. For as much help whereof, as may be in this case, I have endeavoured throughout the body of this whole discourse, that every former part might give strength unto all that follow, and every latter bring some light unto all before: so that if the judgements of men do but hold themselves in suspense, as touching these first more general meditations, till in order they have perused the rest that ensue; what may seem dark at the first, will afterwards be found more plain, even as the latter particular decisions will appear, I doubt not, more strong when the other have been read before. HOOKER.*

On the grounds of government as laid exclusively in the pure reason; or a statement and critique of the third system of political philosophy,—the theory of Rousseau and the French economists.

I PROCEED to my promise of developing from its embryo principles the tree of French liberty, of which the declaration of the rights of man, and the constitution of 1791 were the leaves, and the succeeding and present state of France the fruits. Let me not be blamed, if, in the interposed essays, introductory to this section, I have connected this system, though only in imagination, though only as a possible case, with a name so deservedly reverenced as that of Luther. It is some excuse, that to interweave with the reader's recollections a certain life and dramatic interest, during the perusal of the abstract † reasonings that are to follow, is the

---

* Eccl. Pol. B. I. c. 1, 2.—*Ed.*

† I have been charged in the Friend with a novel and

only means I possess of bribing his attention. We have, most of us, at some period or other of our lives, been amused with dialogues of the dead. Who is there, that wishing to form a probable opinion on the grounds of hope and fear for an injured people warring against mighty armies, would not be pleased with a spirited fiction, which brought before him an old Numantian discoursing on that subject in Elysium, with a newly-arrived spirit from the streets of Saragoza or the walls of Gerona?

But I have a better reason. I wished to give every fair advantage to the opinions, which I deemed it of importance to confute. It is bad policy to represent a political system as having no charm but for robbers and assassins, and no natural origin but in the brains of fools or mad men, when

---

perplexing use of the word *abstract*, both as verb and noun. Novel it certainly is not; it being authorized by Lord Bacon, Des Cartes, and others. The fact is this: I take the word in its proper meaning, as *abstraho*, I draw from. The image, by which I represent to myself an oak tree, is no *fac simile* or adequate *icon* of the tree, but is abstracted from it by my eye. Now this appears to me a more natural as well as more grammatical and philosophical use of the word, than that elliptic construction, by which an accusative noun, and the preposition following it are to be understood, namely, I draw *(my attention from)* the, &c. Thus:—I give the outline of a flower on a slate with a slate pencil.—Now, I would say, I abstract the shape from the flower, or of the flower. But the objector would express the same thing by saying, I abstract the colour, &c. (that is, my attention from the colour, &c.)

Perhaps the latter might be better in familiar writing; but I continue to prefer the former on subjects that require precision. 1830.

experience has proved, that the great danger of the system consists in the peculiar fascination it is calculated to exert on noble and imaginative spirits; on all those, who, in the amiable intoxication of youthful benevolence, are apt to mistake their own best virtues and choicest powers for the average qualities and attributes of the human character. The very minds, which a good man would most wish to preserve or disentangle from the snare, are by these angry misrepresentations rather lured into it. Is it wonderful that a man should reject the arguments unheard, when his own heart proves the falsehood of the assumptions by which they are prefaced; or that he should retaliate on the aggressors their own evil thoughts? I am well aware, that the provocation was great, the temptation almost inevitable; yet still I cannot repel the conviction from my mind, that in part to this error, and in part to a certain inconsistency in his own fundamental principles, we are to attribute the small number of converts made by Burke during his life time. Let me not be misunderstood. I do not mean, that this great man supported different principles at different æras of his political life. On the contrary, no man was ever more like himself. From his first published speech on the American colonies to his last posthumous tracts, we see the same man, the same doctrines, the same uniform wisdom of practical counsels, the same reasoning and the same prejudices against all abstract grounds, against all deduction of practice from theory. The inconsistency to which I allude, is of a different kind: it is the want of congruity in the principles appealed to in different parts of the same work; it is an apparent versatility of the principle with the occasion. If his opponents are theorists, then every thing is to be founded on prudence, on mere calculations of expediency; and every man is represented as acting according to the state of his own immediate self-interest. Are his opponents calculators? Then calculation itself is represented as a sort of crime. God has given us feelings, and we are to obey them;—and the most absurd prejudices become venerable, to which these feelings have given consecration. I have not forgotten, that Burke himself defended these half contradictions, on the pretext of balancing the too much on the one side by a too much on the other. But never can I believe but that the straight line must needs be the nearest; and that where there is the most, and the most unalloyed truth, there will be the greatest and most permanent power of persuasion. But the fact was, that Burke in his public character found himself, as it were, in a Noah's ark, with a very few men and a great many beasts. He felt how much his immediate power was lessened by the very circumstance of his measureless superiority to those about him: he acted, therefore, under a perpetual system of compromise—a compromise of greatness with meanness; a compromise of comprehension with narrowness; a compromise of the philosopher,—who, armed with the twofold knowledge of history and the laws of spirit, looked, as with a telescope, far around and into the remote distance,—with the mere men of business, or with yet coarser intellects, who handled a truth, which they were required to receive, as they would handle an ox, which they were desired to purchase. But why need I repeat what has been already said in so happy a manner by Goldsmith of this great man:—

Who too deep for his hearers, still went on refining,
And thought of convincing, while they thought of dining.*

And if in consequence it was his fate to "cut blocks with a razor," I may be permitted to add, that in respect of truth, though not of genius, the weapon was injured by the misapplication.

For myself, however, I act and will continue to act under the belief, that the whole truth is the best antidote to falsehoods which are dangerous chiefly because they are half-truths: and that an erroneous system is best confuted, not by an abuse of theory in general, nor by an absurd opposition of theory to practice, but by a detection of the errors in the particular theory. For the meanest of men has his theory, and to think at all is to theorize. With these convictions I proceed immediately to the system of the economists and to the principles on which it is constructed, and from which it must derive all its strength.

---

* Retaliation.—*Ed.*

The system commences with an undeniable truth, and an important deduction therefrom equally undeniable. All voluntary actions, say they, having for their objects, good or evil, are moral actions. But all morality is grounded in the reason. Every man is born with the faculty of reason: and whatever is without it, be the shape what it may, is not a man or person, but a thing. Hence the sacred principle, recognized by all laws, human and divine, the principle indeed, which is the ground-work of all law and justice, that a person can never become a thing, nor be treated as such without wrong. But the distinction between person and thing consists herein, that the latter may rightfully be used, altogether and merely, as a mean; but the former must always be included in the end, and form a part of the final cause. We plant the tree and we cut it down, we breed the sheep and we kill it, wholly as means to our own ends. The woodcutter and the hind are likewise employed as means, but on an agreement of reciprocal advantage, which includes them as well as their employer in the end. Again: as the faculty of reason implies free-agency, morality,—that is, the dictate of reason,—gives to every rational being the right of acting as a free agent, and of finally determining his conduct by his own will, according to his own conscience: and this right is inalienable except by guilt, which is an act of self-forfeiture, and the consequences therefore to be considered as the criminal's own moral election. In respect of their reason [*] all men are equal. The measure of the understanding and of all other faculties of man, is different in different persons: but reason is not susceptible of degree. For since it merely decides whether any given thought or action is or is not in contradiction with the rest, there can be no reason better, or more reason, than another.

Reason! best and holiest gift of God and bond of union with the giver;—the high title by which the majesty of man claims precedence above all other living creatures;—mysterious faculty, the mother of conscience, of language, of tears, and of smiles;—calm and incorruptible legislator of the soul, without whom all its other powers would 'meet in mere oppugnancy;'—sole principle of permanence amid endless change,—in a world of discordant appetites and imagined self-interests the one only common measure, which taken away,—

> Force should be right; or, rather right and wrong,—
> Between whose endless jar justice resides,—
> Should lose their names, and so should justice too.
> Then every thing includes itself in power,
> Power into will, will into appetite;
> And appetite a universal wolf,
> So doubly seconded with will and power,
> Must make perforce a universal prey!

Thrice blessed faculty of reason! all other gifts, though goodly and of celestial origin, health, strength, talents, all the powers and all the means

---

[*] This position has been already explained, and the sophistry grounded on it detected and exposed, in the last essay of the Landing-Place, in this volume.

of enjoyment, seem dispensed by chance or sullen caprice;—thou alone, more than even the sunshine, more than the common air, art given to all men, and to every man alike. To thee, who being one art the same in all, we owe the privilege, that of all we can become one, a living whole,—that we have a country. Who then shall dare prescribe a law of moral action for any rational being, which does not flow immediately from that reason, which is the fountain of all morality? Or how without breach of conscience can we limit or coerce the powers of a free agent, except by coincidence with that law in his own mind, which is at once the cause, the condition, and the measure of his free agency? Man must be free; or to what purpose was he made a spirit of reason, and not a machine of instinct? Man must obey; or wherefore has he a conscience? The powers, which create this difficulty, contain its solution likewise: for their service is perfect freedom. And whatever law or system of law compels any other service, disennobles our nature, leagues itself with the animal against the godlike, kills in us the very principle of joyous well-doing, and fights against humanity.

By the application of these principles to the social state there arises the following system, which, as far as its first grounds are concerned, is developed the most fully by J. J. Rousseau in his work *Du Contrat Social*. If then no individual possesses the right of prescribing any thing to another individual, the rule of which is not contained in their common reason, society, which is but an aggregate of individuals, can communicate this right to no one. It cannot possibly make that rightful which the higher and inviolable law of human nature declares contradictory and unjust. But concerning right and wrong, the reason of each and every man is the competent judge: for how else could he be an amenable being, or the proper subject of any law? This reason, therefore, in any one man, cannot even in the social state be rightfully subjugated to the reason of any other. Neither an individual, nor yet the whole multitude which constitutes the state, can possess the right of compelling him to do any thing, of which it cannot be demonstrated that his own reason must join in prescribing it. If therefore society is to be under a rightful constitution of government, and one that can impose on rational beings a true and moral obligation to obey it, it must be framed on such principles that every individual follows his own reason while he obeys the laws of the constitution, and performs the will of the state while he follows the dictates of his own reason. This is expressly asserted by Rousseau, who states the problem of a perfect constitution of government in the following words: *trouver une forme d'association —par laquelle chacun s'unissant à tous, n'obéisse pourtant qu' à lui même, et reste aussi libre qu' auparavant,*—that is, to find a form of society according to which each one uniting himself with the whole shall yet obey himself only and remain as free as before. This right of the individual to retain his whole natural independence, even in the social state, is absolutely inalienable. He cannot possibly concede or compromise it: for this very right is one of his most sacred duties. He would sin against himself, and commit high treason against the reason which the Almighty Creator has given him, if he dared abandon its exclusive right to govern his actions.

Laws obligatory on the conscience, can only therefore proceed from that reason which remains always one and the same, whether it speaks through this or that person: like the voice of an external ventriloquist, it is indifferent from whose lips it appears to come, if only it be audible. The individuals indeed are subject to errors and passions, and each man has his own defects. But when men are assembled in person or by real representatives, the actions and re-actions of individual self-love balance each other; errors are neutralized by opposite errors; and the winds rushing from all quarters at once with equal force, produce for the time a deep calm, during which the general will arising from the general reason displays itself. 'It is fittest,' says Burke himself,* 'that sovereign authority should be exercised where it is most likely to be attended with the most effectual correctives. These correctives are furnished by the nature and course of parliamentary proceedings, and by the infinitely

---

* Note on his motion relative to the Speech from the Throne, Vol. ii. p. 647, 4to. Edit.

diversified characters which compose the two Houses. The fulness, the freedom, and publicity of discussion, leave it easy to distinguish what are acts of power, and what the determinations of equity and reason. There prejudice corrects prejudice, and the different asperities of party zeal mitigate and neutralize each other.'

This, however, as my readers will have already detected, is no longer a demonstrable deduction from reason. It is a mere probability, against which other probabilities may be weighed: as the lust of authority, the contagious nature of enthusiasm, and other of the acute or chronic diseases of deliberative assemblies. But which of these results is the more probable, the correction or the contagion of evil, must depend on circumstances and grounds of expediency: and thus we already find ourselves beyond the magic circle of the pure reason, and within the sphere of the understanding and the prudence. Of this important fact Rousseau was by no means unaware in his theory, though with gross inconsistency he takes no notice of it in his application of the theory to practice. He admits the possibility, he is compelled by history to allow even the probability, that the most numerous popular assemblies, nay even whole nations, may at times be hurried away by the same passions, and under the dominion of a common error. This will of all is then of no more value, than the humours of any one individual: and must therefore be sacredly distinguished from the pure will which flows from universal reason. To this point then I entreat the reader's particular attention: for in this distinction, established by Rousseau himself, between the *volonté de tous* and the *volonté générale*,—that is, between the collective will, and a casual overbalance of wills—the falsehood or nothingness of the whole system becomes manifest. For hence it follows, as an inevitable consequence, that all which is said in the *Contrat Social* of that sovereign will, to which the right of universal legislation appertains, applies to no one human being, to no society or assemblage of human beings, and least of all to the mixed multitude that makes up the people: but entirely and exclusively to reason itself, which, it is true, dwells in every man potentially, but actually and in perfect purity is found in no man and in no body of men. This distinction the later disciples of Rousseau chose completely to forget, and,—a far more melancholy case—the constituent legislators of France forgot it likewise. With a wretched parrotry they wrote and harangued without ceasing of the *volonté générale*—the inalienable sovereignty of the people: and by these high-sounding phrases led on the vain, ignorant, and intoxicated populace to wild excesses and wilder expectations, which entailing on them the bitterness of disappointment cleared the way for military despotism, for the Satanic government of horror under the Jacobins, and of terror under the Corsican.

Luther lived long enough to see the consequences of the doctrines into which indignant pity and abstract principles of right had hurried him—to see, to retract and to oppose them. If the same had been the lot of Rousseau, I doubt not, that his conduct would have been the same. In his whole system there is beyond controversy much that is true and well reasoned, if only its application be not extended farther than the nature of the case permits. But then we shall find that little or nothing is won by it for the institutions of society; and least of all for the constitution of governments, the theory of which it was his wish to ground on it. Apply his principles to any case, in which the sacred and inviolable laws of morality are immediately interested, all becomes just and pertinent. No power on earth can oblige me to act against my conscience. No magistrate, no monarch, no legislature, can without tyranny compel me to do any thing which the acknowledged laws of God have forbidden me to do. So act that thou mayest be able, without involving any contradiction, to will that the maxim of thy conduct should be the law of all intelligent beings—is the one universal and sufficient principle and guide of morality. And why? Because the object of morality is not the outward act, but the internal maxim of our actions. And so far it is infallible. But with what show of reason can we pretend, from a principle by which we are to determine the purity of our motives, to deduce the form and matter of a rightful government, the main office of which is to regulate the outward actions of particular bodies of men, according to their particular circumstances? Can we hope better of constitutions framed by ourselves, than of that which was given by Almighty Wisdom itself? The laws of the Hebrew commonwealth, which flowed from the pure reason, remain and are immutable; but the regulations dictated by prudence, though by the divine prudence, and though given in thunder from the mount, have passed away; and while they lasted, were binding only for that one state, the particular circumstances of which rendered them expedient.

Rousseau indeed asserts, that there is an inalienable sovereignty inherent in every human being possessed of reason: and from this the framers of the constitution of 1791 deduce, that the people itself is its own sole rightful legislator, and at most dare only recede so far from its right as to delegate to chosen deputies the power of representing and declaring the general will. But this is wholly without proof; for it has already been fully shewn, that according to the principle out of which this consequence is attempted to be drawn, it is not the actual man, but the abstract reason alone, that is the sovereign and rightful lawgiver. The confusion of two things so different is so gross an error, that the Constituent Assembly could scarcely proceed a step in their declaration of rights, without some glaring inconsistency. Children are excluded from all political power;—are they not human beings in whom the faculty of reason resides? Yes! but in them the faculty is not yet adequately developed.

But are not gross ignorance, inveterate superstition, and the habitual tyranny of passion and sensuality, equally preventives of the development, equally impediments to the rightful exercise, of the reason, as childhood and early youth? Who would not rely on the judgment of a well-educated English lad, bred in a virtuous and enlightened family, in preference to that of a brutal Russian, who believes that he can scourge his wooden idol into good humour, or attributes to himself the merit of perpetual prayer, when he has fastened the petitions, which his priest has written for him, on the wings of a windmill?—Again: women are likewise excluded—a full half, and that assuredly the most innocent, the most amiable half, of the whole human race, is excluded, and this too by a constitution which boasts to have no other foundations but those of universal reason! Is reason then an affair of sex? No! But women are commonly in a state of dependence, and are not likely to exercise their reason with freedom. Well! and does not this ground of exclusion apply with equal or greater force to the poor, to the infirm, to men in embarrassed circumstances, to all in short whose maintenance, be it scanty or be it ample, depends on the will of others? How far are we to go? Where must we stop? What classes should we admit? Whom must we disfranchise? The objects concerning whom we are to determine these questions, are all human beings and differenced from each other by degrees only, these degrees, too, oftentimes changing. Yet the principle on which the whole system rests is, that reason is not susceptible of degree. Nothing, therefore, which subsists wholly in degrees, the changes of which do not obey any necessary law, can be subjects of pure science, or determinable by mere reason. For these things we must rely on our understandings, enlightened by past experience and immediate observation, and determining our choice by comparisons of expediency.

It is therefore altogether a mistaken notion, that the theory which would deduce the social rights of man, and the sole rightful form of government from principles of reason, involves a necessary preference of the democratic, or even the representative, constitutions. Accordingly, several of the French economists, although devotees of Rousseau and the physiocratic system, and assuredly not the least respectable of their party either in morals or in intellect,—and these too men, who lived and wrote under the unlimited monarchy of France, and who were therefore well acquainted with the evils connected with that system,—did yet declare themselves for a pure monarchy in preference to the aristocratic, the popular, or the mixed form. These men argued, that no other laws being allowable but those which are demonstrably just, and founded in the simplest ideas of reason, and of which every man's reason is the competent judge, it is indifferent whether one man, or one or more assemblies of men, give form and publicity to them. For being matters of pure and simple science, they require no experience in order to see their truth, and among an enlightened people, by whom this system had been once solemnly adopted, no sovereign would dare to make other laws than those of reason. They further contend, that if the people were not enlightened, a purely popular government could not co-exist with this system of absolute justice: and if it were adequately enlightened, the influence of public opinion would supply the place of formal representation, while the form of the government would be in harmony with the unity and simplicity of its principles. This they entitle *le despotisme légal sous l'empire de l'évidence.* The best statement of the theory thus modified, may be found in *Mercier de la Rivière, l'ordre naturel et essentiel des sociétés politiques.* From the proofs adduced in the preceding paragraph, to which many others might be added, I have no hesitation in affirming that this latter party are the more consistent reasoners.

It is worthy of remark, that the influence of these writings contributed greatly, not indeed to raise the present emperor, but certainly to reconcile a numerous class of politicians to his unlimited authority: and as far as his lawless passion for war and conquest allows him to govern according to any principles, he favours those of the physiocratic philosophers. His early education must have given him a predilection for a theory conducted throughout with mathematical precision; its very simplicity promised the readiest and most commodious machine for despotism, for it moulds a nation into as calculable a power as an army; while the stern and seeming greatness of the whole and its mock elevation above human feelings, flattered his pride, hardened his conscience, and aided the efforts of self-delusion. Reason is the sole sovereign, the only rightful legislator: but reason to act on man must be impersonated. The Providence which had so marvellously raised and supported him, had marked him out for the representative of reason, and had armed him with irresistible force, in order to realize its laws. In him therefore might becomes right, and his cause and that of destiny, (or as he now chooses to word it, exchanging blind nonsense for staring blasphemy), his cause and the cause of God are one and the same. Excellent postulate for a choleric and self-willed tyrant! What avails the impoverishment of a few thousand merchants and manufacturers? What even the general wretchedness of millions of perishable men, for a short generation? Should these stand in the way of the chosen conqueror, the *innovator mundi, et stupor sæculorum*, or prevent a constitution of things, which erected on intellectual and perfect foundations groweth not old, but like the eternal justice, of which it is the living image,

———————————— may despise
The strokes of fate and see the world's last hour?

For justice, austere, unrelenting justice, is every where holden up as the one thing needful: and the only duty of the citizen, in fulfilling which he obeys all the laws, is not to encroach on another's sphere of action. The greatest possible happiness of a people is not, according to this system, the object of a governor; but to preserve the freedom of all, by coercing within the requisite bounds the freedom of each. Whatever a government does more than this, comes of evil: and its best employment is the repeal of laws and regulations, not the establishment of them. Each man is the best judge of his own happiness, and to himself must it therefore be entrusted. Remove all the interferences of positive statutes, all monopoly, all bounties, all prohibitions, and all encouragements of importation and exportation, of particular growth and particular manufactures: let the revenues of the state be taken at once from the produce of soil; and all things will then find their level, all irregularities will correct each other, and an indestructible cycle of harmonious motions take place in the moral equally as in the natural world. The business of the governor is to watch incessantly, that the state shall remain composed of individuals, acting as individuals, by which alone the freedom of all can be secured. Its duty is to take care that itself remain the sole collective power, and that all the citizens should enjoy the same rights, and without distinction be subject to the same duties.

Splendid promises! Can any thing appear more equitable than the last proposition, the equality of rights and duties? Can any thing be conceived

more simple in the idea? But the execution — !
Let the four or five quarto volumes of the Conscript Code be the comment! But as briefly as possible I shall prove, that this system, as an exclusive total, is under any form impracticable; and that if it were realized, and as far as it were realized, it would necessarily lead to general barbarism and the most grinding oppression; and that the final result of a general attempt to introduce it, must be a military despotism inconsistent with the peace and safety of mankind. That reason should be our guide and governor is an undeniable truth, and all our notion of right and wrong is built thereon: for reason is one of the two fountainheads in which the whole moral nature of man originated and subsists. From reason alone can we derive the principles which our understandings are to apply, the ideal to which by means of our understandings we should endeavour to approximate. This however gives no proof that reason alone ought to govern and direct human beings, either as individuals or as states. It ought not to do this, because it cannot. The laws of reason are unable to satisfy the first conditions of human society. We will admit that the shortest code of law is the best, and that the citizen finds himself most at ease where the government least intermeddles with his affairs, and confines its efforts to the preservation of public tranquillity; we will suffer this to pass at present undisputed, though the examples of England, and before the late events,

of Holland and Switzerland,—surely the three happiest nations of the world—to which perhaps we might add the major part of the former German free towns, furnish stubborn facts in presumption of the contrary,—yet still the proof is wanting that the first and most general applications and exertions of the power of man can be definitely regulated by reason unaided by the positive and conventional laws in the formation of which the understanding must be our guide, and which become just because they happen to be expedient.

The chief object for which men first formed themselves into a state was not the protection of their lives, but of their property. Where the nature of the soil and climate precludes all property but personal, and permits that only in its simplest forms, as in Greenland, men remain in the domestic state and form neighbourhoods, but not governments. And in North America the chiefs appear to exercise government in those tribes only which possess individual landed property. Among the rest the chief is their general; but government is exercised only in families by the fathers of families. But where individual landed property exists, there must be inequality of property: the nature of the earth and the nature of the mind unite to make the contrary impossible. But to suppose the land the property of the state, and the labour and the produce to be equally divided among all the members of the state, involves more than one contradiction: for it could not subsist without gross injuſtice, except where the reaſon of all and of each was abſolute maſter of the ſelfiſh paſſions of ſloth, envy, and the like; and yet the ſame ſtate would preclude the greater part of the means by which the reaſon of man is developed. In whatever ſtate of ſociety you would place it, from the moſt ſavage to the moſt refined, it would be found equally unjuſt and impoſſible; and were there a race of men, a country, and a climate, that permitted ſuch an order of things, the ſame cauſes would render all government ſuperfluous. To property, therefore, and to its inequalities all human laws directly or indirectly relate, which would not be equally laws in the ſtate of nature. Now it is impoſſible to deduce the right of property* from pure reaſon. The utmoſt which reaſon could give would be a property in the forms of things, as far as the forms were produced by individual power. In the matter it could give no property. We regard angels and glorified ſpirits as beings of pure reaſon: and whoever thought of property in heaven? Even the ſimpleſt and moſt moral form of it, namely, marriage, (we know from the higheſt authority) is excluded from the ſtate of pure reaſon. Rouſſeau himſelf expreſſly admits that property cannot be deduced from the laws of reaſon and na-

---

* I mean, practically and with the inequalities inſeparable from the actual exiſtence of property. Abſtractedly, the right to property is deducible from the free-agency of man. If to act freely be a right, a ſphere of action muſt be ſo too.

ture; and he ought therefore to have admitted at the same time that his whole theory was a thing of air. In the most respectable point of view he could regard his system as analogous to geometry. If indeed it be purely scientific, how could it be otherwise? Geometry holds forth an ideal which can never be fully realized in nature, even because it is nature: because bodies are more than extension, and to pure extension of space only the mathematical theorems wholly correspond. In the same manner the moral laws of the intellectual world, as far as they are deducible from pure intellect, are never perfectly applicable to our mixed and sensitive nature, because man is something besides reason; because his reason never acts by itself, but must clothe itself in the substance of individual understanding and specific inclination, in order to become a reality and an object of consciousness and experience. It will be seen hereafter that together with this, the key-stone of the arch, the greater part and the most specious of the popular arguments in favour of universal suffrage fall in and are crushed. I will mention one only at present. Major Cartwright,—in his deduction of the rights of the subject from principles " not susceptible of proof, being self-evident, if one of which be violated all are shaken,"—affirms (Principle 98th; though the greater part indeed are moral aphorisms, or blank assertions, not scientific principles) " that a power which ought never to be used ought never to exist." Again he affirms that " laws to bind all muſt be aſſented to by all, and conſequently every man, even the pooreſt, has an equal right to ſuffrage;" and this for an additional reaſon, becauſe " all without exception are capable of feeling happineſs or miſery, accordingly as they are well or ill governed." But are they not then capable of feeling happineſs or miſery accordingly as they do or do not poſſeſs the means of a comfortable ſubſiſtence? and who is the judge, what is a comfortable ſubſiſtence, but the man himſelf? Might not then, on the ſame or equivalent principles, a leveller conſtruct a right to equal property? The inhabitants of this country without property form, doubtleſs, a great majority; each of theſe has a right to a ſuffrage, and the richeſt man to no more; and the object of this ſuffrage is, that each individual may ſecure himſelf a true efficient repreſentative of his will. Here then is a legal power of aboliſhing or equalizing property: and according to Major C. himſelf, a power which ought never to be uſed ought not to exiſt.

Therefore, unleſs he carries his ſyſtem to the whole length of common labour and common poſſeſſion, a right to univerſal ſuffrage cannot exiſt; but if not to univerſal ſuffrage, there can exiſt no natural right to ſuffrage at all. In whatever way he would obviate this objection, he muſt admit expedience founded on experience and particular circumſtances, which will vary in every different nation, and in the ſame nation at different times, as the maxim of all legiſlation and the ground of all legislative power. For his universal principles, as far as they are principles and universal, necessarily suppose uniform and perfect subjects, which are to be found in the ideas of pure geometry and, I trust, in the realities of heaven, but never, never, in creatures of flesh and blood.

END OF VOL. I.

C. WHITTINGHAM, CHISWICK.

LaVergne, TN USA
29 November 2010
206609LV00003BA/34/P